I0833695

The Healing of Jena Parker

Lee Blacketer

ISBN: 979-8-218-56600-5
The Healing of Jena Parker
Copyright © 2024 by Lee Blacketer
Publisher: Marjaylin Publishing

Acknowledgements:
Cover Design by Sondra Ortega Cedillo

All rights reserved.
Except for use in any review, the reproduction or utilization of this work in whole or in part in any form by any electronic, mechanical, or other means, now known or hereafter invented, including xerography, photocopying, and recording, or in any information storage, or retrieval system, is forbidden without the written permission of the publisher.

This is a work of fiction. Names, characters, places and incidents either are products of the author's imagination or are used fictitiously. Any resemblance to actual events or locales or persons, living or dead, is entirely coincidental.

Author's Note and Dedication

Although a work of fiction,
this story deals with traumatic loss and grief.

It is a love story of recovery.

So, I dedicate this to all our lost babies.
And to all our lost loves.
And for all who dare to keep living.

Prologue

The echo of American jets blasting off from the NATO airbase in the Italian valley below reverberated off the mountainside and sent a surge of adrenalin rushing through his veins. The view was beautiful from the top of the mountain. He never tired of watching the jets take off from the runway with fire in their bellies, headed for the unknown parts of the world to protect and defend.

His weekend leave would be up in a few hours. Soon it would be time to start back down the mountain. But not yet. He still had things to sort out.

He took a long drink from his water bottle and looked south. He made out the staggered barracks and hangers, roads and commissary, grounded aircraft, and the fencing around his military base home for years. This way of life, service to country, however honorable, weighed heavy nowadays.

He was a pilot in the Air Force. He flew F-16s on occasion, and HH-60G Pave Hawk helicopters, the U.S. Air Force's primary combat search and rescue helicopter used by Air Force special tactics teams. He was one of the bad-ass good guys and gave as much heat as he got. His years of service were laden with danger. He'd seen more than any man should see in a lifetime.

His body, soul, and spirit were now paying the sacrifice.

Yet he was determined in his commitment to follow through all the way. At six-two and two hundred and thirty pounds, just under the weight limit for a pilot, nothing could stop him.

Little deterred him. And no one could make him leave his post until his tour of duty was over.

But when the letter came from her, it ripped his insides out, and caused him to question his own motive for being here.

His ex-fiancé had never understood or appreciated his commitment to country. She had made him wonder if it was worth it at all, if only to go home to no one.

The sun slid behind the hillside and created a soft European glow that inspired poetry and wine and dinners on a terrace of red roses. He wasn't a mush by any means. His mother had instilled in him a core of integrity and stoic fortitude, and the ability to defend himself in any situation. But she had also embedded in him a sense of the romantic, and the nostalgic.

He knew how to woo women.

But he had only ever truly cared for one.

Now, she was gone from his life, having made the decision for them both weeks before, and long before the letter even reached him on the other side of the world. She'd given him no chance of rebuttal, or opportunity for conversation. No time or space to talk, to question, or to understand.

It was over.

She'd made that perfectly and permanently clear.

Perhaps it was for the best. Perhaps he'd seen it coming, but never admitted it. They were ill matched from the beginning.

Perhaps true love would forever be evasive.

But he didn't have the time now, or the heart, to chase it.

Across the Italian countryside, the sound of bells rang out and echoed across the miles. Each little village of this old world had its own chapel, built from the generations of the faithful. The bells in the towers rang out long hallowed sounds that called forth the wandering ghosts of wars long past.

The lost souls seemed to wander aimlessly across the haunted grounds of this whole country. They were the spirits of the young men and women who had fought each other a century ago, for reasons they themselves never quite understood. So many had died in this country before they had even had a chance at life.

And there were some spirits that still roamed, especially in the pitch black of night, not yet accepting that they were long dead and the world war they'd fought so desperately in had ended generations ago.

The abandoned hanger on base was one place they still haunted. And the woods down the barricaded road still whispered of commanding German voices and Italian screams.

He shook his head to clear the thoughts of such atrocities. But the desolate loneliness hung heavy in the air.

It was six o'clock in the evening, with only a whisp of daylight left. He gritted his jaw against his own heartache, carefully strapped up, and climbed back on the road bike. He had a few more miles to ride the old Italian motorcycle before he sold it for much more than he'd paid for it. It wasn't worth shipping back to the states.

He'd go home to the Harley he'd had since college, still safely stored in his brother's garage.

He paused.

Too bad there would be no bride-to-be to welcome him home.

But he was going home, whether he wanted to or not. The military didn't keep the likes of him around longer than they had to, no matter how many medals adorned his uniform.

Twenty years in was long enough, considering, they said. He had the training to do anything in civilian life, they said. While his injuries had not kept him out of the sky yet, they would eventually ground him forever. *They said.*

The Air Force was walking him into retirement, at the grand age of forty-one.

Who was he kidding?

It was time to move on, and just start a new life.

Carefully, he placed his right foot on the far pedal of the motorcycle and then pushed off with his other. It didn't take long for him to pick up speed down the narrow road that switch-backed down the mountainside, gently swerving now and then for a lost shadow still trying to find their way to the light.

Chapter One

Lightening crashed around them, and the thunder reverberated through their black Escalade. Pete Parker glanced over at his wife.

The storm had come out of nowhere tonight and caught them out on the open highway deep in East Texas country. They were thirty minutes from home, coming back from visiting his mother at Hideaway Lake. The day had been warm and sticky, a foreboding heaviness that even weighed their spirits down. They had left barely fifteen minutes ago, having stayed an hour too long, and hadn't been watching the unpredictable spring weather.

They'd left his mother's house as the sky turned a sick shade of green, and lighting cut across the sky. Thunder clapped, then rolled into the distance. Just five minutes after leaving, the sky went black with the storm clouds. Now, it was too dark to see.

But something was out there. Pete could feel it.

From her place in the front passenger seat, Jena Parker glanced over her shoulder at the six-month-old baby twin girls in the back seat. They were strapped securely in their car seats, but the thunder had jarred them from their sweet slumber, and now they were fussing. Jena unbuckled her own seatbelt and leaned through the opening between the driver and front passenger seats. Her graceful hand touched each one of the babies and she cooed soft words to quiet their whimpers.

"Mommy's here," she said. "It's alright. Just a little rain."

Jena turned back around and reached for the diaper bag at her feet. She dug past the diapers and wipes. Their pacifiers might comfort them for a little while longer.

Pete observed his wife. At thirty-five and after the recent birth of her babies, Jena was still amazingly drop dead gorgeous.

She was petite and slender, and had always reminded him of a sexy country star. Her layered shoulder length blonde hair curled in all the right places. Her soft suntan accentuated the tiny freckles on her cheeks. She'd been a cheerleader in high school. But she wasn't a school girl anymore. She owned her own high dollar corporate consulting business and was the Vice President of the Junior League. She was smart, and gracious and a beautiful woman. Her tiny babies were a spitting image of her. They were even starting to smile like her, all lit up from within.

"Are the girls alright?" Pete looked her way again.

Jena glanced over at her husband of five years.

"They are either mad, wet, dirty, hungry, or thirsty. Or all of the above," Jena smiled wearingly. "But I can only address one of those right now. I haven't gotten my Supermom t-shirt yet."

The vehicle hydroplaned in the rain, but only for a moment. Jena braced herself against the back of the seat to counter balance.

"It's getting ugly out there," Pete remarked, slowing the speed down. He was six inches taller than her five foot five, and was baseball player husky. He was waiting for word back from the Texas Rangers regarding a position in the team office. If he got that job, they'd be living the dream. They'd have to move to Dallas, of course, but it would be a great opportunity. He shot her a nervous smile. "It's a nasty storm, but nothing to worry about."

But Jena could see that his knuckles were white from gripping the steering wheel. Wind buffeted them back and forth, and the sound of thunder and wind grew around them and suddenly seemed deafening.

"How much longer in this weather, do you think?" Jena asked loudly. She was about to climb in the back seat with the girls and attempt to feed them. Her breasts were full and tingling, and the girls' crying wasn't helping one bit.

"All I see are flashing tail lights. Everyone's stopping up here," he said. "Maybe we should too. The rain is so hard right now, I can't see the stripes in the road. The water's getting high."

"Maybe we should have waited out the storm, like your mom asked. She practically begged us."

"My mother worries too much. We'll be fine. Turn on the radio. See if you can find the weather. We're so close to home, but we might have to pull over and wait this thing out."

Jena fumbled with the diaper bag for a moment, getting it out of the way. Then she reached over and turned on the radio dial. The babies kept crying.

The storm intensified around them, then the rain suddenly stopped and an eerie, menacing omen blanketed them.

There was static on the radio, then a male voice broke through clear and strong. "*…immediate shelter. Do not attempt to outrun the storm. Again, this is a dangerous tornado. If you are on Interstate 20 near Highway 69, pull off and seek shelter immediately. Do not stop under bridges or overpasses*."

"We're on I-20," Pete said. His expression changed drastically and he swallowed hard.

"Pull off, Pete."

The wind started buffeting their vehicle and rocking it hard.

Pete's voice raised an octave. "Where's the damn storm? Pull up the radar on your phone, Jena."

She reached into her purse and was searching for her phone when the lightening crashed beside them, not twenty yards away. Then it started to hail huge stones. The hail smashed into their windshield and battered the roof. Their windshield cracked with each hailstone and the cracks splintered into tiny webs.

The radio squawked again. "*…this is a tornado warning. Take immediate shelter around Interstate 20 and Highway…*"

"I can't get any reception! Pull off, Pete!" Jena tossed the phone on the floor board and reached back again toward the girls.

"Where is there to pull off?" Pete yelled over the roaring of the storm. "All the cars are stopping ahead and I don't see an exit."

"There's the exit!" Jena answered, frantically.

They both glanced over to see the highway sign billowing in the wind. It said *Highway 69 Ahead.* Then it was ripped from the poles and went flying into the dark.

"Pete!"

"Just buckle in, Jena." he said. "We're getting off this road!" Then the windshield started shattering from the hail and they were pelted as the shards of glass and rain blew across the dash.

Jena glanced back at the babies, then quickly reached for her seatbelt and wrestled it across her body. She fumbled with the buckle until she heard the hard click. From the radio came the horrible, chill-inducing tone of the Emergency Alert System.

"Why is all of the traffic stopping ahead of us, Pete?"

"For the same reason we are. Damn it! I can't see a thing!"

"Just stop, Pete! Get under the overpass!"

"Don't tell me how to drive right now!" Pete shouted. He leaned forward over the steering wheel. The babies screamed louder from the back seat. The hail came harder and faster.

Pete stared ahead. "Oh my god!" The color suddenly drained from his face. "Shit!"

"What?" Jena snapped at him. When he didn't answer, she turned to look at him. But his face was contorted in terror, staring straight ahead. She turned to look where he was looking.

"…oh God," she breathed inaudibly.

Around them, the roar was deafening. Ahead of them, cars were sucked out from the shelter beneath the bridge and slung like Match Box cars across the highway. And with them came flying metal, tires, pieces of the bridge, and uprooted trees. Debris smashed across the hood before it went flying off.

Lightening flashed like rocket mortars, illuminating the black sky and back lighting the rotating monster in front of them. Jena only stared. The freight train rumble of the ghastly vortex permeated the world around them. The pressure suddenly dropped and her ears popped. She opened her mouth to scream, but the scream never made it past her lips.

"Holy Mother of God!" Her husband yelled and slammed on the brakes.

The Escalade swerved on the slick payment and side-winded across three lanes. Then the back end of the vehicle took flight. He fought desperately to gain control.

But it was too late.

Pete Parker had driven directly into the path of the F4 tornado.

* * *

Time stood still.

Jena was in another dimension of time and space. A different kind of place. A twilight zone. But it was peaceful. Strangely peaceful. But so very dark.

Then bright lights exploded through her consciousness and yanked her back into reality. Screaming voices drowned out the roar of the thunder. Cold rain stung her face. And there was agonizing pain! There was a dull sickening reverberation as the sound of death and terror fell away into the night, like the low rumble of a freight train moving away and on down the mountain. There was the grinding buzz of a chainsaw, and people desperately hollering out for loved ones.

Jena tried to open her eyes, but they were matted with blood and skin tissue from her own face. Someone touched her hand. She recoiled away. She felt so cold and started shaking uncontrollably.

Overhead, the oscillating chop-chop-chop of helicopter blades cut through the night. There were a thousand sirens in the distance. Coming closer. More yelling voices. Wailing. Radios squealing.

She took in a labored breath and grimaced from the pain, then she reached out her bloodied hand toward the light.

"Be still, Ma'am. You can't move."

Jena tried to wipe the wet goo from her eyes.

"Please, Ma'am. You've gotta be still. We'll get you out."

She tried to talk but nothing came out, save a deep and mournful moan.

Then hands were all over her. Someone was pulling her leg.

"Be careful!" A frantic voice. "Her leg is pinned!"

Lightening flashed and penetrated through her pain.

The dragon named darkness clamped her between its teeth and shook her violently in its mouth. But she fought against it. It couldn't take her.

She had to… What? What did she have to do? She couldn't remember. But there was no more time!

"Get the jaws! We're going to have to cut her out!"

Flashing red and blue lights reflected off her eyelids. More yelling. More shouting. More pulling. Excruciating sorrow.

"Hold on, Ma'am. We're getting you out!"

She screamed through broken ribs as the jaws of life pried apart the door that was wrapped around her leg.

Then she remembered.

"…my babies," she whispered.

Fire exploded through her body as they lifted her out of the mangled remains of the high-dollar vehicle.

"She's talking to us, but she's bleeding all over the place! Has the Care Flight landed?"

She whimpered again and again. But her words were inaudible.

"Watch her neck. Get the backboard under her!" someone ordered.

Then the world went black as Jena Parker was strapped on the backboard stretcher, her neck immobilized, and her leg wrapped tight to delay the draining of her own blood. Four firemen lifted the stretcher and scrambled precariously over debris to the waiting Care Flight helicopter.

Two minutes later, the chopper lifted off, still cautious of the outflow winds from the killer storm that had passed not an hour earlier. It hovered for a few seconds over the carnage on the highway, now lit by floodlights and the frantic strobe of emergency vehicle lights.

Then the chopper powered up and banked toward the nearest trauma hospital.

Chapter Two

"Incoming from the helipad!"

The automatic doors of the emergency entrance swung wide and the paramedics raced the stretcher through. The emergency room was a war zone as physicians and staff raced to receive yet another victim. There was blood and mud all over the stretcher, and the first responders held the IV lines up over their shoulders. They were covered in blood and mud, as well.

The head trauma nurse stopped them in the hall and looked down at the female casualty. She couldn't tell much except that she was female, blonde, and young, perhaps in her thirties. The victim's face was hardly recognizable, and she was unconscious, probably having sustained some head injury. The victim seemed familiar, but the nurse couldn't make out all her features. She felt strangely connected, and for a moment, her heart broke. Then the nurse backed away and shouted orders, and the paramedics rushed the stretcher down the hall to the main trauma room.

In rapid response, the trauma team took over and moved as one as they examined the horrible injuries. One of the legs was mangled. Obvious internal and head trauma. Bleeding from every limb. They paid particular attention to the gashes on the head and the right leg. Her blood pressure dropped and the patient started convulsing. Then she went suddenly still.

"She's crashing! No heartbeat!" An intern grabbed the defibrillator.

Another intern ripped open Jena's shirt and cut away her bra in lightning speed. Then the intern wiped away the mud and blood, and stood back.

The ER doctor took the defibrillator. "Stand clear!" Then he shocked her.

"Got nothing…"

"Clear!"

Boom! Another shock.

From the heart monitor came the faint beep of a heartbeat grasping for life.

Within two minutes they had the victim stabilized enough to literally race her toward surgery. There was no time to do anything else. She was losing too much blood way too fast. The surgery team was waiting and claimed her at the surgery door.

The charge nurse, who'd been assisting, now stood in the middle of the hall, blood all down the front of her scrubs. The young woman on the stretcher was a nursing mother. The nurse had noticed it when they ripped the bra away to shock her. The stretcher cleared the surgery area doors.

Then the doors closed as another Code Blue sounded.

The nurse turned and ran back down the hall, yelling for someone, anyone, to start calling in reserve medical staff.

Three more ambulances arrived, and the trauma team raced out to receive more victims. But these victims were already gone. One white male. Two female infants.

The nurse followed the stretcher with the babies to the trauma rooms. Two paramedics quietly stood over the stretcher, as if guarding it now, almost not letting her near it. Then they backed away. Their faces were streaked with tears. Slowly, they shook their heads.

"We tried forever to revive them," one whispered.

The nurse went over and pulled back the sheet. She tenderly caressed their faces and the blonde curls on their heads. One by one, she memorized their faces. She followed protocol and checked their vitals.

But she knew they were gone, and had been gone for a while.

Strangely, there were no evidence of devastating injuries to their small bodies. No marks of hard trauma. They looked like two little cherubs who had fallen from the sky.

"Don't leave them here like this," she whispered to no one, for the paramedics had already quietly left. Gently, she wiped off the mud from their dainty innocent faces, and carefully wrapped each of them in a clean sheet, leaving their faces free.

Then she pulled out her phone and called Pediatrics ICU. She couldn't just send them to the morgue. No, she couldn't send them to that dark smelly dungeon in the basement.

She stayed with the babies until Pediatrics arrived. She touched each face one last time, then wiped the tears from her own eyes. She grabbed her stethoscope from the stretcher and followed Pediatrics out the door. They turned left toward the elevator.

The charge nurse, not even out of her thirties herself, stopped, put her hand in her pocket and pulled out the bloody driver's license that had come in with the young woman, now in surgery. She wiped off the picture. Then, she memorized that face, too.

Most likely, the babies were hers.

Another ambulance arrived with two more victims, an older man, and his wife. They were bloody, but conscious and talking, and the nurse prayed they'd make it. They were someone's parents or grandparents.

More and more ambulances arrived. Some victims were in critical condition, some walking, and some were deceased. Even more were brought in via pick-up trucks, by neighbors in SUVs, and by good Samaritans in cars.

The night dragged on, and more and more victims were wheeled into Emergency and rolled over wet, sticky, crimson floors. Radios blared. Orders barked. Extra medical teams that had been called in from their weekend started racing through the doors. Volunteers showed up to help. Family members flooded the ER and waiting rooms for any word of their loved ones. It was mayhem, as the hospital responded to the most devastating tornado in the history of the area.

By morning, forty-eight had died. Four hundred were given medical attention at this hospital alone. Twenty-seven were in critical condition. And one was still in surgery, fighting for her life.

* * *

Jena Parker put her hand on the knob and opened the French doors that led out to the swimming pool. It was a beautiful day with brilliant sunshine and the scent of honeysuckle and roses in the air. Birds sang from the magnolia tree on the far side of the yard. Music came from the other side of the wrought iron fence. The water in the pool was translucent and aqua blue.

"Hi, Mommy!"

Two little girls, around five years old, emerged simultaneously from the shallow end of the pool, their blonde hair slick from the water. Their eyes were alit with innocence and joy. Their little swimsuits clung to their child bodies like plastic wrap. They were laughing as they came toward her.

"Hello," Jena whispered.

"Come play with us!"

Jena looked at them and smiled.

From the far side of the pool, Pete raised his head from a book and gleamed at her. His expression was full of love. Then he stood up from the pool lounge chair and walked toward her, his saunter slow and easy, his arms opened wide. "Hello, Baby."

"Hello," Jena whispered to him.

"Come play with us, Mommy!" the two little girls called again. Then they tagged each other and raced for the pool.

"Stay with us," Pete said. He was almost to her.

Then the timer on the kitchen stove started beeping.

* * *

The surgeon barked orders as the anesthesiologist slipped her farther under the anesthesia. But they couldn't take her much farther under, without chancing her slipping completely away.

A nurse wiped the sweat from the surgeon's brow. They'd been at it for four hours. They'd lost her twice. But the miracle of medicine brought her back each time.

The surgeon was trying hard, but didn't know for sure if he could save her leg, or even her life. She'd lost so much blood. But the morning was still young and he knew she didn't have a chance without him.

* * *

Jena was walking along the nature trail by a lake. It was mid-morning, and the clouds floated by without a sound. But she could hear boats far out on the lake, and the voices of people calling to one another. Laughing.

She heard her name and turned back toward the trees. Pete was walking toward her. He had his backpack on and was carrying his favorite walking stick. Walking alongside of him were two beautiful teenage girls in shorts and halter tops, holding hands and singing the silliest song.

"We thought we might find you down here by the lake," Pete said, his face alight with happiness. "We've missed you."

"…Pete," Jena breathed.

"Come walk with us, Mom," the teenage girls beckoned. "The trail isn't too hard. We've walked it a hundred times."

Pete looked up and waved to someone behind her. He seemed so happy and relaxed.

A young man, perhaps thirty, appeared from the opposite direction. He was clad in old jeans and a t-shirt, and motioned to a Labrador to stay close to him. "Hello. I hope you are enjoying yourselves," the young man said kindheartedly.

Pete grinned. "We are! Look who came to see us."

The young man walked closer and stopped when he got to Jena. "Hello, Jena."

She glanced at him, trying to remember. He was so familiar, but just out of reach of her recollection. "Do I know you?"

The young man grinned. "Yes, you do."

"I can't seem to remember."

"You will."

Pete turned to Jena. "Can you stay this time? We are always hoping you will stay."

Jena stared at her husband, confused.

"It's alright," Pete said, reaching out to her but not quite touching her. "We can wait forever. It's not long at all."

The girls blew a kiss at her, then they went on down the trail and disappeared around the next bend. Pete followed them, glancing only once over his shoulder back in her direction. Then he was gone, too.

Jena turned to the young man, who was still standing beside her. "Why did they leave?"

He smiled. "They didn't leave. You just haven't arrived."

She started to question. Should she feel sad? But she wasn't sad at all.

"All in time, Jena."

Then the young man turned and walked back up the trail he'd come, whistling for the lab to follow.

***

An alarm sounded.

Jena groaned and tried to turn her head.

But it was in a vise grip and any attempt to move at all only sent stabbing pain through her neck and head. Her face burned. She couldn't feel her body. Her throat was raw and on fire. And there was a stick down her throat. Her eyes were swollen shut and, try though she did, she couldn't open them.

"Lie still." The feminine voice was kind.

Jena tried to turn toward it.

A door opened and closed. People whispered in the doorway.

"She's fighting the tube." The female said. "She can't be fighting the tube."

Someone touched her arm.

“I think she might be trying to come back to us.” A different voice. A deeper voice. A man’s voice.

“She doesn’t know,” the female whispered.

Silence.

Finally, the deep voice whispered. “She’ll know soon enough. Let’s get her out of the woods, first. One day at a time.”

A few moments later Jena felt the cool dampness of a cloth on her cheek. A gentle fingertip applied moisturizer to her bruised and swollen lips, and then rubbed a tiny piece of ice across the parchedness there. She tried to breathe. She wanted to breathe. But something was already breathing for her.

So, she stopped fighting and went back down into the abyss.

***

The day was beautiful. The sunlight was coming through the trees. Birds sang. A cloud wisped by above.

Jena felt a cool breeze across her face.

She was in a beautiful park of some kind. So many trees and flowers and stone walls. Stone markers. There was a huge crowd gathering around small tents.

Jena stood a little away from them and watched curiously, yet strangely detached.

Her friends from church were all there, as were her neighbors and her colleagues…her clients…and Esther. They were standing around in the soft new grass under the trees. Why were they all crying? Why were they all hugging each other? So many colorful flowers in all arrays. So many black cars parked along the narrow road that meandered through the park.

Two little girls played by the roses.

Pete was standing by her. She looked over at him and he smiled.

***

The voices were back, soft around her. “How is she doing?”

"It's touch and go." The man's voice again. "I need to take her back into surgery, but I can't risk it. She's too weak. She's barely breathing, even with the ventilator. Her oxygen levels are still low."

"I saw her when she arrived. God, it was awful. I'm shocked they didn't lose her in the chopper." A sigh. "What are her chances?"

"I'm not sure she has any," he replied.

Jena heard them talking from far, far away. Then she felt lips close to her ear. "Jena, you have to fight. Do you hear me? You have to fight."

***

Jena held her dolly close to her chest and cried. They told her Granny died. Now, there were so many people in her house. She scooted farther back in her parents' closet, and hid behind her mother's dresses. The only thing that comforted her was the fragrance of her mother's sweet perfume.

Then, she saw her father's hand reaching through the dresses and she took it. He gently pulled her out and lifted her into his arms. "It's alright, baby girl."

***

"She's got to try and breathe on her own," a male voice said.

It felt like her throat had been ripped out. She tried to scream, but nothing came out. There were growls coming from beneath her bed. Her panic escalated. A mask was slapped on her face.

Then the pinprick. The warm water flowed over her again and she relaxed into the flood. She would go now where it took her.

***

She was late for prom. She checked her makeup and applied lipstick to her lips. Her high school crush had finally asked her.

Maybe he'd kiss her tonight. Her slip bothered her so she stepped out it and threw it on the bed. She heard the doorbell ring, and suddenly hands were all over her. Then the mule kicked her in the chest.

***

Jena groaned and awoke to incredulous pain rocketing through her body. She painstakingly opened one eye. No one was there. The room was dark except for the one light by the door. She was weighed down by ten thousand pounds of penetrating sorrow that she didn't understand. The world spun away. She retreated into the darkness of nothingness.

***

It was dark in space. And so very, very still. Far away, in the distance, she saw the galaxies of the millenniums swirling slowly toward infinity. Time was in no hurry. She was pulled backward into a hole and then went flying across the dark expanse of sky toward a distant light.

Then the light above her flared bright and she squinted against the brilliance. Someone put a mask over her face and told her to breathe. Someone else touched her arm and told her to relax. Her body suddenly had no feeling and she felt her arms fall away. Then the stars winked at her.

***

Her eyes fluttered, and she emerged from the darkness and the dreams. The aroma of coffee woke her. The morning news played quietly above her.

Someone was there with her, by the window. Jena tried to clear her throat. The shadow stood and came close.

Voices out in the hall.

Her feet were cold. She closed her eyes.

***

Jena heard singing.

She stirred, trying for one clear breath.

Her ribs hurt.

Her arms hurt.

Her legs hurt.

She felt buried in cement.

Someone checked her pulse and then reached over her head for something.

"Good morning, Mrs. Parker." A new voice. "It's good to see you this morning."

Jena wanted to throw up.

"A little more pain meds, now, and you can go back to sleep for just a while."

Jena swallowed the bile in her throat and drifted away.

***

The smell of roses again.

She struggled to open one eye.

It was morning.

She slowly turned her head, and winced. There were roses on the table by her bed. Her heart was beating fast.

Her soul hurt horribly.

She didn't understand.

She closed her eyes and passed out.

***

"Time to rouse a bit, dear," came the soft order of a foreign voice.

Nigerian?

"Yes, I see you there trying to wake up."

Jena grimaced against the pain. It was a fire that consumed her body and soul.

"Do you know where you are?" The voice was soothing, but hard to understand.

Jena shook her head slowly. *No.*

"Ok, then," the voice reassured. "It's too early yet." The person behind the voice adjusted the sheet.

Jena tried to speak, but nothing came out.

The nurse bent down to listen.

"Where…am…I?" Jena whispered.

The nurse smiled and covered Jena's hand with her own. "You are safe. Try and rest for now."

Then she was gone, and Jena drifted off to sleep.

***

Jena opened both eyes and looked around.

The room was empty.

The roses were wilting a little. The sun was too bright coming in through the window shades.

She took a deep breath and found she could, for the first time without excruciating pain, breathe. But it still hurt like hell. Her chest felt like an elephant was sitting on it.

She looked at the array of monitors around her, and down at the sling holding her pinned leg aloft.

She was groggy and disoriented and confused. And her heart bore such utter sorrow. She blinked slowly. Another deep breath.

Jena tried to brush the cobwebs and confusion away.

The door opened.

A man came in. He was tall, dark, and carried a chart in his hands. He was reading it when he heard her make a whimpered sound. "Good morning," he said quietly.

She blinked in response.

He smiled sadly. "You've had a tough go, Mrs. Parker. I was hoping we would get you back sooner."

She stared at him.

"I'm Dr. Riley. I've been caring for you."

Slowly, ever so slowly, her body was waking up. And as her body woke up, her heart burned.

"Do you know your first name?" he quietly asked.

She whispered her name. "…Jena."

"Do you know where you are?"

Jena slowly nodded. "…hospital."

"Do you remember what happened?"

Jena was still. Then she said one word. "Water."

Dr. Riley nodded. "I think we can do something about that." He disappeared for a minute, then reappeared with a cup and a straw.

"Don't lift your head, Jena. You've had a major concussion. I'm going to let you have a few drops through the straw."

She looked up into blue eyes.

He looked down into hers. "Let's take this slow."

They did. Each drop was painstakingly administered and received through bruised lips. When he was done, she carefully reached out to touch him.

"You're welcome, Jena. Little sips, ok?"

She nodded slowly.

"You're still in ICU, so everything is in little steps."

She closed her eyes. It was of no use. She had no more fight.

Dr. Riley adjusted her IV drip, then her leg sling. He checked the bandages that were wrapped around her leg like a cocoon.

He watched her closely, then checked her vitals before covering her bare shoulders with the sheet and leaving her to find her way back to the world of the living.

***

"Mommy."

Sweet voices called to her in her dreams. She turned to see where they came from. They were just beyond her sight, somewhere out there in the shadows between life and death and life again.

"We're ok, Mommy. Don't be sad."

"I love you, Babe," Pete whispered in her ear. "Be strong."

***

Two days later Jena woke up….and remembered.

Tears were pooling in her blue eyes when the nurse walked in to take her vitals.

Expecting her to still be asleep or groggy, the nurse went about the routine for a full two minutes before she realized that Jena was awake, looking at her, and suffering so silently.

"Hello, precious," the nurse said, bending down a bit.

Jena slowly reached out to her.

"I know, sweet thing. It hurts. But there are no worries." She gently patted her arm. "We are all here for you. You've got to fight through this and come back to us."

Jena shook her head no.

"Talk to me, precious," the nurse gently urged.

"…fam…lee."

The nurse paused and looked sadly down at the patient. She wasn't the one to tell her. What family she had left was waiting outside in the waiting room. They should be the ones to tell her.

"Let me get your doctor. Give me just a minute. Everything is going to be alright." Then she walked out of the room.

Jena turned her face to the window.

She knew. No one had to tell her.

She was groggy, but she was awake enough to remember what had happened. Heartbreak screamed from her soul and she tried to let it out. But it strangled in her throat.

She lay there alone, in terror of the reality awaiting.

The door of her room eventually opened. Dr. Riley slowly walked in. He was in his late thirties and walked in with a little bit of a swagger. He was in a suit and tie. He looked relaxed and at peace with the world.

"Good morning, Jena. The nurses paged me," he said gently. He checked her vitals, then wrote in her chart. He pulled a chair alongside her bed and sat down. He reached for her hand.

At first, she was still and her hand was lifeless. Then, like a tiny signal of response, she wrapped her fingers around his.

They sat there quietly, but the sorrow welled in her eyes. He took a tissue and wiped one lone tear that escaped. He didn't say a word, but patiently waited for her. He couldn't rush it. He didn't know where she was mentally and emotionally. He needed to tread carefully and monitor her cognitive abilities.

"Tell me," she finally whispered.

"Your mother-in-law is outside. Do you want her?"

"No," Jena said almost inaudibly. She took a labored breath. "You. Tell me."

"We have chaplains to help through these things." Dr. Riley stared into her eyes. "This isn't easy, Jena. For either one of us."

She nodded that she understood.

"You were in the tornado." He reminded her. "It picked up your car." When she didn't respond, he shifted uncomfortably in the chair, but didn't let go of her hand. "You were with your family."

Her eyes could not hold back the terror racing through her.

He wiped her face again, softly, gently. He scooted closer to her bedside and held her one hand now with both of his. "They found you alive in the wreckage."

She nodded once, then squeezed his hand again.

He felt himself getting emotional, and swallowed the lump in his own throat. He'd been determined not to let any of his patients affect him ever again. But this patient was different. She'd gotten to his heart. She was so beautiful and innocent, and injured, and had lost everything.

Time stood still for both of them in that tiny hospital room. If neither one of them said it out loud, there was still hope that what she remembered had all been a nightmare.

"They found your family. Your husband. Your babies."

He caressed her hand, as though that simple gesture might ease the blow of the truth. Then he leaned in to her.

"They didn't make it, Jena."

Jena swallowed. Then the tears flooded from her eyes and raced down her bruised cheeks.

"A lot of people died that night in the storm. You almost did. You were Care Flighted here. It's been four weeks since the storm. You've been in a coma and heavily sedated since."

Jena stared at him, with a questioned look in her eyes.

"Today is April, the twenty-sixth," he said quietly.

She rolled her lips together. He reached around for a cup of water and a new straw and offered her one drop at a time. She took each drop slowly, rolling them across her lips before she let them slip into her mouth.

Then she slowly pulled her hand from his and painstakingly turned her face to the window.

He sat with her for the longest time, not saying a word or moving. And when he was sure that she'd slipped off again, he quietly rose and walked out the room. But not before stopping by the sink counter and studying the 8 x 10 portrait of a beautiful young mother holding two newborn baby girls. A tall handsome man stood beside them.

The young woman in the portrait was smiling and radiant and gloriously happy. A family member had brought the picture, erringly hoping that it might bring comfort one day.

He glanced back at his patient in the bed.

First, do no harm.

But it was too late.

Harm was already done.

Chapter Three

They took her off the critical list and took her out of ICU six weeks after the tornado.

The days rolled into nights and into days and back into nights again. Over and over. It was an endless cycle of excruciating pain and unbearable heartache. Jena tried to die. She tried to let go and let the darkness come and swallow her, too.

She willed herself to die.

She knew her heart had stopped once in the ER, twice in surgery, and once more in the ICU. She set off the Code Blue, but they always started her heart again.

There was no one to help her die.

They were all trying too hard to keep her alive.

Days came and went, just like the storm that killed her family. She had no hope or will to live. The nurses and doctors and chaplains and therapists all came. And then they went away again, when it was obvious they were talking to a shell of woman who had no interest in talking to anyone… or even living.

Dr. Riley came every day. He let her try and use a straw. She was so thirsty, and carefully leaned forward to take the straw between her lips. But the water dribbled down her chin and onto her gown. She groaned and pushed it away.

The black bruising turned to purple, then purple to an ugly dark lavender that covered her entire body.

She didn't speak much. There was nothing to say.

But there was much to say behind that veil of pain. There were so many thoughts and regrets and questions. And there was guilt. But she couldn't speak of it. She couldn't put into words the depth of her loss, or her fear. There were no words to describe the utter devastation of her heart. She had no need for words.

Her mother-in-law came to visit her after a while. She'd been there in the beginning. She was the one who had to identify Pete and the girls. Then all the arrangements for the funerals took her time and effort and energy. The older woman had gone deep down into grief and depression and an unrelenting anger emerged, and she couldn't bring herself to come see her daughter-in-law for the longest time. Not after the storm had taken her only son and grandbabies, and left her daughter-in-law the only one to survive.

None of the feelings made sense. And Esther was ashamed.

When Jena's mother-in-law realized that she was being ridiculously unfair and unloving, she returned to the hospital. Jena had not created the tragedy. So, Esther tried again to visit. But every time she walked in Jena's room, Jena was either down the hall for tests, or asleep. Esther had almost given up and retreated into her own grief and isolation.

But today she'd come again, hoping to see Jena.

Jena was laying there, staring out the window, when her mother-in-law entered the hospital room.

"Hello?" Esther, whispered from the doorway.

Jena slowly turned her head.

"They said you might be awake," Esther stood, waiting. "Can I come in?"

A slow pathetic motion of her hand indicated Jena's permission. Esther closed the door behind her and moved carefully into the room, stopping for a moment to put down her purse by the only chair.

"Hello, darling."

"...Esther," Jena responded after a few long seconds.

They'd been close from the beginning, when Esther had taken Jena in her arms the moment they'd first met.

"They said I shouldn't stay more than five minutes, but I had to see you today. I've come quite a bit, but end up waiting in the waiting room for hours."

"I'm sorry," Jena whispered. She was still hooked up to an array of monitors and tubes and an I.V. And her throat was still raw from the breathing tube. Her voice was raspy and weak.

Esther moved closer to the bed and pulled up the chair.

It was hard to think of what to say. She'd had a little time to process the horrible loss of Pete and the children. She'd be able to weep and mourn and wail, and see their bodies one last time to say goodbye. Esther had had the blessing of friends to help ease the trauma. But Jena had been in a coma all that time, and was now waking up and was just processing the horror of it all.

"I love you, Jena," Esther said quietly. Then she gently took Jena's hand in her own. "They told me that you remembered what happened."

Jena stared at Esther; her eyes void of any life.

Esther's eyes teared up. "I'm so sorry, darling Jena."

An alarm went off in another room. Jena heard the hurried steps of nurses rushing to the emergency. Voices. Then things settled down and the room was quiet again.

"You…," Jena drew in a labored breath, "You lost too."

Esther turned away and stood up out of the chair to retrieve a tissue. "It was a tragedy. So horrible. So many gone."

"It came out of nowhere," Jena whispered. She struggled with her words. "Pete didn't see it. I didn't see it."

Esther was quiet. She knew the pain. Yet experiencing the death of her only son was more than she expected, or on most days, could handle.

Jena slowly reached for her. "Help me."

"What is it, dear?" Esther leaned closer.

"...help me."

Esther looked at her daughter-in-law. "I don't understand what you are asking, Jena."

Jena blinked and one lone tear fell. "Let me go, too."

"Let you go?" Esther felt her own tears rush to the surface. "Why no. I can't let you go, too. You must live, Jena. You must live for them." *You must live for me.*

The tears came rapidly, then, and flowed down Jena's face. She was alert enough to realize the devastated life ahead of her. She was broken. Crushed. Dead, but still living.

Esther slowly stood and let go of Jena's hand. She couldn't stay any longer. "You need to rest, dear."

Jena closed her eyes.

She was trapped in her broken body in a room of beeping machines keeping her alive and monitoring her every move, in case they had to intervene again to bring her back.

There was no family.

Her parents had died, two years apart, when she was in her twenties. She had no siblings. No extended family. Esther was all she had in family, but Esther was not in a place to comfort. And certainly, not in a place to assist Jena in giving up.

Jena felt buried alive in her own grief, and paralyzed by her injuries. She was imprisoned, locked in a hospital bed with tubes everywhere, not even able to reach for a cool cup of water.

"I'll leave and let you get some rest," Esther said. "Don't give up, Jena. You must fight. You are so young. You will make it through all of this. You must." She leaned down and placed a tender kiss on Jena's wet cheek.

Then, she was gone.

And Jena was alone again to fight the desolation.

***

Dr. Riley came by the next morning and was patiently waiting for her to wake up.

"Good morning, Jena."

She slowly opened her eyes.

"I heard your mother-in-law came by yesterday."

Jena slowly nodded.

"She said you're giving up. Is that true?"

Jena looked him in the eyes. She didn't say a word, but let her eyes convey the utter devastation of her heart and soul. Behind her, the morning sun filtered through the window.

She didn't know what day it was. She didn't care.

"Are you giving up?" His voice was gentle and kind. He came to sit next to her by the bed, like he always did.

She didn't answer.

"So," he smiled sweetly. "Are you going to talk to me?"

She didn't answer.

"Are you angry?"

Jena stared at him, before she turned her head away and pretended to go to sleep.

"Look at me, Jena," he commanded. 'Turn your head and look at me. This is important."

Slowly, she complied.

"I want you to listen to me. Can you do that?"

She nodded, but knew that whatever he had to say wouldn't make a difference in how she felt. She felt nothing, yet everything.

"I know what it's like to want to die, to just close your eyes and die," he said. "For every waking moment is torture."

Jena stared at him.

"And you feel so isolated in that torture. Pinned to a life that is holding you captive to emptiness and sorrow."

She nodded slowly, her eyes betraying the truth he spoke.

"I'm three years older than you. I married young." He paused to see if she was still with him. She was. "She was beautiful, like you. My wife. We did everything together. Skiing, hiking, camping, hang gliding. Loving."

He paused to remember and smiled sadly.

"She was the love of my life. She died an hour after our son was born. He was three and a half months premature. I lost her to a blood clot. My son died five days later, the day of her funeral."

Jena lifted her eyebrows ever so slightly.

"My wife. My son. Two funerals in one week." He stopped and glanced out the window, and swallowed hard. Then he turned back to her. "I know what you are feeling. It hurts like hell."

She clenched her jaw and fought the sobs threatening to erupt out of her heart.

"It's going to hurt like hell for a long time,' he said gently. "I can't say anything right now that is going to take away this pain. It is what it is. It stays a long time, buries itself deep into the psyche, and becomes a part of us. It destroys us, or transforms us."

She watched him through her tears.

He nodded, somehow aware of her unspoken words.

"If we're wise, we'll look for the sun to rise and choose to keep breathing," he said. "At first, every breath is an effort. Then, every day is an effort. Some days we are buried in the darkness of it all. And, after a while, the days turn into weeks again. The world keeps spinning around. The sun keeps shining. The birds keep singing. And one day, out of the blue, hope comes back."

He reached out and took her hand.

"You must keep breathing, Jena. You are too young to die. You are too beautiful to let go of this incredible gift of life. There is a reason you are still alive."

She started to shake her head no, but he stopped her.

"I know you don't understand why all of this happened the way it did. You may never understand."

She took a deep breath and then whispered. "Why did it?"

Dr. Riley sighed. He'd asked himself that same question so many times when it had happened to him. He leaned closer. "I don't know, Jena. I don't know."

She bit her lower lip, fighting the grief and the anger. "I love them so much."

"I know." He touched her cheek and wiped a tear away. "Just know that God holds them in safe keeping. Do you believe that?"

Jena turned her face from him. "I dreamed about them."

He was quiet and listened.

"I saw them," she whispered. "They all looked so happy. They kept asking me to stay with them."

Her IV bag alarm went off, and he reached up to turn it off.

"I'm lost, Dr. Riley," she whispered. "They were my only family. My loves."

"But you're not alone, Jena. We are all here together. We are going to get through this bittersweet thing called life."

She looked at him.

He smiled knowingly. "You are going to keep breathing. You are going to get well. You're going to walk again. And, you are going to love again."

She shook her head…no.

"Yes," he smiled. "And you are going to be loved. You cannot quit because of what has happened. You must believe there is more than this…this time…this place…this moment."

"Easy for you to say," she whispered.

"No, it's not easy for me to say. It took five years. Then I met someone. Now, we have three sons and a daughter, two dogs, and three turtles."

She almost smiled. But it never made it to her lips.

"One day at a time, Jena. That's all that is being asked of you. No more. Will you do that?"

"I can't even get past this moment."

"Then one moment at a time. We'll do this together. I'm not going anywhere. But I need you to do something. Promise me."

"…what?"

"Promise to keep breathing." He gently squeezed her hand. "That's all we're asking. Your family would want you to live. Fight for *them*. Live for *them*."

After the longest moment, she squeezed back.

That night, she had another dream. She was walking along a path. It was spring. She was holding hands with two young women, adults now, one on each side. They were quietly walking together. They looked like her. They smiled like she used to.

"Mom," one said. "Life is beautiful. It never ends."

Jena stopped and looked at them, feeling such a sudden joy from deep inside of her.

"Mom," the other said. "What we had together there, where you are, is made perfect here, where we are."

Then Jena woke up and it was morning again. She breathed in. Slowly. And then she breathed in again.

***

They moved her to another room a little farther down the hall from the nurses' station. It was a room with a magnificent view of a ten-acre wooded park. Bike trails and streams meandered through the trees. From her third-floor window, she could see the life there. Birds flew past her window on their way to the pond, and clouds floated by high above.

That same afternoon she started physical therapy, however modified to account for the pinned leg still in the cast. But getting her up out of the bed was a feat, and a triumph. All she could do was drape her legs over the side of the bed and sit up.

It was excruciating, but Jena never said a word.

The therapist cheered and clapped her hands together.

Jena wiped the sweat from her brow.

When she mentioned that she wanted to throw up, they carefully laid her back down again. It was enough that day.

Jena was rewarded with a Popsicle and pain medication.

She slept the rest of the day.

The next day they taught her how to stand with a walker. The doctor monitored her diet of clear liquids and she slowly, methodically ate cherry Jell-O one small spoonful at a time.

They removed the catheter and led her step by excruciating step toward the bathroom. That night, she sipped sweet tea through a straw and watched Who Wants to Be a Millionaire on the television.

The next day, the nurses and therapist wrapped her cast in plastic, led her to the shower, sat her on a stool, and bathed her head to toe. By the time she made it back to bed, she passed out from exhaustion. The TV stayed on through the night.

The next day Dr. Riley came to visit her.

"Hello, beautiful," he said sweetly as he came in the door. "I'm hearing great things about you."

He'd come to visit her every day after his rounds, since they moved her out of ICU. But he'd come in the afternoon after her physical therapy and always found her asleep.

"Hello." Jena replied, glad to see him, but sad to her core.

"I have good news," he declared.

"I could use some good news," she replied, despondently.

He nodded good-naturedly. "Your voice is stronger."

"I don't have a tube down my throat."

"Ah, yes," he grinned. "It was a necessary evil."

She watched him walk across the room and sit in his usual place. "What's the good news," she finally asked.

"We are upgrading your diet. From clear liquids to a soft diet. You can order anything you want…that's soft. Jello. Ice cream. Yogurt."

"I'm elated," she whispered. "I'm already eating Jell-O."

"Thought you would be." He checked her pulse. "Beating strong. That's good."

"I had another dream the night after you left."

He stopped writing on her chart and looked up.

"I saw them again. All three of them."

A game show was on, so Dr. Riley stood up and turned the TV set down so he could listen to her.

"They're gone," she whispered. "But they're not gone."

He watched her closely and saw the exact second the cognitive acceptance of the tragedy came through her eyes.

"What you said…" she whispered.

"And what was that?" He stayed where he was by the window.

"What you shared about losing your family. I don't feel so alone through this." She paused. "Today came again." Her voice was stronger this time. "I watched it from the window. And I kept breathing."

He wanted to hug her, but stayed his distance.

"But what am I supposed to do with it?" she asked softly.

He was still her attending physician, and his place was in surgery and his role was to distance. But he had become her friend.

"What am I supposed to do when tomorrow comes?"

"Just live," he whispered. "…one day at a time."

Jena let one breath escape, and she turned her face away. She felt her heart contract with the full brunt of fear of the unknown.

"Tiny steps, Jena," he reminded.

***

Over the next few days, she was visited by several of the ICU nurses who had cared for her during the weeks she was incapacitated. They brought her little gifts and remembrances and well wishes.

A single rose.

A card.

A balloon.

Her mother-in-law visited, too, never staying long, but always touching her softly before leaving. Friends from her church starting showing up, free to visit her now. No one knew what to say, so they conversed about meaningless things.

After a week, they took her back into surgery and took out the pin in her leg. It took her three more days to recover back to the point of mashed potatoes and applesauce.

Every morning, she spent one hour in the physical therapy room, one hour with a counselor, and one hour with an occupational therapist. By the time she got settled for an afternoon nap, the orthopedic doctor showed up and poked and prodded her to tears.

Her pastor came and reassured her that the church was keeping up on her mortgage and insurance and utilities, so not to worry about losing her house. The next day the insurance agent dropped in to find out more about the life and property loss.

House Hunters and Flip or Flop started repeating shows.

After two weeks out of ICU, another friend, a hair stylist, came, trimmed her hair and did her nails. After they were done, her friend helped her stand with the walker and make her way over to the small mirror over the tiny hospital room sink.

Jena lifted her head to look at herself. Her friend stood beside her and didn't say a word.

Jena stared for a long time. The bruising had all but disappeared. Three scars were still red on her forehead and cheek where they'd sewn her up from the glass and flying debris.

Her eyes were shadowed and guarded, no longer the open vibrant windows to her soul. Her lips were back to normal, although empty of kisses for little babies no longer in her life. And empty of Pete's kisses. But her hair was trimmed, washed, and movie star glamourous as it fell almost to her shoulders.

"Thank you," she whispered to her friend.

Her friend tenderly hugged her from behind, then left a few minutes later to go pick up her children at school.

Dr. Riley came later that afternoon. There'd been a shooting at a convenience store and surgery was over-run with victims.

"I like your hair," he mentioned.

She smiled sadly.

He looked down at her hands. When he'd first seen her, her fingers and nails were caked with blood and mud and flesh that had been sandpapered off her own body by the winds.

"Your nails look nice, too."

She nodded.

He watched her for a minute, then said that he would be right back. When he returned, he had a wheelchair. "Climb aboard. It's time we got you out of here for a while." He helped her with a soft satin robe her mother-in-law had brought up and left hanging in the closet. Then he laid a light blanket across her lap.

"Where are we going?"

"Trust me. You'll like it." Then he took the handles and led her out of her prison and down the hall to the elevator, past the nurses' station. "I'll be back later. I'm taking Mrs. Parker for a spin around the block."

The nurses smiled and waved them on.

An intern held the door and winked at Jena as she passed.

They'd all grown attached to the beautiful young woman who, despite her terrible injuries and great personal loss, was the perfect patient. She was very quiet, gracious and kind and more low maintenance that any other patient they'd ever had.

The elevator emptied them out on the ground floor by the lobby. Dr. Riley rolled her past the reception desk and right out the front door into the sunshine.

"…oh," she whispered, as the sunlight hit her eyes. She covered her eyes for a moment while they adjusted to the light. And the warmth.

It was mid-June and becoming quite warm during the day.

Jena lifted her hand in a motion for him to wait a minute. She looked all around her as her eyes adjusted to the brilliant sunshine.

Then she looked up at him with the saddest of expressions. "I missed the spring, didn't I?"

"Jena," he began. "Today is Thursday. It is the middle of June now. Today is the day you begin living again…for real. Our first stop is that ice cream stand over there on the corner. Then we're going for a walk in the park."

"Can you do this? Take me out of the hospital?"

He laughed. "I have highest security clearance."

She chose lime sherbet. It was cool and tart on her tongue. She savored every tiny lick, and let it melt where it wanted to. He ordered a double dip chocolate chip and devoured it in a few minutes.

"See," he smiled. "I'm honoring your soft diet."

"Can I eat the cone?" she wondered.

"I'll never tell anyone."

She tentatively tried biting into the cone, and carefully chewed three little bites she allowed herself.

"Eat it all," he encouraged. "You've lost too much weight and we need to get a little of that back on you."

She made it half way through before handing it back to him. He offered her a napkin in exchange.

They strolled fifty yards into the park before they stopped at a big tree lining the path.

Leaning her head back, she closed her eyes against the sunshine. "This feels good."

"Good! Sunshine is better than drugs."

"I've missed it. I used to take the babies in the stroller…" Her words suddenly caught in her throat. She swallowed hard a few times, but the lump wouldn't go away. "But it wasn't warm like this. I bundled them up so they wouldn't get cold."

He took her hand. "I used to dream of throwing the football with my son. Before he was born, I went to the sports store and bought a football, a catcher's mitt, and a soccer ball… hoping that one day we'd toss a few back and forth, or kick a few around. Those were the hardest to let go after I lost them."

Jena took in a long deep breath. "We have this little lake by our house. The HOA developed it out and it is quite lovely. I used to take the babies in the stroller around the lake."

He nodded slowly.

"I miss them," she whispered. "It's like they were just here yesterday, in my arms."

"I know."

There was a long silence. The birds were out singing today, and the squirrels frolicked up and down the trees not too far from where they were sitting.

"Tell me about your family," Jena said softly.

"My family?"

"Yes," Jena replied. "Your family…now."

He laughed. "Oh my god. My kids are crazy! And wonderful! And they cost me too much money."

Jena smiled. "And your wife?"

Dr. Riley paused as a tenderness came to his eyes. "She's really something. Gentle. Kind. Gifted. You remind me a lot of her. You two would be great friends."

"I'd like to meet her."

He looked at her. "I can make that happen, my friend."

"Are we friends, Dr. Riley?" she whispered.

He nodded enthusiastically. "Absolutely. You can't get rid of me so easily. I take caring for my patients very seriously. And I think it is time you stopped calling me Dr. Riley when we are together. It's Rick."

"That's a strong name. Do you have any siblings?"

"One brother. And a sister, but she's a missionary in Thailand. She works at an orphanage over there. Those kids broke her heart when she went over there on a mission trip one summer with her college group. She comes home twice a year and stays with me."

"Do you live far from here?"

"Not really." He named the neighborhood.

She turned her head and looked at him strangely. "That's my neighborhood."

"Really," he laughed. "What street do you live on?"

She told him.

"I can't believe this," he exclaimed. "We live three streets over. We're neighbors!"

"Have they fixed the entry gate code, yet?"

"Nope. You still have to ring the security office."

They both let the fact that they lived so close to each other sink in a bit. The squirrels ran across the pathway and up another tree.

"You know, Jena," he began. "I think you and I are destined to be life-long friends. Helping you has really reinforced why I went into medicine in the first place."

She was quiet. How could she express that he was the reason she was still here? He was her guardian angel. The big brother she never had. Her truest friend now in all the world.

"When you get out of the hospital, Jena, I want to stay connected. My wife and I have been praying for you all along. You are a beautiful and brave person. There is so much waiting for you out here. So much life. So much love."

She dipped her head. It was too early to believe that. It was too early to talk of life, or love, or happy ever after again.

"If you don't mind, I think it's time for me to go back. I'm starting to hurt."

He nodded, stood up, and rolled her back through the park, through the front doors of the hospital, and to her room. He left her with the evening shift, said his goodbyes and left to go home to his wife, children, dogs, and turtles.

After he left, Jena slowly curled up in ball and disappeared into the covers.

Chapter Four

Rick came every day faithfully after his duty in surgery and the ICU.

He took her for a walk a few more times. He talked about his dogs and made her laugh once with a story about their antics. He showed her pictures of the kids.

When her diet restrictions totally lifted, he brought her a hamburger and a chocolate shake from Whataburger.

One day he came in and told her not to worry if she didn't see him. His family was going on a short vacation to the gulf coast. They'd be gone for a week. They had a timeshare down there and went several times a year. It was tropical and beautiful with a long beach of sand, he said.

On July 10th, while he was gone, they moved Jena to a rehab hospital across the parking lot. There was a problem with her insurance, but it was quickly resolved. She settled in to a first-floor room close to the therapy room that looked out on a beautiful courtyard.

It was grueling therapy that challenged her. But the therapists were kind and patient and let her go her own pace for the first week.

The second week they pushed her hard. With her cast off now, she walked with the walker everywhere she went. They refused her a wheelchair, encouraging her with words of admiration for her efforts to overcome.

The meals were better at rehab, but she still picked at her food. Esther came to visit a few times. Every visit was the same. A warm welcome, a tiny gift, the teary remembrances, the affectionate departure.

Fully awake now from all the pain meds, Jena not only felt all her heartache, she felt all of Esther's heartache, too. There was nothing she could do to ease her own pain, much less Esther's pain. It was an ever-constant companion that followed her everywhere she went. Into therapy. To the dining room. Out into the courtyard. It followed her into her sleep and tormented her there with visions of babies and swirling winds.

The second week in rehab, a knock came at her door. It opened slowly and a beautiful woman, in her thirties, walked in, her arms full of flowers and a box of chocolate chip cookies. They could have been sisters had Jena had a sister.

"Hello," she smiled. "Are you Jena?"

Jena slowly got up from where she was sitting in the chair by the window. "Yes, I'm Jena."

"I'm Katie. Rick's wife."

"Dr. Riley?"

"That would be him," Katie nodded, placing the flowers on a side table and positioning the box of cookies on her tray. "He asked if I would come by and say hi. He's been swamped in surgery since we got home from vacation. He's talked so much about you that I feel like I know you."

"It's nice of you to come," Jena replied, slowly making her way over to her new visitor.

Katie held out her hand. Jena shook it.

Katie looked down at Jena's leg. "How are things going?"

"It's been rough."

"I can't imagine," Katie smiled knowingly. "But Rick said you were a warrior woman inside and that you'd fight your way back. He said you are resilient."

"That was nice of him." Jena felt strangely comfortable with her new friend, just as she had with her husband who had overseen her care for so many weeks.

Katie looked around the room. "I bet you're absolutely bored in this place."

Jena smiled hesitantly. "I am. There's no one to talk to."

"Well, let's remedy that. But not here. Let's get out of here."

Jena glanced down at her attire. She had on navy blue gym shorts and a white tank top, low cut ankle socks and slippers. "I'm afraid I'm not presentable."

"You're fine!" Katie reached out and touched her arm. "We're not going far. But let's see how much trouble we can get into in the next hour. Grab that cane."

Jena checked herself out at the front desk and slowly followed Katie out to a red Mustang convertible parked under the awning in front. Katie assisted her as she maneuvered into the front seat and put on her seatbelt. Katie placed the cane in the back seat.

"It's a little warm, but a beautiful day," Katie said. "I thought we'd take a drive. Is that alright with you?"

Jena hesitated. The last time she'd been in a vehicle was the storm. She wrapped her arms around herself, as if to ward off a silent threat.

"It's alright, Jena…" Katie waited patiently. "We don't have to go. We can go back inside."

Jena finally answered. "I'm ok. Just maybe go slow for a bit."

Katie climbed into the driver's seat, put the convertible in gear and slowly headed out of the parking lot. They cruised down the street and Jena felt the warm wind in her hair. A few minutes later, Katie turned into a Sonic, drove through to the order box and ordered two corny dogs and two large Strawberry Limeades. Soon, they were back on the road.

Katie didn't say much but let the afternoon sun speak for her. It was another beautiful day, more unseasonably mild than most east Texas summer afternoons. A rain shower had passed a couple of hours before, and the few remaining clouds sent wispy swirls through the sky.

This part of the state was home to native forests. The scent of the East Texas piney woods permeated the day around them and filled the soul with faith of another day.

The road out from town wound through one of those areas and took them deeper into nature. Katie turned down a country road and pulled off at a state park. She parked the car next to a small lake that was surrounded by old trees and was home to mallard ducks. A few moments later, the song of birds and the occasional splash of jumping fish were the only sounds around them.

Jena sipped her Strawberry Limeade.

Katie reached into her purse. "I've got some OFF wipes if you need them to ward off any mosquitoes. But I think we'll be fine here for a while."

Jena put down her drink and stared out across the small lake. Campers lined the far side under the trees, and a few people were swimming in the secluded lake.

Katie finished the last of her corny dog. Then she wiped her hands on a napkin and turned toward Jena. "Beautiful, isn't it?"

Jena nodded. "I never knew this was here. I live so close."

"How long have you lived here?"

"Not long. We moved here a couple of years ago from Oklahoma after Pete finished his Master's Degree."

Katie smiled sadly. "Well, I grew up here. My family used to come camping here every month. We used to camp on the other side of the lake. There's a road that takes you across that little dam and winds around through a group of campsites."

Jena looked around at all the surroundings. The sun beams were coming through the trees. The grass was emerald green. It was beautiful and wild and surprisingly peaceful.

"Thank you for bringing me here," Jena whispered.

"I thought you might like it."

"You're very kind, Katie. Kind like Rick."

Katie laughed. "We all have our good days."

Silence fell around them again and they both let it join them.

Finally, Jena turned and asked. "Why are you doing this?"

"You mean kidnapping you?" Katie turned to her and smiled. "I want to be friends."

"Why?" Jena had no malice or suspicion in her question. Just curiosity.

"I needed to get away for a while. I thought you might need to, as well. No hidden motives. Just looking for a friend to share the day. Rick speaks so highly of you, that I wanted to meet you."

Jena nodded. "Thank you for the corny dog and drink."

Katie slurped the last of hers. "They are wonderfully sinful, aren't they?"

Out on the lake, the ducks practiced their take offs and landings. The fish jumped again. The water rippled in gentle rolls across the surface.

Finally, Jena spoke. "I didn't want to live for the longest time."

Katie was quiet, but kept her eyes trained on Jena.

"The counselors have helped. Rick has helped. Thank you for sharing him."

"He's good at what he does," Katie replied.

Jena nodded. Another sip of her drink. "What do you do for a living, Katie? Do you work?"

Katie paused and carefully set her drink in the holder. Then she turned in her seat to face Jena. "I'm a charge nurse. I work in the emergency room."

Jena turned and looked at her. "At the same hospital?"

"Yes," Katie smiled. "It's where I met Rick. He may have told you. You may have forgotten."

"I remember now."

"It was a cold night and rare snow and ice roared in from Dallas. We had a lot of patients that night. They called in reinforcements. He was running down the hall in his scrubs, with that stethoscope flapping across his chest. I was a goner. It was love at first sight. For both of us."

"Sounds like a scene out of a romance novel or a Hallmark movie."

Katie laughed. "Not at all. He was barking orders to all of us and I was furious at first. I thought he was the biggest narcissistic jerk I'd ever met. But things settled down and we worked together through the night"

Jena smiled.

"He kissed me the next morning at 3 a.m. in a stairwell where we'd both escaped for a few minutes. And, that was that. We got married three months later, with half the staff at the wedding. Every day has been a flurry of adventures, laughter, and love."

"Was he your first love?"

"No," Katie frowned. "I broke up with my fiancé after I found out that he was making a move on my cousin. Lost some wedding venue deposits on that one. And Rick, well, he lost his first wife and son pretty early on."

Jena swallowed. "He told me."

"He did? Sad story, isn't it?"

The silence came again and wrapped itself around them.

"Katie?"

"Um?"

"Where you in the ER the night of the storm?"

Katie lowered her eyes and took back her cup. She stirred the ice with her straw. "I was."

"Did you take care of me?"

Katie looked into Jena's eyes. "I was there."

"Did you…," Jena began, her voice suddenly tight and emotional. "Did you take care of my babies?"

"I was there all night."

Jena paused, then whispered. "Did you see them?"

"I held them," Katie whispered. "They were beautiful."

Something passed between them in that moment. An unspoken question in Jena's eyes. A whispered, compassionate answer from Katie's lips.

"They didn't suffer, Jena. The paramedics assured us of that. It happened so fast. They were gone in an instant."

Jena felt the tears coming again. She hated the tears.

"What were the babies' names, Jena?"

Jena wiped a lone tear. "Jana and Alexis. We called her Lexi."

"Beautiful names."

"How did they…?"

"Don't do this, Jena. It won't help. It won't bring them back."

Jena struggled against the grief.

Then she took a deep breath and looked at Katie again. "Thank you for taking care of them."

"I think they bonded us somehow. You know, I came to see you early on, when Rick was taking care of you in ICU. But you were in the coma. We prayed for you, together, standing over you."

"Why?" Jena whispered.

"For every reason." Katie reached over and touched her arm. "You and I are going to be friends, Jena, if you'll have me."

"I don't want anyone feeling sorry for me," Jena declared.

"I don't feel sorry for you, Jena. I admire you. You are strong and resilient, beautiful and smart. You don't need to be alone, and I want us to be friends. I know this sounds crazy, but when I saw you there on that stretcher when they brought you in, it was like I knew you. It was intuitive. It felt like we were friends but I didn't recognize you because of all your injuries. I even had them double check your driver's license. Perhaps we are spirit sisters."

Jena looked up and smiled sadly. "I feel that, too."

"Then it's settled. It will be our secret pact that every Tuesday we will sneak off and get our corny dog fix and Limeades."

Jena let out a soft laugh. "Deal."

"Do you like new country music?"

"I do."

Katie started the convertible, turned on the radio, and slipped in a CD by the late Toby Keith. They drove slowly back to the rehab hospital.

* * *

Katie and Rick visited her often after that, together and separately. Every Tuesday Katie took them to Sonic and for a short drive in the woods. They talked for hours and shared childhood stories. Jena eventually started opening up about Pete and the baby girls. Then one day on one of their outings she opened up about the storm.

"We never saw it."

Katie stayed quiet. She'd been waiting patiently for Jena to get to the point of talking about that night.

"We drove right into it. I don't remember anything. I just remember the dreams."

"The dreams?" Katie asked. They had driven to a city park that day and were sitting at a picnic table. Katie timed it each time so they had an hour and half from the end of her shift in ER to when she needed to pick up their children from daycare.

"The first dream they were little girls, not babies. The second dream they were teenage girls. And Pete was always there. They looked so happy. And they kept asking me if I could stay with them."

"What did you say to them?"

"I don't remember. I just remember how happy they were and that they kept telling me they loved me." Jena looked out over the park. "Do you believe in heaven?"

"I do. You can't do what I do day in and day out without believing in a place of love after."

"I think they are in heaven," Jena said.

Katie nodded.

"They wanted me to stay with them."

"You had a choice to stay, Jena. Why didn't you?"

"I couldn't."

"Why not?"

Jena shook her head. "I don't know. I just couldn't."

"Maybe your heart knew something that you still haven't discovered."

"What do you mean?"

Katie touched her shoulder. "Maybe your heart or soul, or both, knew that there was a reason you needed to live. You had a will to live, even when you were dying. We all watched you fight. Maybe you were fighting for your true destiny."

Jena bit the inside of her lip, then brushed her blonde wild hair from her face where the wind had blown it. "Well, I'm not sure about all of that. But I believe in heaven."

Katie smiled. The journey back had begun.

Chapter Five

Jena was released from rehab the second week in August and finally went home. It was raining that afternoon, a soft rain that touched her face and wiped the tears away. Katie drove her home and offered to go into the house with her, but Jena politely refused. She needed to do this alone.

The grueling weeks of therapy had prepared her to live alone. She'd done it before.

Carefully, Jena took her house key out of her purse. Her real keys and purse had been sucked up by the tornado and were in Arkansas somewhere. One of her friends had a lock smith come and put in new locks, then brought her the key.

They'd left the house a mess that Saturday in March when they went to Hideaway Lake to visit with Pete's mother. The dishes had been left in the sink. There were dirty diapers still in the pail. The floors had needed mopping. There were towels on the couch that Pete had meant to fold before they left, but he never got around to it. The fireplace ashes had not been cleaned out.

Jena took a deep breath.

Her heart was pounding.

She didn't want to go in and see where they all had left off. She waited a full five minutes on the porch.

Then, she slowly opened the door and just stood there. Then she took a step back into her home.

Someone had come in the months since the storm and cleaned the three bedrooms up, two bedrooms down mini mansion. Her dishes were all washed and put in their place in the cabinets. The laundry was all done. The floors were swept and mopped. The carpets had been cleaned. The baby toys were carefully placed in the bin by the TV. Pete's tennis shoes were placed side by side by the back door, where he'd left them. But they'd been washed.

The furniture was dusted. The mail was neatly stacked on the counter by the phone. The refrigerator had been emptied and scrubbed and left with only bottled water and a bowl of fresh fruit. All the linens were washed and the bed in their bedroom was made. The tubs and showers had been scrubbed.

It smelled like clean linens throughout the house.

She walked into their bedroom closet and put her face into Pete's jacket. She felt of each of the shirts hanging there. She lifted his bottle of cologne and breathed deeply.

Her heart was breaking.

She put the bottle of cologne down and kept moving through the house.

The girls' room was spotless. The linens had been changed there, too. The diapers were neat on the changing table. The blanket was draped over the back of the rocking chair. She touched their stuffed animals, and embraced their pillows, breathing in the scent of baby detergent and baby powder.

Everything was clean and in order. Other than being cleaned, nothing had changed. But everything had changed.

She slowly walked, with the help of her cane, from downstairs room to downstairs room, taking in the smells and the memories. A few moments later, she heard the front door open. She went toward the front of house to see who was coming in.

Esther was coming through the front door, her arms full of groceries and a bucket of laundry soap.

"Hello, Esther."

Esther looked up surprised. "Oh my. You scared me, dear. I was hoping to finish before you got home."

"You did all this?" Jena looked around again at her home.

"Yes," Esther said quietly. "I hope you don't mind. I should have asked."

Jena went to her mother-in-law and opened her arms. Esther set the soap bucket and groceries on the floor. They held each other tight for the longest time, each trying desperately to hide their tears from the other. But the sobs broke through and both wept unashamedly.

Esther ended up staying overnight and slept in the upstairs guest room. The next morning, she woke late and made her way to the kitchen. Jena was already up and sitting at the table sipping a cup of hot coffee, staring out to the back yard and pool. Someone had even kept up the mowing and edging and pool care.

"Good morning, dear."

Jena turned. "Good morning, Esther. I made us some coffee."

"Ah, that sounds wonderful." Esther poured herself a cup, and added one teaspoon of sugar and a dash of powdered creamer from the cupboard. She stood by the counter for a moment longer then came to sit across from Jena. She sat quietly, lost in her thoughts for a moment.

"You look good, Jena."

Jena smiled self-consciously and pushed a strand of hair behind her ear. "I look terrible."

"Perhaps I should say it is so good to see you, dear."

Jena looked at her mother-in-law and hesitated. Then she turned and faced Esther. "I'm so sorry, Esther. I know you begged us to stay with you that night and wait out the storm."

Esther looked down.

"We didn't know."

"No," Esther said softly. "No one knew."

"I know it's been hard on you."

"Yes, on both of us." The older woman took a sip of her coffee. "I want to bring them all back for you, dear. But we cannot bring them back. We were blessed to have them for the moments we had them. There are secret rooms in our hearts where they will live forever."

"They were my life."

Esther took a sip of coffee. Yes, they were her life, too. Her only family. Her only bloodline. Her only hope for joy in her aging years.

Jena reached out her hand and held the hand of her mother-in-law. "Tell me about the funerals."

"Oh, my," Esther breathed. "The funerals were at your church. The service was for all three of them, together. The building was full. All your friends were there. A young woman sang and, oh my goodness, she sounded like an angel."

Jena caught her breath.

"So many people came. And your pastor offered touching words." Esther took a long sip of coffee. "Then we buried them." There were the tears in her eyes. "When you're ready, I'll take you where they are. You need to say goodbye to them."

Jena looked away. "Not today."

They sat there for the longest time before Esther ventured forth. "What are you going to do, Jena?"

"I don't want to stay here. Their memories are everywhere I turn. I can't breathe."

"Where will you go?"

"I don't know. I don't care. I just want to go away."

"You must face this, dear. It is part of your journey. It is part of the pain. But it is part of the healing, too."

"I don't know where to begin."

"I want to help you where I can and where you will let me," Esther said quietly. "You don't have to do anything today. But tomorrow, you must begin. Or you will drown in the sorrow of it all, and you will never make it out again."

Esther stayed the day and into the evening. She made a simple dinner and watched Jena pick at the food. Her petite frame had withered and Esther worried about her.

Esther decided to stay one more night. The next morning, she left after breakfast, promising to call and come back the next day. After she left, Jena went outside and sat on the patio under the awning. It was early, but the sun was already hot and beating down on the yard. Jena hardly noticed.

But when the heat became unbearable, she picked up her cup of long forgotten coffee and walked back into the big lonely house of sorrow and started packing up the study.

It took her three weeks to go through everything.

Her resolve to put her life in boxes was interrupted every other day when Katie or Esther arrived to take her to physical therapy. But it would begin again once they dropped her back off at the house.

Esther brought dinner over every few nights and sat quietly as Jena pushed her food around on the plate and daydreamed. After washing the dishes, Esther left again for her own home an hour away to be alone in her own grief.

Jena threw away more than she boxed up for charity, or packed to take forward with her to wherever she went next. Her bedroom was excruciatingly difficult. She would pack a box and then sit on the floor and cry for an hour. Then she would rise, wash her face, and tape another box together. His clothes were the hardest. He didn't have a lot, as he was a minimalist. But everything he had said something about him. Every suit, every pair of jeans, every shirt. His hiking boots, his bathrobe.

She felt like she was packing him up and giving him away.

She kept his bottle of cologne and his walking stick, his camera, and his old worn leather jacket he'd worn on winter nights when they went out on date night. She kept his razor and comb. And she kept every picture.

When she finally made it to the nursery, she was emotionally empty and so deep in grief that she was numb to all feeling. She'd had them for so little time, they seemed like a distant imagining. Had they been real? Had they ever lived at all? But the sweet little baby dresses and sleepers reminded her that they had been alive, however short a time that was.

She kept their baby blankets, their rattles, and the sleepers that they had worn, and still somehow carried their scent.

She kept the blankets she had wrapped them in to rock them.

She kept their special Teddy bear.

And she kept the hospital birth book with their tiny footprints.

But everything else went in a box. One by one, the little things were laid carefully in the cardboard tomb, and with them went tiny little memories that were so young they had yet to imprint into her soul. She cried when she was done. She hugged Teddy to her breast and wailed aloud. She was a wounded doe crying alone in the vast wilderness for tiny creatures who were taken from her by a monster in the night.

She fell asleep on the floor of their nursery, so exhausted and frail that she didn't hear her phone going off. It vibrated repeatedly deep into the night.

***

The doorbell rang.

Jena opened her eyes. She was on the floor, still dressed in worn jeans and a wrinkled t-shirt. She looked around. The open boxes sat where she'd left them, full of lost dreams and dashed hopes for a future. But a new morning had come, all the same.

She sat up and struggled to get her legs under her. She held on to the rocker and pulled herself up to a standing position. The doorbell kept ringing.

She was stiff and in pain. She reached for her cane and walked out the room, down the hallway, and opened the front door.

"Good morning." It was Katie. Rick was behind her. They glanced at her ragged appearance, disheveled hair, and tear-streaked face. Then they looked at each other with disconcerted expressions.

Jena didn't say anything, but opened the door wider and turned to walk back through the entryway toward the kitchen.

Katie came carefully through the threshold. "I think she wants us to come in," she said to Rick. He slowly followed. They closed the door behind them and followed Jena through the house to the giant kitchen.

"Look," Jena said, turning toward them. She felt her heart pounding. "I'm not ready to make good on any promises. I feel like I'm having a heart attack every time I breathe."

Katie and Rick stared at her, not saying a word. Their silence was empathetic and they waited for Jena to go on.

"I just can't get over them like that," Jena walked over to the back door. "You can't just switch off love like that. Flip on! Flip off! One moment they're here. The next moment they're gone!"

Rick slowly walked over to the kitchen island and put down a small bag of groceries. Katie stood still by the kitchen table, watching her friend.

"The whole world keeps going around. I want to scream and make it all stop!" Jena looked at them. "I want off this madness."

Rick and Katie were in jeans and t-shirts, having come straight to her house after dropping the kids off with his parents for the day. It was the weekend and they wanted to check on her. Their eyes betrayed the worry, but they remained quiet, watching Jena. Waiting.

Jena sank into a chair.

Slowly, Katie sat down in the chair by her side. The silence was deafening. No one said a word.

Behind them in the kitchen, Rick found a frying pan and put it on the stove. There was rustle of plastic as he opened the bag and retrieved the slab of bacon. He turned on the back burner and sliced open the bacon package with his pocket knife.

"I miss them so much, Katie," Jena whispered.

"I know, sweetie."

"I can't do this."

"You are doing this," Katie responded, her voice soft and kind. "You're grieving. You're hurting. But you're alive. *Breathing*."

From the kitchen came the sound of bacon sizzling on low heat. The smoky scent filled the kitchen. Rick took the coffee pot and filled it with water, poured it into the coffee maker, filled the filter with Starbucks Verona, and closed the lid. Then he pressed the ON button.

Soon, the aroma of the brew permeated the kitchen and Jena closed her eyes. The perking of the coffee brought back memories of her and Pete around a campfire, sharing dreams and wishing upon the stars. Now the stars refused to shine.

"When does it stop hurting?" Jena wept. "When can I wake up and breathe again and not feel my heart being ripped out?"

"Over time," Katie said, still not moving to comfort her friend. She glanced over the counter at her husband. He smiled sadly and reassured his wife with a look of love. There was nothing either one of them could say to make the pain go away. It had to go the cycle, run its course, and eventually morph into something else.

Jena cried, with her face in her hands, for ten full minutes. No one moved to stop her. They let her grieve. And when the crying let up, Katie handed her a tissue.

From the kitchen, an egg shell cracked. Then another. And another.

Jena blew her nose into the tissue.

Katie reached out then and took her hand, and smiled. "Good morning, my friend."

Jena looked up at Katie. She hadn't welcomed them well. She was sorry for that. So, she apologized with her eyes and a slight tilt of her head. "Morning."

Rick came around the kitchen counter and set a glass of orange juice in front of Jena. "Drink."

She looked up at him, and then reached for the glass and sipped the juice. The smell of the smoked hickory bacon and coffee wafted through the air. Her tummy growled.

A few minutes later, Rick brought each of them a plate of bacon, fried eggs, toast, butter and jam. Rick and Katie waited until Jena finally picked up her fork and stuck it into the egg. Then they picked up their forks and began to eat. They all ate quietly, washing it down with orange juice and coffee.

When they were done, Rick removed their plates and glasses and took them to the sink. Then he refilled their coffee and joined the ladies at the table.

Katie looked over at him, and he nodded.

"Jena," she began. "Rick and I want to talk to you about something."

Jena's blue eyes were clearer now, with the wave of grief past her for now. "I'm so sorry I fell apart on you like that."

"It's natural," Rick said. "Nothing surprising. In fact, it's good to cry. And it's good to be angry. It means you are progressing through. Just don't cry over my bacon."

Jena looked over at him and finally smiled.

Katie took her hand. "So, we've been talking and we want you to come to Galveston with us next month, four weeks away. We have the beach house for ten days. Part of that is fall break for the kids. You'd have your own room and can come and go as you'd like. It's a huge house and it has a small elevator from the living quarters down to the beach level."

"You need a break from all of this," Rick commented. He, himself, was more familiar with the grief process than he cared to remember. But getting away occasionally had helped him clear his mind and given him a new perspective.

"Let us help you finish packing the house, and then come with us to Galveston," Katie implored.

"The fresh air and sand will be good for you," Rick said. "And when we all come back, we can help you decide what to do about the house, and your things."

Katie smiled. "The weather will be nice."

Jena nodded. "I appreciate the offer, really, I do. I'm just not ready for crowds and the whole vacation thing. I'm not good company. And, I'm a mess. I can't even walk without help."

Rick shook his head. "You can walk the beach. You just need to be careful."

"The house is way down the island, away from all the tourist traps. The only reason we ever go back into town is to buy groceries," Katie said. "There are no people where we will be. Just sand and surf. And a few wayward sea turtles. And it'll be cooler there. All the tourists will have gone home and back to school by then."

Jena paused. Her house had become a tomb of grieving and memories that followed her as she roamed the empty rooms and halls. She needed to get away, away from the swirling of echoing laughter, baby giggles, and Pete's soft voice in the night. She needed to escape. To anywhere. "Alright. I'll come."

"Good!" Katie exclaimed. "We're going mid-October. We'll leave on a Friday morning. We'll pick you up in the morning and we'll be on the beach by dinner time. You can sleep in the car all the way down, if you'd like."

"With your kids in the car?" Jena grinned.

"All four," Rick reminded her. "But no dogs this time. We're boarding them with my parents."

Katie followed her back to the bedroom and helped her make a short list of the things she might want to bring. But she and Rick were bringing everything else. They let themselves out thirty minutes later and Jena closed the door after them.

Who was she kidding?

It was a Band-Aid on a mortal wound.

No vacation could mend her heart. It could only put off what was inevitable.

She walked back toward the kitchen and looked around. She and Pete had bought the house new when they'd moved from Oklahoma. Jena had picked out everything new. The furniture. The curtains. The carpet. The tile. The paint. The only scents and memories in the house were theirs. So, the thought of selling and letting others come in and establish a presence was heartbreaking. But she knew that it was what she had to do. She couldn't live here anymore without them.

She looked at the trip list she and Katie had made, then laid it on the table. Then she reached for her computer and started to Google realtors.

Chapter Six

The months since the accident were an eternity. Jena had been in a coma in the spring, and in the hospital all summer. Then, her life had transitioned to the grueling routine of physical therapy, day in and day out, first at the rehab hospital, then from home. It was the summer of her hell. The next two weeks were no different.

She tried to keep herself busy and pre-occupied, but everything she did was connected to Pete and the girls. She turned away repeated offers by friends to come over and help with the daunting task of loading her life into cardboard boxes and letting them go. She insisted on packing every box herself and taking her time to touch and feel every single item she placed away. Little things of no significance or value became treasures and the U-Haul boxes became physical caskets of memories.

With every item that she finally allowed to slip through her fingers into a box, a piece of her heart and soul followed.

Her pastor came by and sat with her for a long time, most of which was in total silence. He offered to pray with her, then quietly revoked his offer when Jena glanced over at him with a look that bespoke of the undersurface anger that he knew was all a part of the process of grief. He was gentle with her, and followed her lead in the intermittent conversation that went all over the place and down a hundred rabbit holes.

He and his wife had known Jena and Pete for only a short time, and not that well. But she was one of his flock, and he felt responsible to aid in the healing that he knew she so desperately needed. But, today, he seemed at a loss as to where to begin.

But he'd been through this more than once over the years, and he was smart enough to know that there was really nothing he could say to make it better.

So, he just sat with her, and listened intently when she did speak. And after an hour, he looked at his watch, then put down his glass of tea she'd offered him earlier.

Jena walked him to the door.

He smiled and handed her a card. Then he left.

Jena closed the door behind him, and glanced down at the card. *Little Thicket Grief Recovery and Support Group.* She bit her lip, and tossed the card on the entry table. Then she went back through the house to the back patio and sat alone until the sun set.

The next few days, she withdrew even more, and waved off both Katie and her mother-in-law when they called to confirm they were picking her up for her therapy sessions. After the fifth time Jena pushed them away, Katie showed up at her door.

"Hello, Jena."

Jena stepped outside on the porch and closed the door behind her. "I thought I told you I wasn't going today."

Katie smiled gently. "That's not why I'm here."

"Then, why are you here?"

Katie took in Jena's disheveled appearance. There were dark circles under her eyes. Her hair was unwashed and stringy around her face. Her t-shirt had a coffee stain. Her feet were bare.

"Let's go for one of our drives," Katie said, matter of fact, more of a sweet order than a suggestion.

"I don't want to go anywhere."

Katie reached out and took her friend's hand. "You need to get out of that house. I know what you're doing in there, and it's not healthy. You're isolating. And you're drinking, aren't you?"

Jena looked up. "Wouldn't you?"

"Not on the medications you're taking, I wouldn't, no."

"I'm not drinking that much," Jena replied, looking away. "Just at night." Her eyes teared up. "The evenings are the worst."

"…I know." But with those words came a soft grace and whisper of true understanding.

"It's when the world stops and the night goes quiet, and this darkness fills the house, and I can't sleep. So, I have a glass of wine. It helps me sleep."

"Does it?"

Jena looked up at her friend, no words for the spoken truth.

"You are going to get through this, Jena." Katie's voice was gentle. "But you can't go to that place where you are doing things to deaden the pain. Because the pain will still be there in the morning. You have to make choices to process the pain."

"Coming from the head charge nurse…who gives morphine at the drop of a hat."

Katie slowly pulled her hand away from Jena's. "I wish I had the medicine that could cure what you're feeling. I truly do. But there isn't any. There is only time."

Jena looked away and bit back a flood of anger. "And time heals all wounds, right?"

Katie didn't miss the undercurrent of sarcasm. "No. Time doesn't heal all wounds. But it lessens the intensity of the heartache to a level you can bear."

"If you came here to cheer me up, you're doing a terrible job, Katie."

Katie paused. "Actually, I came by to see if you'd go for a drive with me. I had to put one of our dogs down this morning, and I need a friend."

Jena looked up quickly. "Oh." She took a deep breath. "I'm so sorry, Katie."

"Death and saying goodbye are hard, Jena. Even when it's your old deaf dog. So, I get it. I really do. Call me when you're ready to get back into physical therapy. Don't wait long. It'll be three times harder."

Katie turned to leave.

"…wait," Jena reached out to her. "I'm sorry. I truly am sorry. You've been there for me all this time, and I am treating you so badly."

Katie stood still. For once she let Jena hear her own words and let the reality of them sink in.

Now paying attention, Jena could see the puffiness around Katie's eyes, and suddenly Jena felt horrible. "I'm sorry about your dog."

Katie stared at her.

"And I'm sorry I'm…not in a place where I could even see you are hurting."

"Don't worry about it," Katie said.

But Jena could tell that she'd deeply hurt Katie. But she didn't know what to do to turn it around.

Katie waved her hand in dismissal. "We'll go for a drive another day. Or we can talk in Galveston. And you're still going."

Jena started to say something, but she couldn't think of any words to say except what came out of her mouth next. "I love you, Katie."

Katie swallowed. "I love you, too, Jena."

"I'm really sorry about your dog."

"Thanks. I'll call you tomorrow, ok?" Then Katie turned and walked back down the driveway to her car that she'd parked by the curb.

Jena watched her friend drive away. Then she went back into the house and closed the front door. She paused when she saw the card still lying on the entry way table. *Little Thicket Grief Recovery and Support Group.* She picked it up and walked toward the kitchen where her phone was still plugged in the charger. She reached for her cell phone and dialed the number.

***

She went to group the next night. She didn't know a soul.

So, she sat quietly, while the small group of participants introduced themselves and who they'd lost and how. It was a diverse group of grieving survivors. But Jena wasn't really listening. She was lost in her own thoughts and sorrows.

After forty-five minutes, it was her turn, and she pulled herself back to the present. "Hello," she said with great reserve.

"Hello," they all answered back.

She looked around. There were twelve in the group tonight. All ages. Men, women, and a teenager. She'd barely heard what any of them had said. She hadn't paid attention. But looking up now, she could see her own face mirrored in their pain.

"I'm Jena Parker."

There was silence, but a few understanding nods.

"Who did you lose, Jena Parker?" the facilitator gently asked.

"My family. I lost my family," Jena quietly replied. "They're all dead. "

A few of the participants looked up.

"My husband. Peter. My baby girls. They're dead."

She could have heard a pin drop.

"Oh my god," she whispered. "They're dead. That's the first time I've ever said that out loud."

The facilitator leaned forward in his seat. "How did they die, Jena?"

Jena grinded her teeth. "The tornado killed them. On the highway."

The older woman next to her began to silently sob. A deep silence filled the room.

"So, why are you here, Jena?" the facilitator asked. Then he waited, not saying another word.

"I don't want to be here," Jena replied.

"But you are."

"That's kind of obvious," Jena deflected. She shifted in the folding chair, then cleared the knot in her throat that was strangling her. She wanted to bolt. "I guess…I guess I'm lost in a darkness and I don't know how to get out of it."

The facilitator nodded.

"I lost my husband in that storm," the woman next to her said, as she wiped her eyes with a wadded tissue. "He was trying to bring the horses into the barn."

Jena turned toward her. Jena now saw the deep sadness in the woman's face and the bags under her eyes. The woman's sorrow, a grief wrapped in grace, was now obvious to Jena.

The teenage young man on the other side of the circle spoke up next. "I lost my mother that night. The damn thing just sucked her out my arms. We were parked under the overpass. We'd been fighting about me being on the internet and gaming too much. I was driving and wasn't paying attention. It was my fault."

Jena stared at him.

The room fell quiet again.

Then the facilitator stood up. "So, we are all here together to process through the pain we all feel. Let me remind you that grief is a long process. But with friends and support, that journey is made easier."

Everyone nodded.

"Our time is up for this evening," he continued. "We'll meet again on Thursday night. Same time. In the meantime, please take the time to love on one another before you leave. Goodnight." Then he slowly walked away to leave the participants to find their way, together, out of the darkness.

Jena reached for her purse.

The older woman leaned over. "He's one of the pastors of this church. He lost his wife that night. It was a horrible night, wasn't it?"

Jena looked into the old woman's eyes. They were weary. And sad. "Yes. It was."

"Will you be here Thursday?"

"I don't know."

The older woman reached out and patted Jena's hand. She could have been her own grandmother. "We need you, dear."

Jena grimaced. "This sucks."

"…like hell," the old woman nodded. "But we can't heal alone." Then she painfully stood up and made her way over to the punch and cookies.

Jena went back to the group later that week. That time was as painful as the first. But, in listening, she learned more of each story of loss and pain. And somewhere in all of that, she realized that, even though these people were in the same room, they were still all very lost in their own grief. They were *all* alone.

For grief is the great isolator. And grief is a monster. Jena was only now realizing how powerful a foe it was. It was a dragon that breathed fire in the day, and roared at night through endless and mournful dreams. And it kept coming back, attacking day after day after day, tormenting souls who'd lost the loves of their lives.

It was merciless. It was brutal and relentless.

The only way to conquer it, Jena had heard, was to climb on its back and ride it all the way back down into hell. Once there in that solitary despair, one found themselves faced with critical choices… either the will to fight, or not. The will to live on, or not.

In the lonely hell…that was where the real battle was.

In the pit of sorrows.

And that is where Jena found herself in mid-October when Rick and Katie pulled up in her driveway to pick her up for the trip to Galveston.

Chapter Seven

Daylight was waning when they pulled up to the timeshare beach house on the southern tip of the island. They would have been here sooner, but they stopped at Joe's Crab Shack near the causeway and had dinner.

Jena stepped out of the car and walked toward the end of the driveway that jutted toward the ocean. The smell of salt air and waft of rotten fish permeated her senses. In the distance she heard the crashing of waves against the shoreline and the faraway horn of a cruise ship echoing across the vast open water. She started to walk toward the sounds of the sea but then stopped and turned back toward Rick and Katie. "Can I help carry in the groceries or the luggage?"

"Go ahead, Jena," Katie called out. "The beach starts on the other side of the fence. We're going to unload the kids and the groceries. Just don't go far. It gets dark quick out here."

"You don't mind if I explore for a few minutes?"

"That's why we're here," Rick answered as he lifted one of the sleeping children into his arms. With his free arm, he held out her cane. "Use this and be careful. I'll turn the deck lights on for you. We'll be the only house lit for a way."

Jena came back the few steps and took her cane from him. "Thank you."

"We'll join you on the deck in thirty minutes," Katie said. "I need to unload the groceries and get the cold stuff put away in the refrigerator."

Jena turned back toward the water and slipped off her shoes. In ten steps she was in the sand. She walked slowly toward the sound of lapping waves, using the cane as a precaution, more than a crutch. Her leg was healing nicely. In thirty more steps she felt the ocean water, still warm from the summer, roll over her feet.

The mid-October evening was pleasantly warm.

Behind her in the giant beach house, built twelve feet up on concrete piers, lights came on and soon lit up the beach below with their glow. Jena walked a little way down the beach, maybe fifty yards. She stopped and breathed in the evening air. It was dusk. The sun was gone now beyond the horizon and the darkness slowly rolled over her, too.

She took in a breath.

It caught in her throat.

Suddenly, she felt them all there beside her. Pete and the girls. They were standing quietly, patiently, reverently waiting for her to let them go.

But she couldn't. Not yet. She just couldn't. It was too soon.

She crossed her arms across her breasts and fought the grief. It was like the ocean. It came in waves now, ebbing and flowing. High tide. Low tide. Turbulent waters. Crashing wave. Soft lapping of gentle reminders of them.

Sometimes the grief just sat beside her, like an old gray- haired woman, bent over at the waist, with the weight of the world on her shoulders. Sometimes, it was a baseball bat that knocked her legs out from under her.

Tonight, the grief was quietly walking beside her, an unseen dark and powerful entity of heartache.

She waded in a little deeper. The water rushed around her ankles. The water was still warm weeks after the scorching summer sun, a summer sun that had given way to the changing of seasons.

She looked up.

A few stars had come out. She looked south down the beach. She saw a few large beach houses scattered a quarter of a mile apart. Some were lit up. Others were dark.

She waded a little deeper still. The water lapped at her knees. It was like the ocean was talking to her, communicating some age-old code of life and death, ebb and flow, the changing of energy.

She was lost in her thoughts.

The heartache paused, breathing in and out, as it led her farther into the water, step by step. Hand in hand. Deeper and deeper. It could lead her deep enough so that she would not return.

What would it be like to keep wading deeper, Jena thought? To lose herself in the warm ocean? That was the choice suddenly before her, wasn't it? To turn back now, or be slowly drawn away and swept out to sea? To be safe yet tormented one minute, or be lost, but at peace, the next. To claim some hope on the shore behind, or to give in and let go and let the pain claim her.

To live. Or die.

She was up to her waist then, and her shorts were soaked with the salty sea. She was totally lost in her thoughts of them. She felt the energy of the ocean pulling her deeper into its embrace. The current was stronger against her legs.

There was something to be said for just giving in. To just stop fighting. To let go. To will her own fate.

The water was up to her breasts now.

Maybe she could just dive in, and let the waves crash over her. Maybe she could just lie back in the water and the tide would take her out. She would make no effort to fight it.

The waves lapped around her shoulders, plastering her blouse to her skin.

She wanted to go where life couldn't hurt her anymore. She wanted to go to them.

"You're past the shallow now," came a deep masculine voice right behind her. "You don't know what's out here. I wouldn't go any farther out without a life jacket."

Slowly, Jena turned.

A man was standing not five feet behind her in the waves.

"Swimming in the ocean is not the best of ideas," he grinned. He was over six feet tall and good looking as hell. "You shouldn't be here. Especially at night. Especially alone."

She stared at him. Surprisingly, she was not alarmed that a strange man should be standing so close to her in the middle of the ocean off a strange beach in the dark of evening.

"Why not at night?" she asked.

"Sharks. Their attack is vicious. Lots of blood and guts… a violent end. No one will know what happened to you."

The spell that grief had on her quickly broke.

"Oh my god!" she whispered, but her words were caught up in the wind as she slowly turned against the rising current and carefully pushed herself back through the water toward the beach.

She pushed past him. But she could feel him right behind her, following her back in to the shore. Like a quiet escort.

When she reached the beach, she sat down in the wet sand. He sat slowly down beside her, a respectful distance away. His clothes were soaked, as were hers.

"I didn't realize I'd gone so far out," she said.

"You were up to your neck. Lucky that I came along, and saved you from the rip tide and the sharks. You might have never been found until you washed up past the Mexican border. Or, you might have never been found at all. You're welcome, by the way."

Jena didn't say a word.

"It's not a good idea to be out on the beach at night alone, much less going for a swim out there. Some strange drug lord might kidnap you and sell you into human trafficking. You should be afraid. The cartels are active in this area. Anything could happen out here at night. Anyone could come along."

She turned her head and looked at him.

His short dark hair, cut in a military high and tight, was wet from the ocean. His blue eyes reflected the glow of the moon above them now. His whole demeaner spoke of strength and integrity and…a powerful aura of protection.

"You came along," she whispered. "Should I be afraid of you?"

"No." He smiled genuinely. "Should I be afraid of *you*?"

She smiled.

He leaned back. "Wow. That's a beautiful sight."

His tender voice caught her suddenly off guard. “What is a beautiful sight?”

“Your smile.”

She pressed her lips together, and briefly turned her face from him. “I haven’t done much of that lately.”

“Why not?” he wondered, so very disarming and gentle. “Smiles look good on you.”

“It’s been a hard few months.”

He watched her.

The full moon had risen above them in the ten minutes that they sat on the beach. They were two strangers in the night lost in the mystery of the beach and the sea and the moonlight. The breeze had died down, and the sand was warm under them.

“What are you doing out here all alone?” he asked softly.

“I’m with friends. It was a long drive down. I just needed a few minutes to myself. I guess I ventured out a little too far.”

“Yes, you did. I was a little worried.”

“You were watching me?”

“Not intentionally...but yes. I was watching you.”

She glanced at him again. “You and I don’t know each other.”

“No.”

“So, why do you care?”

He leaned back and looked up at the stars. He smiled to himself. Then he looked back over at her.

“A beautiful woman. A moonlit night. An ocean full of sharks. An area with a notorious history of pirates and thieves. It was my duty to save you, Bella. I had no other motive.”

She smiled. It was a tiny smile, barely noticeable, but he saw it and embraced it.

“I don’t need saving,” she whispered. “Especially by a stranger.”

He was astounded that she was not exhibiting some kind of caution with him. But maybe she just wasn’t afraid of anything or anyone. Or, maybe she just didn’t care about her own safety.

“I assure you that if I had evil intent, you would not be here right now,” he responded.

"So," she said, her eyes raking over him again, studying him more closely. "Why are *you* here?"

He sat up. "I'm visiting family. I haven't seen them in a while. Got the invite, so I decided to meet up. So, I packed up and hopped on my motorcycle and fought the traffic down."

"It must be nice to have family."

"You don't?"

She bit her lip and slowly shook her head. "Not any more. They were all killed. My husband. My baby girls."

The silence was deafening and only broken by the sound of the soft waves gently crashing in the surf.

"I'm so sorry," he whispered. He wanted to know how and why, but he didn't ask.

She turned toward him. "Me, too."

They looked at each other for the longest moment, strangely connecting at the deepest level of the heart. Then the moment was gone. She stood up and reached for her cane.

"I think I might be in trouble, as I was supposed to meet back up with my friends. It was nice meeting you. Thank you for the shark warning." She reached out her hand toward him.

He slowly stood. He reached out and took her hand. "It was nice saving you from them."

They held their handshake just a little too long. Then Jena pulled back.

"Have a good time with your family," she said as she turned and slowly walked away, back down the beach, favoring her leg and occasionally balancing herself with her cane.

He watched her walk away. In her absence, the moon pulled at the waves and they lapped over his feet. The melancholy silence rushed in around him and filled the void where she had just been.

He breathed deeply. There was something about her… something so deeply profound and tender and needing to be saved.

For a moment, he felt part of his heart go with her.

Then he turned and walked down the beach the other way to where he left his motorcycle parked on the cement area down by the jetty.

***

"We were about to come looking for you," Katie said, coming out of the door that opened out to the top deck of the beach house. "Why are you all wet?"

Jena glanced down at her shorts. "I went wading."

Katie took in her wet clothes. "Wading or swimming?" She handed Jena a beach towel, which Jena wrapped around herself.

"Don't do that at night," Rick gently commanded. "It's too dangerous. There's no way to see what's in the water."

"Want a cup of tea?" Katie asked, handing her a cup of chamomile.

"Yes, thank you," Jena replied, taking the cup. She met her friend's gaze and nodded that she understood the gentle reminder for sobriety. Then she sat in one of the deck chairs that lined the railing and looked over the ocean. She took off her sandals. "It's beautiful here."

"Wait until morning when you can see the sun rise to the east," Katie smiled, settling herself in a chair beside Rick.

"What do you do when you come here?" Jena asked, taking a sip of the tea. She was a little chilled so the towel helped, and the warm liquid warmed her a bit.

"Whatever we want, whenever we want," Rick answered, sipping on a Dr. Pepper. "Mainly, we relax and hang out with the kids. Go see a few sites. Build sandcastles, swim in the pool in the summer, and eat a lot. We might go to downtown, or the next day we'll go to Moody Gardens. Maybe take in a movie."

They all sat quietly for a few minutes, letting the day ease away and watching the moon. Rick stood up and turned off the deck lights and they were quickly swallowed up by the evening and the sounds of the waves and a wayward seagull.

"Thank you for inviting me to come," Jena whispered.

Rick and Katie glanced at one another and smiled. The deck stairs creaked and in the corner of her eye, Jena saw a shadow coming up the steps. Rick stood up. Katie put her drink on the table and smiled.

"Hey! I thought you weren't coming," Rick said jovially, as he reached out his hand to the stranger almost at the landing.

"After you guys left, I sat around for a couple of hours, brooding," the stranger said. "It wasn't working for me, so I changed my mind and headed down. I can use a little R and R."

Jena stared.

It was him. Her savior. *The man from the ocean.*

"Glad you're here," Rick said, and opened his arms to envelop the stranger in them.

"Mark," Katie beamed. "Your parents alright? Our dogs ok?"

"They're fine," the stranger smiled at Katie, as they hugged.

"You look good," Rick said. He took in his brother's appearance. "But why are you all wet?"

The stranger looked down at himself. "I took a little walk on the beach and decided to cool off. It was a long trip down. And I met a woman. We talked for a while."

Mark saw her then, in the dark corner of the deck. He stared incredulously into her eyes. Jena's mouth dropped open ever so slightly at the surprise of seeing him again. Rick grinned, reading between the lines. Intuitively, Katie detected something else, and glanced over at Jena in her wet clothes. But Jena had turned away and was looking out to sea and sipping her tea.

"Well, we're glad you came," Katie said. She hesitated a moment, thought the best of it, then slipped into her hostess mode. "Let me introduce you two. This is our friend, Jena Parker. Jena, this is Rick's brother, Captain Mark Riley. He's stationed in Italy with the Air Force and is on leave."

Slowly Jena put her cup on the table beside her chair and reluctantly rose. She reached out her hand, holding the towel around her. "Hello."

Mark smiled at her. "Hello."

They touched.

Something happened then, again. She'd felt it on the beach when they'd first touched. It was not a bad thing, but a surprising thing. It was warm. Kind. Kindred. But it scared her, and she pulled away, just like she'd done on the beach.

"It's nice to know your name." he said, looking briefly down at the hand she'd pulled away.

"Same here," she whispered, glancing away.

Rick and Katie looked at each other as if to say, "what the heck?" Then the moment was gone and the reunion flared back up between the two brothers.

Jena quietly excused herself to change into dry clothes. Katie followed her with pretense to check on the children.

"Are you alright, Jena?"

Jena turned. "I'm sorry, Katie. I didn't know I was intruding on your family."

"Are you kidding? I'm the one that's sorry. I should have told you that we invited him at the last minute. He's on leave for a short time. We didn't know he was coming until he showed up just now. And I thought if I told you he might be here, you wouldn't come. And you needed to come, Jena. You need this time away. And Mark's a good guy. He and Rick will just hang out together."

"Oh, that's fine," Jena smiled. "I just don't want to be in the way. This is your vacation time and I know how important it is for you to be together as a family."

Katie reached out and touched Jena's shoulder. "But you're our family, too. Sisters of the heart, remember?"

Jena nodded. "Yes. Sisters of the heart."

"It's all good. Everyone just kind of does their own thing on these vacations. I want you to feel comfortable to do the same."

"Thank you, Katie." Jena looked down at her wet clothes and shivered slightly. "I think it's time to get out of these. Which room do you want me in?"

Katie showed her the way to the room, on the other side of the house from her, Rick and the children. Jena had a beautiful bright room and a private bathroom.

"Katie," Jena turned back toward her friend. "What did you tell him about me? Did he know I would be here?"

Katie tilted her head in question. 'Who, Mark? We didn't mention you. Your story is not ours to tell."

Jena nodded. "Ok."

"You're tired, Jena. Go to bed. We'll talk more tomorrow." Katie touched her arm endearingly.

Jena said her goodnights and went into her room and closed the door. She saw her suitcase on the bed. In the bathroom, she slipped out of her wet clothes that were now clinging to her like sticky sugar, and stepped into the shower. She put both her hands on the shower wall to balance, and rested her head against the tile. She stayed there for the longest time, letting the hot water run over her body and wash away the solemn and dangerous contemplations of the last hour.

The moments alone in the ocean had brought her too close to the brink of no return. Had it not been for *him*, she might have…

She couldn't go there again. Not ever again.

She had promised to keep breathing for *them*.

Then Jena cried softly, so that no one else could hear.

Chapter Eight

The morning came early for Jena. She woke before the sun came up, threw on sweat pants and an old t-shirt from high school, and walked quietly out to the kitchen to make coffee. She waited patiently for the coffee to finish. Then she poured herself a cup, slipped in a teaspoon of sugar and a splash of milk.

She swept her blonde hair up and secured it with a large clip, then tiptoed across the wooden plank floor to the deck door and opened it. Stars still were visible in the predawn sky. She stepped outside and softly closed the door behind her. The air was calm, almost still.

"It's beautiful early in the morning." His voice captured her attention and she turned to see him standing on the far side of the deck. "I was worried I frightened you away last night."

"I don't scare easily," she quietly responded.

"I didn't think so. Not you, the woman who swims with sharks." Mark looked out over the ocean. "It used to be we swam in the ocean and never thought twice."

"We used to do a lot of things and never thought twice," Jena answered. She took a sip of coffee.

"True," he replied, watching intently as she walked over to the opposite side of the deck and leaned against the railing. "I'm sorry I surprised you last night. I didn't know who you were or that you were here with Rick and Katie. I would have introduced myself had I known."

She glanced over her shoulder at him. "There's nothing to apologize for. I'm the intruder here. If you'll excuse me. I think I'll go down to the beach and watch the sunrise."

He watched her go down the stairs, taking them one at a time and grasping the rail with white knuckled hands, while favoring one of her legs.

It was a full sixty seconds before he realized she'd taken his breath away.

The morning broke quietly as the dawn spread the early sunshine across the ocean like a dimmer switch slowly increasing the power for a new day.

Jena sat in the sand, warm coffee in her hands, and watched as the sky turned from purple to pink to baby blue. Above her, seagulls floated in the gentle breeze, occasionally dipping toward her as though she might provide them with a treat. She was alone as far as she could see on either side.

She took a sip of coffee.

It had been almost seven months since the storm. Yet it seemed like last night.

It was so hard to be alone with her thoughts, yet she preferred it that way of late. People suffocated her with their good intentions. She didn't feel of use to anyone, and was sensitive to the fact that, once the life of the party, she was now a recluse.

She hadn't gone back to her consulting practice, or regrouped with the Junior League, or even gone back to church since that night. She lived in constant grief and residual shock from the devastating loss of her family.

But she'd kept her promise to Rick and kept just breathing.

From behind her, she heard steps in the sand, and looked over her shoulder.

"I hope I'm not intruding," Mark said, motioning toward the sand beside her. "May I?"

"Knock yourself out."

Mark bent down and settled himself in the sand beside her. He smiled but didn't say a word.

They sat there together for a long time, just allowing themselves to be a part of the world that was still going on. The waves lapped softly ten yards out. The tide was going back out. Occasionally, a tiny sand crab popped itself up out of the sand and scurried away.

"There is this beach in Italy," Mark whispered, pulling Jena out of her deep thoughts. "It's beautiful like this. Isolated. I went there sometimes on the weekday when the Italian locals went back to their jobs in the larger towns. The water is crystal blue. And rainbows sometimes appear out of the mist in the evenings."

Jena turned and glanced at him.

He smiled back and took a long drag on his coffee.

"Do you miss it?" Jena finally asked.

He nodded. "Sometimes. But it is another world there. It is a whole different way of living.'

"How so?"

He looked into her eyes. They were as crystal blue as the Mediterranean waters. "People savor life there. In the northern part of Italy, where I am stationed, there aren't cities, but more little villages and hamlets. Very little commercialism. No big box stores, or chain groceries. Most businesses are still small and family owned. Everything shuts down for a few hours in the afternoon, and people go home to take a nap, or hang out with their family, or just sit in their gardens with a glass of good vino. They make time to enjoy their life."

Jena watched him as he spoke, noting the slight grin as he recounted what attracted him there.

"Why don't you stay there and live?" she finally asked.

"It's time to move on. The Air Force is discharging me this coming year." He reached down and massaged his knee.

"What happened to your knee?"

He put his coffee cup in the sand. "I blew it out on a rescue mission to extract a few of our guys from deep behind enemy lines. That was several years ago. It healed up enough. I've been on active duty since."

The seagulls multiplied above their heads, calling out in the early morning as they dipped their wings and sailed lower and circled around Mark and Jena.

"How long have you been in the Air Force?" Jena asked, brushing back a strand of wild blonde hair that the wind had caught and flipped in her face.

"All of my adult life. Twenty years. I went into the military. My brother went into medicine. Our sister went into the mission field, a faith-based Peace Corps."

"So, you've seen a lot of action?"

He nodded. "Yep. Most of which I can never talk about.

She hesitated before she uttered her next words. "What can you talk about?"

He grimaced slightly. "Not a lot. There is a sworn code that forbids military from divulging information."

She watched as he continued to massage his knee.

"Let's just say," he glanced out at the ocean where a shrimp boat was headed out to sea. "This knee isn't my only war wound."

Jena stretched out her own bad leg. "I would think that you've seen and done a lot in the years you've been in the military."

"I shared some things with my ex-girlfriend, but she never got it. She called me some awful names, spit on the flag, and finally left me for someone else who tickled her fancy of entitlement."

"I'm sorry."

"Oh, I'd do it all over again."

"The girlfriend?"

"Not the girlfriend. But the military… yes. Despite the lack of morality in war, there is a cost to keeping the free… free."

"Thank you for your service," Jena whispered.

He looked at her for a long time before he finally spoke. "You're welcome."

For a moment, however brief, they were locked onto each other's souls.

"Walk with me?" He stood and reached out his hand. She took it and he helped her up from the sand.

They stood still for one moment, looking at one another.

Then they turned and walked side by side along the beach in the opposite direction from all the other beach houses. The seagulls flew over them. Little sand creatures scurried toward the water to get out of their way. They both were barefoot and the sand was wet and cool beneath them. The sun's rays danced across the water and touched their faces with warmth. In the distance, an oil tanker sat balanced on the horizon. The waft of beached marine life permeated the early morning around them.

They walked silently for a while, still side by side, going at a snail's pace, with a few feet between them. Jena used the cane to ensure her balance and she got lost in her own thoughts. And Mark was lost in his thoughts of her. It was a natural quiet between them that neither felt the obligation to fill. Finally, Jena broke the silence.

"Are you staying the full ten days?" she asked, stopping to pick up a lonesome shell.

He waited for her to stand back up. "If you don't mind."

She glanced over at him, then out at the ocean. The sun was fully up by now. "Why would I mind? I don't mind."

The air was electric around them.

"Would you tell me about your family, Jena?"

She stopped walking.

He did, too. But he didn't withdraw his question.

"We drove into a F4 tornado one night. We never saw it."

"…my God," he whispered.

"I would have thought that Rick and Katie would have told you…especially if they thought you might join them here."

"They didn't."

"…well," she breathed. "They all died. My family died."

"I'm sorry, Jena. How long ago?"

"Seven months. Last March."

He stopped again and stared at her. "Is that what happened to your leg? Why you limp?"

"Yes," she nodded, looking down at her leg. "I almost died. I was in ICU for weeks. Your brother was my surgeon."

"…wow," he said. "You must be someone very special, because my brother never gets socially involved with any of his patients."

"They've adopted me, I think. Katie was there when they brought my family into the ER. But they were already dead." She looked over at him. "It's been a devastating time. I question why I was the one that survived, and they didn't."

"You're still grieving," he whispered. He reached over and gently touched a scar on her face. "…and still healing."

"Is that what this is?" She looked over at him. "I used to think it would pass. I used to think that grief was this sad time that would pass. But it never goes away. I thought if I pushed hard enough, I could push through it…to the other side of it."

He looked out over the ocean. "There is no pushing through. It's more of an absorption, an adjustment to the emptiness, an acceptance of what we've lost."

"Maybe," she breathed, pushing the hair from her face. "But I think it is a monster that wants to kill me, too."

He gently reached out and turned her to him. "Jena. Last night, in the ocean. You weren't wading. Were you?"

Her eyes teared up, but she held his gaze. One tear finally overflowed and slipped down her face. "I got lost in the moment. That's all. It was so peaceful. I didn't mean to go out so far."

He touched her hand and she let him. "Then it was fate that I came along."

"Perhaps," she whispered.

"Your loss is so fresh, Jena."

She wiped her tears away, suddenly embarrassed that she'd allowed him to see into her like that, or that he'd even witnessed those moments last night when she was unconsciously ready to give it all up.

"It's hard," she quietly said.

He stared down at her. "Yes, I imagine it is. But you're not alone in this. You have Rick and Katie."

She glanced up at him.

"And I'll be here. I'll watch for the sharks. And the pirates."

"…and the drug lords and sex traffickers." She let a tiny smile escape from the corner of her lips. The moment lingered between them before a seagull dove for them and sent them both ducking.

They released their nervousness with a laugh.

"Come on," he reached out his hand to steady her until she got her balance. "Let's go make some breakfast."

They walked back down the beach toward the beach house. The sun warmed their skin as they walked slowly side by side, never touching. Ten minutes later the bacon was frying and the coffee pot was dripping a fresh hot dark brew. Jena scrambled eggs while Mark popped open two cans of biscuits. By the time Rick woke up and walked into the kitchen, breakfast was ready.

"You two are up early on the first full day of vacation," Rick greeted them as he came into the kitchen. "God, that smells good."

"Beautiful morning, Bro. Didn't want to miss a minute of it."

Rick filled his cup with hot coffee. "We were hoping the two of you would join us today. We've decided to go into town and explore. There are a million things to do. Museums. The Tall Ship Elissa. And the Strand. We might go to Moody Gardens tomorrow, but today we were wanting to just explore. You guys up to it?"

Mark glanced at Jena. "You game?"

"Sure," she replied.

Rick grinned. "Great. Then I'll get the family up and rolling."

They spent the morning strolling through the historic downtown district, then through the Railroad Museum, followed by the Texas Seaport Museum. Finally, they paid the admission, went through the gate and boarded the Tall Ship Elissa.

"She's a beautiful ship," Jena commented after the touring.

"She's more than iron, wood, and canvas," Mark said. "She's not a replica. She's the real thing, built in 1877 by the Scots."

"I would have loved to have sailed on her."

"She was a cargo ship for a while, then commissioned by some royalty. She's worn, but a survivor, for sure. She was rescued from a ship scrap yard in Italy and restored to her full beauty. She's fully functional again and sails in the Gulf Coast trials."

Jena slowly rubbed her hand over the polished wood railing. "She's come through a few storms of her own, I'd say." She spoke the quiet words more to herself than anyone else.

Mark came alongside her, and looked down into her face. "And here I stand…admiring her beauty and courage."

Jena turned towards him. Their fingertips touched on the railing.

"Such a beautiful sight," he whispered, from where he was standing face to face with her. "What a survivor."

His bare touch on her fingertips was a simple heartbeat of hope.

"She's a beautiful ship," Jena said quietly.

"That she is."

Jana slowly pulled away. "Where to next?'

"Lunch!" the children yelled as they emerged from the ship's belly.

Ten minutes later, they were back on the Strand and walking into a quaint little family-owned Mexican food restaurant, where all the adults ordered street tacos and sodas. The kids ate off the children's menu.

The rest of the day went at a leisured pace, but Jena was tiring quickly. They called it an afternoon and headed back to the house.

The four gathered on the deck before dinner.

Jena was exhausted, but relaxed as she leaned back into the porch rocker. She watched at a distance while Rick and his brother bantered back and forth about a sports team. Katie went back and forth from the kitchen preparing dinner.

The breeze was soft and gentle as it blew across Jena's face. It had been a good day, and there'd been small blocks of time where the grief stepped back long enough for her to breathe unhindered.

That moment on the ship with Mark had imprinted her.

That touch. His words to her.

She took a sip of iced tea.

It'd happened so unexpectedly. And so preciously. Like a breath of fresh air. Now, it was just a little keepsake of the day.

***

The third day on the beach was slow and relaxed.

Jena read a novel on the deck while Rick and Katie took the children to Moody Gardens. Mark finished up the breakfast dishes, then settled in on his computer after having quietly joined Jena on the deck.

The sun was warm on their faces. The seagulls stayed close to the water and dove now and then for small fish. The beach was empty of vacationers. The weekend would see more people up and down the sand, some playing Frisbee, others laying on long towels just soaking up the sunshine. But for now, they were alone.

By lunchtime, Rick and Katie and the children were still not back from the Moody Gardens. Maybe the pool was still open. Jena had seen Katie pack sandwiches and chips before they'd left, so she assumed they were eating lunch as a family.

Mark closed his computer.

Jena looked up from her book to see him watching her.

"Are you hungry?" he asked.

"Yes," she answered. "I shouldn't be after such a huge breakfast, but I am famished."

He stood up. "Come on, let's go for a ride."

She laid her book down. "Where are we going?"

"I've got an extra helmet. I want to take you to the best hole in the wall for shrimp in Galveston. Then I'll show you the island. You're not allergic to shell fish, are you?"

"No." She went inside and changed into jeans and a t-shirt that said Texas Rangers. He changed from his sandals into size 14 Nikes, and wrote a quick note for Rick and Katie.

His Harley was parked in the drive and she paused when she saw it. A wave of anxiety rushed through her.

"I've never ridden before."

He glanced over at her. "No problem. Just hang on. I'll do all the work. Don't lean to the outside of the curves. Follow my lead and we'll balance just fine."

She hesitated.

Then, gingerly, she swung her bad leg over and climbed on behind him and reluctantly wrapped her arms around his waist. He started up the motorcycle and it roared to life. Using his legs, he pushed them backward for just a moment, then steered the handle bars into a turn. Then they were off, speeding down the two-lane road back toward downtown and the hole in the wall.

Jena closed her eyes as the wind hit her face. The bike swerved slightly and she tightened her grip around him. They rode a few miles toward the east side of the island. To the right was the Gulf and to the left was the bay. Shrimp boats cruised up and down the waterway, occasionally blowing their horn. After a few more miles, she relaxed against him and enjoyed the wind and view. On the north side of the island, Mark slowed the bike and carefully made a U-turn. He drove slowly then and finally pulled into a family-owned store front restaurant with a picture of a shrimp boat on the old weathered door.

They parked and Mark turned off the bike. Next, their helmets came off and Jena felt the gentle ocean breeze in her hair.

"The place is a dump," he said. "But the food is great."

He held the door for her and they went in.

The place smelled of cooked fish and tangy beer. It was small but surprisingly charming. The couple that owned the joint had lived here for decades. They'd bought the property when they'd first married in the late seventies, and redone it after each storm that passed through. They were slower nowadays, but friendly and efficient.

Mark and Jena got in line and ordered, then found a table in the corner. There were others there, but the place would not be packed until the weekend.

Jena ordered a tea.

Mark asked for a lite beer.

"I'm glad this place is still here," he smiled. "It took a hard hit from the last big storm."

"It's a fun place. Very quaint. How long have you been coming to the island?" Jena asked, wrapping her hands around the cold glass.

"My brother's had this timeshare for years. The owners rebuilt after Hurricane Harvey. I've come a few times."

Their food came and they both devoured it. Fried shrimp, homemade fries, coleslaw, and sweet butter pickles. The butter biscuits topped off the meal and they were both stuffed by the end. Their waitress removed their plates and Mark leaned back in his chair.

"I was engaged," he said, out of the blue. "We broke up."

"Really?"

"Not too long ago, in fact."

Jena watched him for a few seconds, as he glanced out of the window by their table. She didn't want to ask the natural questions, so she sipped her tea again.

"She didn't want to be married to military."

"I'm sorry, Mark."

He looked at her, then shrugged. "I'm better off. But that breakup with her was worse than anything I've been through in the military. It was rough. Still hurts. I'm still trying to process it."

Behind them, someone dropped a tray in the kitchen.

He took the last sip of beer. "I understand losing someone you love through no fault of your own. It sucks."

Jena swallowed hard. "So, she left you?"

"Yep. I wasn't expecting it. When she left me, well, it was pretty much one-sided. I thought she loved me."

"Were you in Italy when this happened?"

"On a mission, in fact. Got her letter when I got back to the base. But it took three weeks for her Dear John letter to get to me. At least she didn't just break up via a text. By the time I got her letter, she was already involved with someone else. A cowboy from Oklahoma City. She said they'd met at a rodeo."

"How long ago was that?"

"This last spring. March, I think."

Jena stared at him. "So, we lost them about the same time."

He nodded. "I guess we did."

"I wonder what's harder," she whispered.

"What?"

She paused, then she looked into his eyes. "To lose someone through death or through rejection."

"Hurts like hell, all the same, doesn't it?" He reached for the check. "Let's get out of here."

He paid the bill and they walked outside. Jena hadn't really been paying attention until now as to how tall he was. Now he seemed to tower over her as he handed her the helmet, then put on his own. They climbed back on the motorcycle and started off.

He took them back down the island the way they'd come. The bike roared at full throttle and Jena relaxed against his back as she watched the ocean speed by to her left. The traffic was light. They passed the timeshare neighborhood and kept going. The houses thinned out, and finally gave way to the vast beach and sand dunes.

After a while Mark slowed and turned onto the beach. The wind was picking up and a few clouds were gathering above them. They parked and got off.

They hadn't said a word since leaving the restaurant. Now he turned to her and smiled.

"The beach is prettier here." He led her down to the water's edge. They walked along the surf, occasionally picking up a shell or two. She took his arm several times to balance herself through the sand.

"By chance," he grinned. "Did you bring a swimsuit?"

She smiled back at him. "Under my clothes."

"Want to go in?"

She grimaced. "Are there sharks?"

"Maybe. But we can probably see them."

"Mark!"

"Risk a little, Jena. We both know that life is too short to be afraid anymore."

She hesitated. "Turn around."

He did.

Quickly she stripped off her jeans and the t-shirt. When she looked back over at him, he'd stripped too, down to swim trunks.

"I'll race you," he teased.

"That's not fair," she grinned. "My leg..."

"I'll give you a head start, but not a big one. So, make the best of it."

She looked out at the water, then back at him. The other night the ocean had called to her, like a siren calling the sailors. But today, it seemed more threatening, even in the daylight.

"Go on, Jena," he urged softly.

She started walking toward the water. He waited behind her in the sand. Her feet touched the water and she paused.

"I'm right behind you," she heard his voice over her shoulder.

She waded deeper up to her ankles. Then her knees. Then her waist. The water was clearer here than anywhere on the island and she could see through the water. She dropped her hands and swirled the water around her. She waded a little farther in, and the water swirled around her breasts.

"Go all the way in."

"I can feel the current," she said.

"It won't take you. I'm still here behind you."

She could tell he'd followed her out every step of the way and was closer than she thought. She pulled her knees up and felt the water lift her up in the surf. For a moment, she was weightless. A waved crashed into her. She went searching with her feet for the bottom. Another wave crashed into her and she was swept under.

She panicked for a moment before she felt his arms around her pulling her up out of the surf and against his chest. She gasped and spit out the salt water that had gone into her mouth.

"I've got you, Jena."

She relaxed and found her footing again.

They were right on the sandbar by then and she stood in the waves. "I'm ok."

He slowly released her and smiled gently. "Being out here is cathartic."

"It's a little intense."

"I surfed down here once right before a tropical storm. Now that was intense."

"So, you're a dare devil?" she grinned at him.

"Gave it away, did I?"

Another wave crashed through them and it knocked her back into his arms. She laughed self-consciously.

He let her hold onto him long enough for her to get her balance back. Another wave hit again before she finally let go.

He laughed down at her. "Maybe we should head back?"

He took her hand and they waded side by side toward the shore. "Do you mind drying off before we head back? I hate driving in wet clothes."

"Actually, I think I'd like to get a little sun," she replied. "I can't believe it's still so warm in October."

"Well, it's Texas."

They reached the beach and sat down in the wet sand. He dug an intact sand dollar out of the sand with his long fingers and handed it to her.

She smiled.

The sun was directly overhead and beat down on them.

"So," she began, glancing up at him. "When do you get out of the military?"

"I'm still on active duty, even though I'm on leave. I should be discharged by this time next year. My tour will be over. They are sending me forth with a medical discharge, full honors, and a very nice retirement package."

"Is it hard leaving after so long?"

He nodded and looked away. "Yep."

"What will you do now?"

"Don't know. Probably something dangerous. I'm an adrenaline junkie."

She shook her head. "That doesn't surprise me about you."

"What about you, Jena?" He handed her a tiny shell the color of rainbows. "What will you do now?"

"I don't know, either."

"It would be nice to just disappear for a while."

Her expression grew solemn. "I tried that."

"What?"

"In the hospital. I tried to die. But they wouldn't let me."

He reached out and touched her hand. And she let him.

"I did die. Four times. In the ER. Twice in surgery and once in the ICU. But they resuscitated me." She dug out a small conk shell and handed it over to him. The ocean churned in front of them.

"I saw a guy die in front of me," he said. "Mortar attack. I tried, but I couldn't do anything to save him. He had a girl back home and was expecting his discharge when we came back from that mission. He bled out with me trying to plug the hole in his gut."

A seagull called out above them and they glanced up to watch it glide on the wind and hover just over their heads.

"Katie was in the ER when they brought my family in. She said they were already gone. She said they died suddenly." Jena turned toward him. "How could she know that?"

"She's a nurse."

"They were so tiny."

He leaned toward her.

"And Pete. He didn't mean to drive into that tornado. He didn't see it. No one saw it until the lightening flashed. It was too late. It was right on us."

"How many died that night?"

She frowned. "A lot. A lot of people died that night."

"Do you remember any of it?"

She shook her head and bit her lip. "I don't know. I can't tell the difference even now, if it is a memory of reality or a memory of a nightmare. I just remember the smell of mold and dirt and that metal taste of blood in my mouth.

He sat quietly.

"There were flashing lights. Everyone around me was yelling. I remember the pain. I remember the sound of the helicopter. I was air lifted out, they said. But I don't remember that."

He waited for a few minutes. Then he asked. "When did you know your family didn't make it?"

She teared up. "They came to me while I was in the coma. That's how I knew." She shrugged. "Sounds weird, I know."

"Wow," Mark whispered, and grew tense. Then he took a deep breath and let it out slowly. "My buddy, the guy that died in my arms, came to me in a dream. He told me he loved me. That I was the best friend he'd ever had. And he told me to let go of it. Let him go."

Jena turned her face toward him.

"There was this incredible light behind him. And he looked happy. At peace. And he had all his parts."

The tide was coming in and the water rushed toward them.

"Why couldn't we save them, Mark?"

"It was their time."

"I don't believe that. It's not right."

He held her hand. "I don't blame God, though. I blame greedy men and world powers who wage war against the innocents for the cause of oil and territory."

"But who do I blame, Mark?"

He looked at her. "I hope, Jena, that even in the middle of all this loss, we can both come to that moment when we get past the anger of having to blame at all. We can't change what has happened."

The next wave rolled in to their knees.

He stood up and reached out his hand. "Come on, kid. Let's get back to the others. They're probably back by now." He pulled her up. She brushed the sand away from her clothes.

Halfway back across the sand dunes he reached out, and they walked hand in hand back to the place he'd parked the Harley.

***

"Enjoy the ride?" Rick asked as Mark and Jena came through the front door. It was four o'clock in the afternoon.

"I'm going to go take a short nap," Jena replied.

Katie watched her. "Jena, are you alright?"

"Let her go," Mark said, walking into the kitchen and grabbing a bottle of water out of the refrigerator.

"…ok," Katie replied, puzzled. "Everything good?"

"Yep," Mark said, guzzling down the cool liquid. "Hey Bro, do you want to take a run before dinner."

"Sounds like a plan," Rick answered, glancing over his shoulder at Katie and shrugging his shoulders. "We'll be back in a bit and then we'll start up the grill for the steaks."

Two hours later Jena opened the door and stepped out onto the deck. The guys were laying corn on the cob and whole onions on the top grill, and dropping thick steaks and hot dogs closer to the flames. Katie was sitting in the corner chair, sipping on a bottle of water, watching the children play in the grass below.

Katie looked up. "Welcome to the sunburn club, Jena. You are red, sweetie."

Jena smiled. "I'm starting to feel it."

Katie handed her a bottle of After Sun lotion. "It becomes you."

"Is it bad?"

"You're a little past pink," Katie grinned.

"She's medium rare," Rick laughed. "Where did you guys go today?"

Mark looked up from the grill. "Down to the State Park."

Katie shifted in her chair and adjusted her t-shirt. "I got burned, too. I think I have to take a bath in Aloe Vera tonight. I keep forgetting how brutal this sun is, all year long."

"She lathers up the kids in UV Protection 50 and uses suntan oil on herself. Oil. At the beach." Rick laughed.

"Don't laugh," Katie moaned. "It hurts."

Mark grinned. "Serves you right, nurse. You need to practice what you preach."

"Shut up," Katie responded. "You've never burned a day in your life. You just tan. I hate you."

Jena poured herself a glass of iced tea from a pitcher on the table and listened to the good-natured bantering.

"How was your motorcycle ride?" Rick asked.

"It was…adventurous," Jena said as she glanced at Mark and they shared a smile. It had been a good day.

Rick nodded. "It's a wonder he didn't take you on the motor cross circuit. He's a crazy man on that bike. Mark rides all across Italy and Europe."

"Hey, now," Mark defended himself. "I was gentle."

"And a gentleman," Jena added, sipping her tea. "My only injury is this silly sunburn."

"Well, suck it up buttercup," Mark grinned. "Because we have been challenged to a game of…"

"Watch Your Mouth." Rick warned.

Jena squinted. "A game of what?"

"Watch Your Mouth," Katie warned.

"I'm sorry…" Jena said, confused.

"That's the name of the game," Katie beamed. "Watch Your Mouth. Ever play it?"

"No," Jena replied.

"You're on my team," Mark declared.

They ate dinner inside because it started to sprinkle as Rick pulled the meat off the grill. Katie put the children to bed afterward. The littlest one had fallen asleep between bites of her hot dog. After the children were settled, Katie brought out the game.

At ten o'clock, they were still laughing through the game, but decided to end it as the next day was loaded with activity. Rick and Katie went to bed. Mark and Jena finished putting dishes in the dishwasher, and then silently walked out to the deck together, closing the door behind them.

The night was calm. The light drizzle had moved off.

The stars were bright, and Jena felt like she could reach out and touch them. They sat quietly for five minutes before either of them said a word.

"It's beautiful…" Jena whispered.

"Yes, it is."

Another few minutes passed.

"My mom used to sing me a song when I was a kid…about the stars."

Mark turned toward her. "How did it go?"

Jena smiled sadly. "I'm a little self-conscious. I'm not the best singer."

"We're not on American Idol, so I think it's safe here."

Her eyes lit up when she looked over at him. "Uh," she began. "Let me remember."

He waited.

Softly, almost inaudibly, she started to sing.

"*The stars shine over the mountains. The stars shine over the sea. The stars look up to heaven...*"

Jena paused.

Mark could tell she'd choked up. So, he quietly finished. "*And the stars shine down on me.*"

She turned to look at him, surprised.

He smiled. "Right up there with Rock-a-bye Baby."

"So…you're not all blood and guts, soldier?"

He shook his head. "Never was."

"…more of a savior?" she whispered.

He turned and looked tenderly at her. "Don't put me so high up on a pedestal, Bella. I'm just a man."

"A good man."

"I try to be," he shrugged his shoulders. "I want to be."

She looked at him for a long time, then slowly looked away. Then back up at the sky.

"What's that constellation?" she pointed south.

He leaned closer to her and followed the direction she was looking. He took her hand, leaned closer to her head and, with his other hand, pointed her across the sky. He named each constellation one by one, telling her the story behind each one.

He was so close she felt his breath on her cheek.

It was after 1 a.m. when they said goodnight to each other and went back inside for the night.

Chapter Nine

They woke to clouds and thunder on the horizon. The wind was coming out of the south in irregular gusts, kicking up small vortexes of sand on the beach. Not unusual for an autumn tropical storm, that ramps up fast and roars through unexpectedly.

Jena laid in her bed listening to the shutters rattle against the wind. It was early still, but light outside. She reached over and turned on the bedside lamp and checked the weather app on her phone. The screen was lit up in red and purple to the south of them, with a great expanse of the radar indicating incoming heavy rain.

So much for doing anything outside today, or at least on the beach or in town.

But she could still be outside, below, under the covering of the deck and house. The owners had made sure to include an open area for relaxing or playing card games under the protection of the huge pier supported house. The area even had a wet bar, TV screen, and fireplace.

Jena rose and put on her jeans and a light sweater and walked into the kitchen. Someone was up, as the coffee pot was on but half full. She filled her cup. Her leg was hurting this morning, so she rode the lift down to the ground level. The door slid open and she saw Mark standing at the edge of the covering looking out toward the ocean and the brewing storm.

"Morning," she whispered.

He turned. "Hey."

"It's building, isn't it? The storm?" She came beside him.

"Yep. And picking up speed. It's that time of year when these things pop up and go nuclear quick. This storm has finally gotten itself organized while we were sleeping."

"Thanks for the coffee."

"Sure."

They stood together watching the clouds roll in and silently counted the lightning flashes to the rumble.

"It was fun last night," she commented.

He smiled at her. "It was good to hear you laugh, Jena."

"You are funny, Mark. A real sarcastic asshole."

"Watch your mouth," he whispered, winking at her.

She answered by gently nudging him with her elbow.

"I'm stir crazy already, and the day hasn't even begun," he said. "I wanted to ride today. I was hoping you'd go with me."

"Tomorrow, maybe," she looked up at him.

"I'm afraid this thing is going to get worse before it gets better. I've been watching it build."

"Will it be a hurricane?"

"Maybe. Certainly, a tropical storm. But we need to stay alert so we have time to leave in case it does. We don't want to get caught out here with a storm surge."

She paused a long time. "At least we have some warning and can see it coming at us."

His eyes were out to sea. "Are you afraid?"

"A little," she softly admitted. "No. Actually, a lot."

He gently wrapped his arm around her shoulders, and together they watched the lightning strike the open sea. Jena felt his comfort and easy reassurance, and didn't pull away.

"I know storms are hard for you," he said quietly.

"An understatement." Jena took a breath. She felt the anxiety building around her heart.

A melancholy silence stood with them for a few minutes.

He finally glanced down at her. "After my fiancé broke up with me, I wondered what it would be like coming home. What it would be like trying to create a different life, after so long."

"You have Rick and Katie. Your sister. Your parents."

He frowned. "Lately, I think a lot about coming home to no one to put my arms around, or hold. No one to grow old with. No one to really talk to. I understand loneliness, Jena."

She lowered her eyes. "How do you handle it?"

He paused a long time. "Not so well. It tends to handle me."

"What do you mean?"

"It's overwhelming. It comes in waves. Like that ocean."

"When does the grief end from losing them?" she whispered.

"Depends. But never really," he answered. "It just changes form and becomes something else altogether. Some people take medication. Some people drink. Some people overeat. Some people take lovers. Some people leave it all behind."

She glanced up at him.

"And some people," he said quietly. "Some people hope and pray someone out there will throw them a lifeline."

"A lifeline…"

He nodded. "A reason to live. A reminder that they still have something to hope for. A friendship, perhaps, with someone who's also in the water, hoping for the same thing."

"I'm scared, Mark."

"We all are, to some extent."

She looked up at him. "I would have never thought you'd be afraid of anything."

He nodded slowly. "I didn't used to be. But now? Yeah."

"What are you afraid of, Mark?"

He looked into her eyes and took one full minute to lose himself there before he answered. "I'm afraid of losing my heart again, and never getting it back. I'm afraid of walking through life without the love of my life. This upcoming retirement has me thinking about a lot of things I've never paid attention to. I'm having to face some inevitabilities."

"It's a lot to face."

"Hmmm. It is. For both of us."

The wind kicked up and whipped around the corner.

Jena fought the wind for a moment, then swept back her hair into a ponytail to keep it out of her face.

"Six months isn't long, Jena. But then it becomes a year, then two, then a lifetime. I don't want either of us to find ourselves at the end of this journey alone, still afraid."

The moment was suspended in time, amid absolute calm. They both stared toward the sea. Then the lightening crashed a mile offshore and the thunder rolled toward them.

"You're pretty wise for not having any gray hair yet."

He grinned. "Oh, I have gray hair. I just keep it cut short so no one sees. And I've earned every one them." He turned toward her and tenderly touched her hair. "But you…your hair is the sunshine."

She took in her breath.

"I'm enjoying every moment with you," he said.

"Me, too… with you," she whispered. Then paused. "And Rick and Katie and the kids, of course."

He nodded. "Of course.

They held each other's gaze and each felt a soft shifting in their new friendship. Then the moment was interrupted by the annoying siren of her weather app warning them of turbulent weather ahead.

It was a depression now, but coming onshore as a tropical storm, with landfall in twelve hours. The eye was to hit spot on just miles east of them. That meant that the storm surge would focus eastward and possibly leave them out of immediate danger. A tropical storm was wicked, but most people stayed and just boarded up. The danger was in two things: would the storm track more west, and would it continue to build into a Cat One or something stronger.

"I can't run my bike in this," Mark commented to her as she fumbled to silence the warning notification. "But Rick and Katie and the kids… and you… might want to head back inland until this storm passes."

"I'll go wake them," she said, turning toward the lift.

"We're awake," Rick said as he took the last step off the stairs. "We've been watching the storm on cable. Getting stronger."

"Yep," Mark said. "What's your game plan, Bro?"

"We're going inland and getting a hotel till it passes. I don't want to take a chance on getting stuck on the island. You both should get packed so we can head out. We can come back here after the storm."

"There's not room in your SUV for everything and everyone," Mark notated. "I'll stay here."

Rick turned on his brother. "No one is staying. We leave the stuff. Just take a couple of bags. Katie's already calling around for a hotel. We'll be back tomorrow. You'll need to pull your bike up under here and secure it."

"I got us a few rooms at the Hyatt," Katie announced as she descended the stairs to the covered area. "It's an hour inland. The kids are up and packing their things. Jena, you and Mark need to go do the same."

"We leave in an hour," Rick announced.

Mark nodded. "Ok then. Mission commencing." He held out his hand to Jena. She took it. Then they packed into the lift and ascended upward.

Rick and Katie watched as they went out of sight.

"Did you see that?" Rick asked his wife.

"The hand holding thing?"

They glanced at each other and shared a knowing look, then went toward the stairs to start their own packing.

***

They weren't the only ones leaving the island. A portion of the population was on the road by the time they hit the causeway. After Hurricane Harvey, most didn't want to risk it. It was always Russian Roulette with these storms, and people were tired of gambling on the storm dying before it made landfall.

Rick and Mark sat in the front, while Katie, Jena, and one of the children sat behind them. The other three children were strapped in the back third row seatbelts. Bags were stuffed at their feet and in the back storage area. They left most of their things, toys, food, and ice chests in order to pack everyone into a seat.

Crossing the causeway was slow and tedious, and Jena tensed as the wind picked up and battle rammed their vehicle. Katie watched her from the other seat and slowly reached out. But their vehicle kept moving forward and they were soon on the mainland.

"I wish we'd boarded up before we left," Rick said. "I'm not sure those shutters will hold."

Mark shook his head. "I looked around for materials to do that, but there was nothing."

"Can we go swimming at the hotel?" one of the children inquired.

"If it is an indoor pool, sweetie," Katie answered.

After battling traffic for two hours, they pulled into the Hyatt and parked in the covered parking garage. They got everything in one trip and walked together to the elevator that took them to the lobby. There, Rick checked them in and Mark put his room and Jena's room on his credit card.

Jena tried to argue with him, but he told her they'd settle later. So, she left them to finish the check in and meandered through the lobby until they were done.

"We're on the second floor," Rick announced, as he passed out the room key cards. "You two have rooms on the third floor. They couldn't get us together."

"That's fine, Bro."

Jena thanked him as she took her key card.

"Ok, we're going to chill for a while with the kids. Do you want to meet for dinner at the restaurant?"

Jena nodded. Mark agreed.

But by two o'clock, plans changed.

The storm stalled offshore and was upgraded.

Katie and Jena took the kids swimming in the indoor pool, while Rick and Mark made a Walmart run before the storm hit. They loaded up on groceries, flashlights and batteries, a couple of Styrofoam coolers, a board game, a few decks of cards, candy bars and the last two cases of water. Then they filled up the SUV with gas, anticipating a shortage once the storm passed.

By dinner, everyone was famished and exhausted.

Revised predictions forecasted the storm was to make landfall at High Point Island, which would bring the backside of the hurricane across them.

That night at dinner, the four of them talked about preparations.

"We could go home," Katie suggested.

Rick shook his head. "It's way too late. We'd be driving all night in the dark, rain, and wind." He glanced over at Jena.

She met his stare, and the look in her eyes was enough to solidify his decision.

"We'll stay put here. This hotel was built to take a hard blow. It's high enough above sea level and we're far enough inland to avoid the storm surge. "

Mark agreed. "Glad that's decided. I'm starved. Let's order before they shut down and kick us out."

Jena barely touched her food, while everyone else devoured theirs. They paid the bill and left and the restaurant closed its doors after them. They separated at the elevator, and went to their respective floors.

When the elevator opened on Mark and Jena's floor, he reached out and touched her arm.

"Hey…"

She turned toward him.

"Want to play couple of games of gin rummy?"

"Sure," she smiled. Anything to take her mind off the storm.

They stopped at his room first and he grabbed a couple of decks of cards, some water and snacks, a flash light, his phone charger, and a couple of emergency candles they'd picked up at Walmart.

By the time they got to her room, her leg was killing her, so she sat down in the lounge chair and propped her leg on the bed. Her shorts rode higher on her thighs.

Mark noticed again the long series of scars where his brother, the surgeon, had worked his magic. He sat down in the second chair and leaned back, propping both his feet on the bed next to her.

"We'll be fine here, Jena. Just once the wind kicks up, we'll have to keep the curtains closed and stay away from the windows. Not to scare you, but to prepare you."

"Ok."

He reached for the TV remote control and flipped to the Weather Channel. They were tracking the storm and one of the reporters was stationed just outside of their hotel. They were close enough to the action, but still a safe distance from the eye.

"The storm is shifting again and will come ashore as a CAT One hurricane. Evacuations along the coast have been underway all day. But time has run out to evacuate. If you are inland, you should stay where you are."

"This will all be over by tomorrow," Mark reassured.

She nodded, her eyes glued on the TV.

"Want to deal the cards, Jena?" He handed her the deck. "I must warn you. I'm the card shark champ at the base in Italy."

She smiled. "Well, you've met your perfect match."

They played for an hour, then the wind started picking up outside. The hotel management had moved everyone down to the lowest levels, so Mark was confident they were good where they were. He stood up and stretched, and helped Jena to her feet. Then he moved the table and chairs across the room from the windows. There was ample room, as it was an upgrade and resembled more of a small suite than a regular hotel room.

They played for another hour, as the eye of the storm tracked east of them. But the winds were wild and howling and they both knew the hotel was taking a beating.

Mark's phone rang. "Hello? We're fine. We're in Jena's room, playing cards. Ok. Will do. Thank you for letting me know. I'm good. Probably not." He glanced over at her. "She's good. Sure. You, too. Take care." Then he hung up.

Jena watched as he put his phone on the desk and plugged in the charger.

"That was Rick. The kids are asleep in the bathroom. They made a tent for them and they're making an adventure out of it."

"They're great parents," Jena said.

He nodded in agreement as he shuffled. They played yet another round of cards, quietly talking about trivial things, when the lights flickered.

"…Mark?"

He reached over and turned up the volume on the TV just as the weather alert posted

The weather channel gave way to a local news cast. "*There are confirmed reports of tornadoes on the ground in the South Houston and Sugarland area. Take cover immediately.*" The newscaster gave the exact location, and Mark stood up.

"*Move to an interior room or hallway, and if you are in your car, pull off the road and seek shelter immediately. Again, there are confirmed reports…*"

"Let's go," Mark commanded, reaching for her hand. They quickly moved to the bathroom and Mark pulled the pillows from the bed and tossed them in the tub. "You take the tub. I'll take the floor."

He stepped out of the bathroom and returned a moment later with her bags, the water and food, his phone charger, and candles.

"Stay put, Jena. I'm going to my room and get my stuff. I'll be right back."

"We're staying the night in here? Don't we need to move to a lower floor? They said there are tornadoes, Mark."

He took her hand for a moment. "We are safe, here, Jena. We're low enough. I'll keep you safe." Then he was gone.

Jena sat in the tub surrounded by pillows.

The wind rattled the windows. Then the lights went out. Something forcefully crashed against the glass panes and shattered them. She could hear the roar of the storm through the blown opening. She covered her ears and squeezed her eyes closed.

Suddenly, time shifted. She was no longer in a tub, but in her car on the highway. The howling of the storm was deafening.

Chaos swirled around her. The radio was full blast with the warning for them to get off the road! Seek shelter! Debris was hitting their vehicle, splintering glass and denting metal.

Pete was yelling at her to "hold on Jena!"

The babies were crying. Something else smashed into the windshield. Then the windows of the SUV exploded and the imploding pressure sucked everything from the car. Something heavy hit the back of her head. A brick smashed her in the face.

She grabbed her head, saw her own blood, and screamed.

Her ears popped.

Metal ripped from the roof. Then, there it was! The monster. It was violently rotating all around her, its force trying to pull her from her seatbelt. She looked up and into the vortex as the SUV was spun up into the very evil of its core.

She looked over at Pete, but he was gone, as was the driver's door. Part of a tanker truck flew over her head. She was flying. Torrents of water pelted her like BB shots, and lightening crashed around her like rocket mortar. She was going around and around, and nausea pulled vomit from her stomach. Still strapped in what remained of her seat and the car, she went careening through the air until she was slammed against a soft muddy hill, landing with a crunching thud. Her body rammed up against the dashboard. Her ribs snapped. Her leg was crushed between her seat and the crumpled door.

She heard herself screaming, and gasped for air to scream again. But there was no air. Her body was on fire! Then everything went deadly quiet, save the whoosh of spinning tires and her own groans.

***

He heard her screaming from his room and ran down the dark hallway back to her room. He fumbled with the door key and practically busted down the door trying to get to her. He found her where he'd left her, huddled in the tub, her hands covering her face, groans now a heartbreaking whimper. Behind them in the room, the wind whipped the curtains and flung the window's shattered glass across the room.

He said her name. But she was not there. She was trapped in metal debris on the side of muddy hill in the depths of horror.

She started rocking back and forth, crying now like a mortally wounded animal.

He gently pulled her hands from her face. "You're ok, Jena." He grabbed a washcloth and wet it in the sink, then rung it out and gently wiped the tears from her face. "You're safe. I've got you."

"You're safe. I've got you." Jena opened her bloodied eyes to see the fireman, suited up in protective gear, reaching to clear the debris from her face. "Stay still. We're getting you out."

Above her, the chopper cut through the silent aftermath of the storm and descended in front of her.

"My babies," she whispered. "My babies."

"I've got you, Jena," Mark whispered. "Come back to me."

The roar of the storm outside their shattered hotel window dissipated, leaving only the noise of splattering rain.

Jena felt the cloth on her face.

"…my babies."

The fireman was talking to her. "Come back to me."

She slowly opened her eyes.

It was dark, save one lone flickering candle in the far corner.

A man was bending over her. She looked up into his eyes, and blinked twice.

"Jena…breathe."

Her heart pounded in her chest. She couldn't breathe. Something was strangling her. She raised her hand and felt the back of her head.

"Jena…I'm here. You're safe."

She wiped the wet from her face. Then she took a breath, then another and another. Then the tears fell. Whimpers turned to crying and then to heartbreaking sobs.

Mark wanted to climb into the tub with her, but he was too tall and his legs too long.

She retreated to the back of the tub, with her arms wrapped tight around the pillow as though she were trying desperately, hopelessly to hold on to babies.

Mark knelt beside the tub. With his hand on her knee, he let her cry, occasionally touching her face with the warm cloth.

She wept for the longest time. And then, the sobs turned back into a soft cry, and finally to quiet whimpers. Eventually it all subsided, and was replaced by occasional sniffing and the catching of her breath. Finally, Jena looked up at him.

He smiled empathetically, and wiped the remaining tears from her cheeks.

When she was ready, he gently pulled her up out of the tub and just held her to himself.

He held her for a long time.

After a while, she lifted her arms and wrapped them around his waist and held on to him, too.

He brushed the back of her hair.

"My head hurts," she whispered, pressing closer into him.

He understood. It'd happened to him a hundred times. Triggered by some innocent sound or smell, or a movie on the TV, he'd been catapulted back into the war zone. Machine guns blaring. The choking smell of smoke. The metallic taste of blood. The pungent odor of sweat and fatigue. The paralyzing fear. The screams of men and women dying in war. The horror.

He understood, so he just held her until she was fully back to reality, and to him.

"Oh, god…" she breathed against his chest.

"Breathe, Jena," he whispered. "Just breathe."

"That's never happened."

He didn't answer, but held her tight.

"I guess they're coming back," she murmured.

"The memories?"

"Yes."

"It's the trauma coming back." He caressed her shoulder.

"I know how they died now."

"I'm so sorry, Jena."

"I think I'm going to throw up." And then she suddenly did. All over him, and the toilet, and the floor.

He held her hair back, and let the emotions rip out her insides. Oh, yes. He was very familiar with the process of PTSD, grief, and a hidden demon called anger.

Anger at the storms. Anger at the world. Anger at self because they couldn't save the ones they loved.

When things settled down, he wiped her face again. After a while, she pulled away slowly and leaned against the doorframe.

Mark then threw a couple of hand towels on the floor and wiped up her vomit.

Jena saw his shirt, where she'd thrown up on him.

She took in a deep breath. "I'm so sorry, Mark."

He turned to her. "Never, ever apologize for something like this. It is part of life, and truth be known, it was probably good for you to let it all go. It happens to the best of us."

She said nothing, but simply watched him.

He finished cleaning up, washed his hands in the sink, and then slowly came to stand in front of her. He looked down into vulnerable blue eyes, crystal clear from the purging of heartache.

"You ok now?" he whispered. He grazed her cheek with his fingertips.

She stared up at him and nodded.

"Come on, Jena. Let's move to my room and get cleaned up."

They gathered all their things and left the room, locking the door behind them. Once in his room, he suggested she take the shower while there still might be hot water.

She did.

Standing in the warm water, she let the tears wash away the remembrance. Then she dried off, changed her clothes, and brushed her teeth by candlelight.

He took his turn in the bathroom while she huddled on the floor by the room door, as far from the window as she could be.

When he came out, it was in gym shorts and a t-shirt, and barefoot, like her. "If you've got to pee, do it now. I'm making a pallet on the floor in the bathroom. I've got to get some sleep, and so do you."

"I'm good," she whispered.

She watched as he dragged the mattress from the double bed and squeezed it into the oversized bathroom. It barely fit. Then he tossed the pillows on top, followed by blankets and a quilt.

The electricity came back on, but he kept the lights low and kept the candles lit. They crawled onto the mattress one by one, giving each other space to maneuver and get comfortable.

The storm kept up outside, but the violence was diminishing.

"Mark?" she whispered.

He turned to face her on the pallet. "Yeah?"

She hesitated.

He sensed it.

She was watching him in the reflection of the candlelight.

"Do you have flashbacks of the war?"

"Yes."

"How often," she whispered.

"A lot," he answered. "I throw up, too, when I'm coming out of them."

She took a deep breath. "I'm so tired."

He thought, then, if he could just wrap up this precious tiny moment and capture the truth and purity in her eyes, he would be able to make it through anything that life might throw at him.

"Me, too," he replied. He opened his arms to her and she looked at him for the longest time, as though she were contemplating the most important decision of her life.

Then she slowly moved closer and laid her head on his shoulder. He wrapped his arms around her. They fell asleep that way and slept through the night.

***

She woke up to the aroma of coffee.

He was gone.

She stood up off the pallet and went into the room. He was standing by the window with the curtain drawn open, watching the rain.

"The storm is over, Jena."

She walked over to him.

He bent down and kissed the top of her head. "Help me move the mattress back, will you?"

Together they wrestled the mattress back on the box spring and threw all the covers on top. Then they got the pillows out of the bathroom and tossed them on the bed.

"I've got to pee," he announced.

She laughed softly. "Me, too."

"You go first, then."

She did, then quickly came out and motioned that it was his turn.

Jena sat on the bed, flipping through the news channels while Mark took his turn in the bathroom.

Someone knocked on the door.

Still in her sweat pants and braless t-shirt, her blonde hair wild from sleep, she rose to answer the door.

"Well!" Rick exclaimed, surprised to see her in his brother's room. He paused, taking in her disheveled appearance head to toe. "Good morning. Rough night?"

She followed his eyes as they took in her appearance.

"Not what I was expecting." She swung the door open. "Mark's in the bathroom."

Rick stepped into the room and saw the one still made bed, and the one that looked like a war had taken place on it. The sheets, blanket, and bedspread were hanging off the mattress, and the pillows were tossed over them. He tried to push back everything that was rushing through his mind.

"We were, uh, going to go down to breakfast and thought, uh, you might like to join us," Rick said.

Jena went over to the full-length mirror and roughed her hands through her hair. Not missing Rick's strange expression, she realized what he might be thinking.

"I'm famished," she said. "It was a long night."

"So, it seems," Rick replied. The candles were still lit throughout the room.

The door of the bathroom opened and Mark stepped out, his face and hair wet from a quick shower. He was dressed only in a pair of boxer shorts. He stopped when he saw his younger brother standing there. "Morning," Mark murmured.

Rick didn't answer but kept scanning the room around him. A thousand assumptions ran rampant.

Mark walked over to his bag and took out a black t-shirt and quickly put it on.

Jena looked away.

Then, Mark pulled on a pair of jeans.

"We're going down for breakfast," Rick commented, looking from one to the other. "The kitchen is up and running. There's coffee and a small buffet."

"Sounds great," Mark replied. Then he turned to Jena. "The shower is all yours."

"Thank you," she whispered. Then she reached for her bag and retreated to the bathroom and closed the door behind her.

The brothers watched her, then turned toward each other.

Rick was first to speak. "What exactly went on here last night? Because Jena's not ready for you, or anyone."

Mark glared at him. "You're a little out of your lane, aren't you, Rick. I'm surprised you think so little of me, and her."

Rick motioned toward the unkept bed. "I'm protective of her. What went on here last night?"

"So am I, dude!" Mark reached for a room card. "You want to know what happened last night? Come with me."

Mark led him down the hall to Jena's room and opened the door. The curtains still flapped in the wind. Glass was everywhere. The carpet was soaked.

"What happened last night? I'll tell you." Mark was clearly agitated, as he advanced toward his brother, his jaw clenching. . "I kept her safe."

Rick stepped back.

"And for you to suggest anything else is a dishonor to her and me," Mark growled.

"Sorry, Bro. I meant no offense." Then Rick said nothing.

"It was a long night for everyone," Mark calmed.

"Understood," Rick finally answered. "I'll leave the two of you to get ready. Would you like for me to report the damage?"

Mark shook his head. "I already did."

Rick reached out his hand then, in a silent apology. Mark looked at it, then grasped it. "We'll see you downstairs."

Mark closed the door and made his way back down the hall. Once inside his own room, he put his things together and closed his bag. Jena came out of the bathroom, her hair washed and dried, but still wild around her shoulders. She was in jeans and a pink top that fully outlined her breasts. She'd applied light chap stick and a little blush.

"Rick looked like he walked into Fifty Shades of Gray," she said, distracted by putting her own things in her bag. She took out some socks, and zipped her bag closed. Then she turned to him.

But he was just standing there. The look in his eyes made Jena take in a quick breath.

"Mark. Why are you looking at me that way?"

Mark slowly rubbed his hand across his stubbled face. He was fighting the urge to cross the room and kiss her. Finally, he found his voice. "You're just beautiful, Jena."

"Oh, god, I'm a mess," she stumbled over her words. "It was a long night." She tried to avoid his eyes. "For both of us."

When he didn't respond, she glanced over at him, then couldn't look away. They stood staring at each other for the longest time, not saying a word.

In that moment, something changed between them. Perhaps it already had. They both felt it. They weren't just acquaintances anymore. The night had made them friends, and taken them to a new level of vulnerability and trust.

"Are we going back today?" she finally whispered.

Mark slowly nodded. "Probably. Everyone still has their things there and, depending on the damage, we might have to pack out and cut the vacation short."

Another long pause of silence. "What did Rick want?"

"There's breakfast downstairs."

"Good thing. I'm…I'm starving."

"Let's go, then." He walked over and opened the door for the door for her. They left the room, leaving their bags sitting side by side on the disheveled bed.

Chapter Ten

The hurricane had shifted to the east at the last minute and come ashore in Port Arthur. It was a much smaller storm, however intense in nature, so the residual weather cleared by lunchtime.

They got back to the beach house to find it unscathed. No windows were broken. The guys had closed the shutters from the outside before they'd left, so their quick thinking had saved the remainder of the vacation. Rick called the timeshare and reported in. All was good. Even the electricity had stayed on and they'd lost nothing, but one and half days' time.

Mark checked out his bike and wiped it down. Rick picked up dead wood and debris off the beach and tossed it in a pile for a bonfire later. Katie unpacked their bags and threw a couple of loads of laundry in, including a load of beach towels. And Jena swept the deck of damp sand and shell bits.

Mark took out some hamburger meat and fired up the grill. By dinner, they were ready to stop and regroup. They fed the children and put them in front of a Disney flick, then all the adults retreated to the deck for a simple meal of burgers, chips, and fruit.

"I saw your hotel room, Jena," Rick said as he bit into this burger. "What a mess."

She looked up, then over at Mark. "The wind was bad."

"Good thing you stayed away from the window."

"Pass the ketchup, please," Mark said, shooting a look at his brother."

Katie stopped mid-bite. "What happened?"

Mark put down his drink. "The storm blew out Jen's hotel room window, so we sheltered the night in my bathroom. Just like you guys did. There were several rooms with damage." He reached for the chips. "Glad we got off this island when we did." He pulled a handful of chips and dropped them onto his plate. "So, what's on the agenda for tomorrow?"

Rick raised his eyebrows as though in deep thought. "No plans yet. Hopefully the sun will come out."

Mark glanced at Jena and she smiled at him.

"I think it just did," he whispered. Then he bit into his double stacked burger and chowed down.

***

In the days following, life took on a simple routine. Rick and Katie spent most of their time with the children on the beach, at nearby parks, or exploring town.

Jena spent her early mornings sitting on the beach. Sometimes, she journaled. Sometimes, she just watched the sea. Mark gave her the quiet time alone before he made her a fresh cup of coffee and came to join her. It became their ritual.

They would then sit on the beach and talk for hours, sharing the stories of their lives, unfolding each layer like an onion. Sometimes they walked together. Jena told him all about her consulting business and the Junior League, and her church. She shared about life with Pete, how they met, and their marriage. She told him about the babies, the day they were born… and the day they died. He shared about the military and his missions, as much as he could. His childhood, his college years, and his ex-fiancé.

The days ambled by.

They went for an occasional motorcycle ride to town for lunch, or treasure hunting in old town. Another day they went to the park with Rick and Katie and the kids. They spent the days on the water and beach, ate too much, and laughed together so freely.

They were the days of unexpected strangers becoming good friends, and then good friends becoming…more.

On the day before they were to leave to go home, Jena woke up especially early, made coffee, rode the lift down to the beach level, and grabbed a beach towel. She sat on the sand looking out to the ocean before dawn even appeared. Stars were shining still. The waves were calm and lapped quietly in front of her.

The dark despair was starting to lift from her soul and her heart was beating strong again. Her time alone on the beach had been deeply reflective, and strangely soothing. She felt more at peace. Less strangled. Her body was healing faster now, and her spirit detected a slight breeze in her sails.

On this morning, she felt Mark before she heard him. He came quietly and sat beside her.

Good morning, he said, without words. She smiled at him.

They sat that way a long time, and watched dawn break over the water.

"Do you believe in God, Mark?" she finally whispered.

"Yes, I do," he replied. "All good soldiers believe in something greater, or else fighting for liberty has no reason."

She looked into his eyes. "Who is He?"

"Ah. The question of the millenniums." He took a deep breath. "I'm not a philosopher or a theologian, but I'm sure He can't be described. He's beyond any of my comprehension, and way beyond my ability to even begin to understand."

"But you have some idea," she asked.

"As do you." He nodded. "A lot of people describe Him as a father. But Rick and I never knew our real father. He left our mom when we were very young. Rick doesn't remember him at all. I remember him drunk and hitting our mom. So, I can't relate to the father figure."

Jena stayed quiet.

"I remember my step dad more. He's a good man. But he and my mom married when I was a senior in high school. I left for the Air Force several years later after I finished college."

"I had a good dad. He died."

"I remember you saying, Jena."

"So, how do you see God, if not a father?"

Mark leaned back in the sand. "I envision him as this king or warrior, someone greater than me. Someone I'd follow into a war."

"Hmmm."

"A protector of sorts. Someone who has my back. Someone who knows what I'm up against and makes a way for me to go. Makes a way for me to survive, and maybe win occasionally." He turned to her. "How do you see God?"

She shifted in the sand and drew her legs up close to her chest, and wrapped her arms around her knees. "I grew up in church, so I know all the things the Bible says. And I believed those things. But my mom got sick. And I prayed for Him to heal her. But He didn't. Then my dad got sick, and I prayed for Him to heal him. But He didn't. And then the tornado. And I prayed it was all a bad dream, and that Pete and the babies would be there when I woke up. But they weren't."

Mark didn't say a word.

She turned to look at Mark. "If there is a God, I don't think He hears me. I'm not sure what to believe anymore." She lost herself in thought, and then glanced toward the sunrise. "I believe in heaven, though. It's where they all are."

He nodded, a little choked up, as he listened to her reveal so much of her hidden soul.

"I think that night," she continued. "That first night when you followed me into the ocean, I was lost. I was looking for a way to follow them there." She turned to him. "But you pulled me back."

"Are you angry at me for pulling you back?" he whispered.

She nodded. "I was. Who were you to decide whether I lived or died? You didn't even know me."

"So why did you come back to shore with me?"

She shrugged. "Probably for the same reason I came back when they resuscitated me all those times."

"And why was that?"

She looked him in the eyes. "Maybe there *is* something more for me here. But I don't see it yet."

He reached over and gently squeezed her hand.

"I don't know where to go from here, Mark."

"You'll find the way," he whispered. Then he leaned over and placed a tender kiss on her forehead.

From the house deck high behind them, Rick wrapped his arms around his wife as they witnessed the tender moment between the couple on the beach. They'd been praying, but never had imagined that the answers would look like this.

***

Everyone hated to leave. But the vacation was over. It was time to get back to reality. Rick and Katie loaded up the SUV and the children as Mark and Jena took one final stroll along the beach.

When they walked up the path toward the house, Katie could tell that Jena had been crying, and yet she looked amazingly at peace. It was the first time she or Rick had seen that expression on her face.

"Rick," Mark called. "Ready to go?"

"Yeah. Hate to break it up, but it's a long drive." Rick finished putting Jena's bag in the back and was starting to close the hatch.

"Mind giving me that bag? Jena's riding with me. We'll follow you."

"Got room on that bike of yours?" Rick reached in the back of the car and retrieved Jena's bag.

Mark leaned toward his brother and whispered for his ears only. "Back off. I'll take care of her, Bro."

Rick looked his brother in the eye. "Ok. Be safe. We'll see you back, whenever." He walked over to Jena. "Take care of yourself, my friend," Rick said, pulling her in for a hug.

"Thank you for everything, Rick."

He nodded, then glanced over at Mark. "You couldn't be with anyone more protective than him. You guys enjoy the trip back. Be careful."

Katie hugged Mark. Then she hugged Jena, holding her in her arms like a keepsake. "Take this time. It is a gift."

Then Rick and Katie climbed in the SUV and drove away.

Mark handed Jena a helmet, then strapped her bag on the back of the motorcycle. He donned his own helmet and climbed on. She carefully swung her leg over and climbed on behind him, wrapping her arms around his waist.

"Ready to roll?" he asked, smiling.

She nodded.

The motorcycle roared to life and powered down the road, increasing speed as they went. It was a beautiful morning, unusually cool as the wind came off the Gulf. They talked to each other through the speakers in the helmets as they cruised the road. Then they were in town and turned toward the causeway.

Once inland, Mark stayed on the highway for only a short while before pulling off an exit and rolling into a gas station. He bought them two waters and they stood there drinking them while the gas tank filled.

"Jena?"

"Yes," she smiled up at him.

"We have a choice to make right now, you and I."

She pulled the water bottle from her lips. "What's the choice?"

He looked at her for a long time. "Choice number one is to follow them home and be back by dark tonight."

"Or?" She stared at him.

"Choice number two. Something unexpected. Unplanned. Unchartered territory."

"A road trip?"

"Yeah, that." He nodded.

Slowly, she screwed the bottlecap back on the water bottle and stowed it in the side saddle bag.

"I'm not ready to go back," she stated. When she turned back to him, her eyes were alive and brilliantly blue.

He waited.

"Choice number two," she said. "But text Rick and Katie and let them know so they don't send the National Guard out after us."

He winked and strapped on his helmet. He climbed back on the motorcycle, then helped her on behind him.

"Let's do this thing," he said.

She answered with a slight hug around his waist. The motorcycle roared to life and they pulled out from the gas station.

They never got back on the highway, the straight shot home. Instead, they took another direction. They had no map. No plan. No itinerary.

They were just two friends on a Harley letting their hearts take them down the backroads less traveled.

Chapter Eleven

The few extra hours on the road home turned into a three-day road trip that meandered along country roads and through small towns. They stopped off at a state park, explored an old forgotten bridge and took shelter in a farmer's barn during a sudden storm. Each night, they pulled off and found a place to eat before finding a motel with separate rooms that Mark insisted on paying for.

He sensed Jena's inner struggles and allowed her the time and space to sort it all out. He was a perfect gentleman on the way back, respecting the turbulent process going on inside of her. He was still experiencing some of it himself, in more ways than one.

Mark knew that the grief process was like an iceberg.

Different counselors had told them both in the previous months. At first, the pain visible seemed to be the only pain. It might certainly seem that way to the outside world. But the real depth of pain went fathoms deeper and spread out in many directions. And it wasn't until the mammoth reached warmer waters did it begin to dissipate.

The last months had them both trapped in open Artic waters. But they'd moved to warmer waters these last ten days together. Their separate pain had transformed to waves of turbulent froth, and then quieter still to a soft but constant lapping of the tide.

They shared their individual losses of the people they'd loved, baring their souls and emotions as they did. They both knew the technical process for grief. Denial. Isolation. Bargaining. Anger. Depression. And, finally acceptance.

But grief was the hardest and longest process of all, for it encompassed so many strong emotions. And going back and forth among the stages was not unexpected.

Mark had processed his anger. But it was still fresh for Jena.

He knew she was angry at God for not answering her prayers.

She was angry at Esther for inviting them that day.

She was angrier still with Pete, her husband, for not heeding his own mother's pleas to stay a while longer and let the storm pass. She even expressed anger at Rick for saving her time and time again. She was angry that she would never see her babies grow up. But the most unforgiving anger was the anger at herself for being the lone survivor.

Some of it made no sense. But the anger was real for her.

It seemed to help her to talk it out. So, Mark listened and held her when it was appropriate. He made her laugh in moments when he sensed her slipping back into the oblivion of sadness.

He created adventures out of small moments and wayward backroads, and sat with her.

She did the same for him.

They kept talking all along the trip, giving each other a safe place to peel back memories and reveal their individual personalities. They shared dashed hopes and dreams, and experiences that had them laughing. They shared meals, and ice cream cones, a park bench at the zoo, and held hands and ate popcorn through an action-adventure matinee film one afternoon.

But every night, they slept in separate rooms, and were alone again with their own thoughts.

It was three days of best friends discovering each other, helping each other process the loss and still see a new day.

Mark wanted to kiss her. And he suspected she wanted it, too, from the way she looked at him at times. But he held back and just let things happen, if they ever did.

But every day brought them closer. There was something wonderful and safe and fascinating and terrifying to be said about whatever this was between them.

The last night of their road trip found them in some small town in deep East Texas. There was one modest hotel, so they stopped and he paid for the rooms. Then they got a bite to eat at a local steakhouse that was loud and messy and full of life.

The meal was good, the drinks cold, and the music country sweet enough for the prettiest rodeo queen and her cowboy.

Mark watched Jena across the table as she dipped her fries in ketchup and brought them to her lips.

It was in that moment that he realized he didn't care anymore about the woman he was going to marry just months before. There was no more angst, or regrets, or heartache like before. There wasn't any anger, either. Or resentment. Not even a void.

He took the last gulp of his water.

Behind him the band was coming back on stage after a short break. The waitress, in her red checkerboard apron, cleared their dishes away and refilled their drinks. Soon the music was playing and couples took to the sawdust dance floor.

"Dance with me, Jena," he said, holding out his hand. She took it and they moved together as one to the dance floor.

"Now I know," the band leader spoke into the microphone with a laid-back good ole Texas boy drawl. "This next song is for someone out there tonight. So, hold her close, cowboy."

The guitar and bass opened with the intro.

Mark pulled Jena close to him and took her hand in his, placing it over his heart. She hesitated, then relaxed into his embrace. He looked down at her at the same moment she looked up to him. Her eyes resembled a young child not quite sure if they were in trouble or about to enjoy a moment of joyous recklessness.

"Relax," he whispered. "Just go with the music."

The band leader stepped up to the mic and softly starting singing.

She closed her eyes against the music and let it take her to a place of promise. The song was about love offering a heart another chance. Mark pulled her closer still, pressing his body into hers. He reached up and caressed her hair, then tangled his fingers in it and pressed her head against his heart.

She wrapped her arms around his body, as he wrapped her in a protective embrace. Her heart beat faster.

The guitar played quietly behind the lyrics.

Mark bent his head down and kissed the top of hers. He was singing quietly along with the song, singing only to her.

He so understood what she was going through. The isolation. The deep fight for survival against the lie that said she had no right to live again, or love again. His lips were so close to her ear. He was a strong soft baritone and his voice carried deep into her wounded heart, and breathed life again.

She inhaled the scent of him. His arms were around her, and their hearts were pounding so wildly, each could feel the other's.

"Just close your eyes, Jena," he whispered to her. "Just be in this moment." She pressed her face into his shirt.

The guitar strings took up the refrain. Jena felt like she was walking on a cloud, and inside of a fire. She pulled herself closer to him, and he gently held her. But she felt herself fighting against the weight of the world, the weight of her sorrow, and the weight of her own guilt. Mark felt her tense ever so slightly.

"Let go," he whispered into her ear. "Just be in my arms."

The band sang the second verse. But Mark and Jena were lost in each other's embrace, and lost in a power neither one of them could explain. He didn't let her go. She didn't want him to. So, they held each other and slowly swayed to the words and music.

The country singer let the words fade into hope for another chance at love. Mark and Jena stayed locked in the intimate embrace a full minute after the lyrics ended. The small band of the guitar, piano, bass, and snare picked up on the romantic dynamics of the couple dancing, so they kept playing quietly in the background, not letting the song end.

Then Mark tenderly tipped her chin upwards toward him, and he bent down to kiss her. She looked up at him. At the very last moment before their lips touched, Jena turned away and lowered her head. He didn't press after her.

As the song faded away, Mark and Jena pulled apart and silently stared into each other's eyes.

They'd just breached a boundary, and found themselves in a new realm neither one of them were ready for. It was a place broken hearts avoided at all costs. A place where wounded souls steered clear of. Yet, somehow, they were suddenly here, in the rebound. In a place called *falling...*

The music ended and they slowly stepped away from each other. He felt her hand slip out of his.

She shook her head. "I can't do this. I'm not ready for this, Mark," she whispered, her eyes full of regret and unexpected tears.

"I know," he answered. He took back her hand and led her to the table. He paid the check and they left.

Out in the parking lot, there was an awkward silence that had never come between them. It was dark by then, so they drove back to the hotel and he walked her to the door of her room.

"Look," he said, looking into her blue eyes. "What happened tonight..."

She reached up and touched his face. "Don't."

"Don't what?" he asked quietly.

"Don't apologize for it."

He didn't say anything to that.

"Mark, I don't want to lose you. But there are too many ghosts in my heart. And I don't know how to let them go."

"I know. It's too soon," he shook his head. "Maybe it's too soon for me, too."

"I never expected to meet you."

"And, I never saw you coming, either."

Jena smiled and shook her head. "I've loved Pete for almost half of my life. I can't betray that."

"I get it."

"And you've had your heart broken, too."

"I have," he agreed. "So, where do we go from here?"

She took a long moment before answering, then she simply said "Home."

"Home. Back to Tyler?"

"Yes."

"Probably best. I have to go back to Italy. My leave is over in a couple of days. I won't be back until the end of my tour." He rubbed his hand through his hair. "I'm so sorry, Jena."

She was silent. "I don't want to hurt you," she finally replied, putting her hand upon his chest. "But I need time. And space."

" And, I don't want to hurt you. You've come so far."

"I'm stronger now. But I have to do this on my own before I can go forward anywhere, or with anyone. My family is still so much a part of me."

He bent his face close to hers. "I don't want to leave, Jena. I don't want to lose you."

She pressed into him and felt her own heartbeat pounding. And that terrified her. It was too soon. Pete still held so much of her heart. But Mark had come into her storm and stolen her very soul. And that kind of connection to him would make it hard to see him go.

"Thank you for the dance," she said quietly, her heart in her throat and every ounce of her courage holding back tears. "You don't know what it meant to me."

"Yes," he clenched his jaw to hold back his own emotion. "I do. I do know what it meant."

"Mark…"

"I know where you've been, Jena. And I know where you are. We are on parallel journeys. I get it. So, I won't hold you back. And I won't push you forward. When we're both ready, if it's meant to happen at all, it will happen."

"Friends?" she whispered.

"Always friends," he replied. He stepped back then. "Good night, Jena. We'll leave for Tyler in the morning."

Then he turned and slowly walked away, and she watched him until he turned the corner and disappeared.

Jena went into her hotel room and closed the door behind her. She kicked off her shoes and laid across the bed, pulling the two small pillows to her breast.

Then she wept.

***

They pulled into her driveway late morning of the fourth day, and he turned off the motor. The day was warm and they both were sweaty. He untied her bag off the back and walked her to the door. He held her bag in his hands, hesitant to hand it over to her.

They hadn't talked at all on the two-hour ride back to reality. There was nothing much more to say. They'd said everything last night. Any more words would only make it harder to say good-bye, and harder still to let the other go.

"Well, Rick and Katie are waiting for me."

She nodded. "And I need to unpack and get a shower."

He hesitated. "I leave on Friday."

She swallowed hard to alleviate the raw emotion rising. "Stay safe. Will you write or email?"

"I'll be pretty busy."

"Ok." She wasn't expecting that reply. "Well, then, thank you for everything."

"I wish you happiness, Jena."

"You, too. Take care of yourself, Mark."

They stood face to face, looking at each other, remembering the beach, and the storm, the long walks, and the road trip home. Recalling that first night he saved her from her own heartache, and the long talks at dawn. The way he held her, and protected her from the pain, and the way he rode it with her.

And the dance.

"Can I hug you?" he asked.

Oh god, she couldn't bear it. She suddenly flung herself in his arms. They stood on the porch clinging to each other until the neighbor drove by and slowed down at the sight of the young grieving widow in the arms of a mountain of a man, holding on to each other for dear life.

"Take your time through this, Jena. But know I'll miss you."

She nodded, and brushed her hair from her face where it had fallen during their passionate embrace.

"I can't make any promises to anyone, especially to you. You deserve more than I can give you right now," she whispered.

"I know," he said, hugging her one last time. "I've got to go. They're waiting for me."

"Give them my love," she said.

Then he got on the motorcycle and drove away.

And she watched him go.

Chapter Twelve

She put her house on the market the night before Thanksgiving, eight months after the storm, and turned all her attention to purging the house of reminders. She kept all the pictures, and the things she'd already packed away for safe keeping. But she called the local non-profit and donated all the furniture, except the refrigerator.

She was going to look for a smaller house in the older part of town, where the trees were old and the streets were brick and cobblestone. Where the breeze made a sound as it rustled through the trees, and the birds could be heard singing in the early morning.

She thought Mark would have come back by before he left again for Italy. But he didn't. She understood why. Still, she missed him terribly and ached for their long talks, and the way he would just sit and hold her hand. And she missed the way he looked at her, and how he walked as though he owned the world. She found herself thinking more and more of Mark, and less and less of Pete. She thought that should bother her.

Then, she felt guilty because it didn't.

She tried going back to church, and friends there were overjoyed to see her. But it was harder than she'd imagined. She found herself at the mercy of well-intended people who wanted to console her but had not a clue how.

She called a few of her old clients trying to reconnect.

The insurance money was a huge amount, and still nestled in her bank account. She didn't have the heart to touch it yet. It felt almost tainted.

But Jena knew she needed to get back to work again, if for no other reason but to keep her from wallowing in the grief of what *had* been, and pining for what *might* have been.

She was caught between two worlds. A heart wrenching past and an uncertain future. And, it was the uncertainly that had her frozen in time.

After a couple of weeks, she got an offer on the house and took it. The equity alone would keep her afloat for another year, and provide a hefty down payment on a quaint little house in the older part of the city. So, she sold her giant custom four-bedroom home in the gated community, and moved into a small two-bedroom house with a wraparound porch and huge trees in the backyard. She even thought of getting a puppy.

She bought a few new things like a couch and bed, and added that to the few things she moved over.

She went out with friends occasionally, and met Rick and Katie every other week for dinner. Mark was fine, they reported. But his correspondence was limited. He was still on active duty, and transitioning his responsibilities. There was no more news.

Christmas arrived like an unwelcomed guest.

Jena had done nothing to prepare for it.

It was the first year she had no tree or decorations, or presents waiting to be wrapped, and then unwrapped. There were no lights, or music, or angel music boxes playing softly from her mantle.

Her mother-in-law took her to dinner Christmas Eve afternoon at a quaint Italian Villa downtown. Then Jena begged off going to Christmas Eve services at the church. So, Esther went alone, then drove home to her empty house.

Rick and Katie invited Jena over Christmas morning. She went for a few hours, and pretended to take joy in their family frolic. But then she went home to her empty house, drank three full shots of vodka, watched an old Betty Davis movie, and passed out on the couch while the late-night talk shows shifted to news to the upcoming New Year's celebration in. She woke up crying.

She spent the day after Christmas organizing her cabinets and painting the bathroom.

She wondered where Mark was and what he was doing. Was he on another mission in the cold mountains behind enemy borders? Or was he alone in his apartment, thinking of her?

Then she found a box she'd forgotten about and started to unpack it. It was the box of photo albums. She sat on the den floor in paint-stained jeans, and wept as she turned each page. It was her punishment for forgetting for a moment about Pete and the babies, and thinking of another who was across the world from her. The loneliness and sadness threatened to pull her back under.

It was cold and raining New Year's Eve and New Year's Day, so she drove to the store and bought some frozen pizzas and three bottles of wine, and turned on the TV and stayed up for 18 hours watching a Netflix miniseries. Then she fell across the bed and slept for twelve more hours.

There was no describing what it is like during the holidays after losing someone you love. It is the loneliest, most desperate feeling of isolation and heartache imaginable. But Jena did her best to keep busy around the house during the day. At night, to numb the pain, she drank herself into a stupor.

By the second week of January, she's slipped back into her isolation. But she'd painted the entire interior of the old house she'd bought, and racked up $150 from Specs on her credit card.

The only time she came out of the house was to run to the grocery store, or check the mailbox for a letter from the war zone.

School started back around town, and everyone transitioned back into normalcy. Friends from church called occasionally. Esther came by once a week for dinner. Katie dropped by after work a couple of times.

Jena had no compass to guide her through the days and weeks. She felt lost and alone, even though people were reaching out to her. She had stopped going to the grief support group before Thanksgiving, and ignored the calls of the members.

Each day was an ordeal just to get through.

The storm of emotions – grief, guilt, loneliness, anger and fear consumed her. Jena missed Pete and the babies so much. And she desperately missed Mark. Perhaps she missed her old herself, too.

She worried about Mark, and if he was safe, and if he felt like she felt… confused, longing, remembering their ten days together by the beach, and the road trip home. During it all, wondering *what if*, or *if ever*.

She was torn between two worlds…two lives…her past and her future. Yet she tried to keep secret what everyone could see. Her heart was still inconsolably broken. And she didn't know how a woman was supposed to live and carry on with a heart so utterly ripped apart, useless to anyone, like a puzzle with lost pieces.

By the end of February, Katie knew she had to intervene. She'd seen this cycle before in the patients they worked with, and in her own family. Jena kept brushing off her invitations for girl time. Katie's texts and calls went unreturned, sometimes for days.

So, Katie and Rick showed up one Saturday morning unannounced, surprising Jena in torn jeans, a sweatshirt, her hair in a pony tail, and bags under her eyes.

They came through the door with Chick-Fil-A, and made themselves comfortable at the new kitchen table in Jena's small house. Only this time, they were not as gentle and tactful as before.

Katie shared about a seminar they'd gone to at their church. It was a weekend retreat, she said. And she and Rick would like to pay for Jena to go, if she wanted to. Katie handed over the brochure and Jena glanced at it.

"An emotional healing retreat?" Jena questioned.

"Yes, it's an awesome program. It was great, Jena. So unexpected and powerful. We'd like to sponsor you for the weekends."

"Weekends? There's more than one?"

"Well, there are three weekends. Part one, two and three. Each weekend is different, but it really takes you from where you are…" Katie hesitated.

Rick chimed in. "It takes you from where you've been to where you want to be. You need it, Jena. We think you should go. It's time."

"Time to?"

"Time to move on, Jena," Katie said gently.

Jena frowned. "You mean, just put everything, and everyone, in a box, and hurry and bury them again, and just move on? As though none of this ever happened? As though Pete and Jana and Alexis never existed?"

"That's not what I meant," Katie said softly.

"Am I supposed to get over them," Jena shot back. "Like they were the chicken pox?"

Rick leaned toward Jena. "Ok, I'll not be so tactful. You've been going through the motions for months. You've filled your time with projects, and moving. You're working hours into the night on your consulting business, and locking yourself away on the weekends. You're stalled in the process."

"Forgive me, please." Jena felt the anger rise. "That I'm not meeting your timeline for recovery."

Rick and Katie looked at each other, exasperated.

"Your wall is back up. You're the one who never wants to talk about your own babies, or Pete," Rick admonished. "Or even Mark."

Katie nodded. "You're pretending, Jena."

Jena was taken back. "Now I'm pretending? Pretending what?"

"You're pretending it doesn't hurt anymore," Rick looked her square in the eye. "You're pretending that you're over them all. And you're not. You're faking it. And we can tell. You say the right words and you're doing the right things, but we can still see it in your eyes."

"We love you. You are our dearest friend," Katie chimed in. "But Rick is right and we are calling you on your bullshit. You're getting good at illusions and might have others fooled. But not us."

Jena stared at them as though they'd slapped her in the face. But she knew exactly what they were talking about. And they were right. She'd been pretending. Faking it. Acting like she was over the roughest part. But she wasn't. The loss and grief were as tormenting as a runaway cancer in her gut.

She was still grieving. She was still in heartache and trapped in it deeper than ever before. And her own eyes betrayed her.

"We want to pay for the weekends," Katie said. "You'll thank us when it's over."

Rick took a breath and steadied his resolve. "Jena, we both were there when they brought you in by Care Flight. I saw how mangled you were. And, I saw the devastation of death that night."

He paused, then finished his entreaty. "I know what you've been through. And I know how hard you are trying. But you are still in the middle of the tragedy."

"It's been almost a year, Jena," Katie reminded her. "You've done so much and you've come so far."

"But now you're stuck." Rick paused only for a moment. "And now we're intervening."

Jena glanced at both of them. "Ok. I'll admit it's been tough. It's been very hard." She felt the emotion choke her. "I thought the trip to the beach and being with you guys… and Mark… really helped me."

"It did!" Katie reminded her.

"But Mark's not here." Rick reminded her. "And, however you leaned into him, or depended on him to help you in the process, it's months later, and you are regressing. And we love you enough that we are not going to let you go backward."

"Take the weekends," Katie entreated. "Please. You have to commit to this, though, or it won't help you."

"What is this program? A support group?" Jena asked quietly.

"No," Rick answered. "It's not a support group. It's a kick in the ass."

"The next one starts tomorrow night," Katie said sweetly.

"Tomorrow night," Jena shook her head. "Wow. Nothing like throwing me into the fiery furnace."

Rick leaned over and got in her face. "I've always been straight with you, Jena, from the moment we first met and you wanted me to let you die. Well, the answer is the same then and now. Do you remember what I said to you?"

Jena nodded. "You said to suck it up and put my big girl panties on. You said to get up and get it done."

Katie turned to her husband. "You told her that?"

He shrugged. “It worked. It got her out of bed and into therapy.”

“So, what are these weekends about?” Jena asked quietly.

They looked at each other. “We can’t tell you.”

“Excuse me?”

“That’s part of the program. You have to experience it for yourself. Each of three weekends is different, for a different reason, with a different emphasis. If we told you, it would ruin it for you, or make it less impactful.”

“So,” Jena started, brushing the hair from her face. “This weekend. Where is it?”

They told her.

“Ok, I’ll commit to one weekend.” she finally answered. “I’ll go for you.”

Katie shook her head. “No, go for *you*, Jena.”

“Am I going to hate it?”

They looked at each other again, then faced her.

Katie leaned into her. “These weekends are grueling. But you must promise yourself you will go and stay and participate. If you do, and give all you have, you will come out the other end…”

“Changed,” Rick said. “I know I was. It’s made all the difference in my life.”

“How much does it cost?” Jena asked.

“It’s our gift to you,” Katie said. “But it’s a lot.”

Jena looked at them. She knew they were right. She knew she needed something to jolt her off center and to pull her out of the mire she’d known since the tornado. She knew that, more than anything now, she wanted to be free of the pain that still haunted her even in her sleep.

She wanted to be free.

***

The next night, she changed into jeans and a dress top, got into her car, and drove to the seminar location.

As she walked in to register, she noticed over a hundred people were completing paperwork on clipboards. She checked in, was handed her clipboard of forms, and told to take seat and fill them out.

She didn't want to be here.

But she'd promised Rick and Katie, and they had an enormous amount of money invested already.

From the moment it started, she regretted being there. She stayed angry and withdrawn the entire first night. She went home afterwards and drank a glass of wine.

The next morning, she was ten minutes late, but they let her in the doors. The morning was full of interaction and sharing. By lunch she was exhausted and thought to slip out when no one noticed. But they sent them to lunch in small groups, and she had no choice but to play along. By late afternoon, she was choking back raw emotion of which she'd never known. That night, she went home and had a vodka and a hot bath, then fell exhausted into bed with her housecoat still on.

Sunday morning, she went to church with a slight hangover. But, keeping her promise to her friends, she was on time for the one p.m. start of the final day of Part One. Sunday was the hardest day of all. She fought her emotions all weekend, never having given in to the tears or the show of pain. But at 5:30 p.m., the counselors had them all line up and hold hands. The lights went dim. They were told to close their eyes and keep them closed. Then the music started.

The song was about letting go and believing in love. As it ended, they were told to open their eyes. That's when Jena lost it. Standing in front of her, cradling an armful of flowers, were Rick and Katie. The tears flowed and her sobs finally broke through as another song played. It was as though a dam burst and the months of pain escaped like a torrent through her well-designed façade. She cried then for the first time all weekend, and wept in Katie's arms for five minutes.

That was the end of the first weekend.

The next session was two weeks later. Jena had bonded with her small group over the first weekend, and in the days following, as was the plan of the program. So, when Part Two came along, she was there to register again.

Part Two was grueling, even more so than the previous weekend. She found the counselors challenging them to dig deeper and pull up the pain.

But her pain was shrouded in anger, and that anger made its nasty appearance halfway through the weekend. The program challenged her more than anything she'd ever gone through and they had her guts ripped out by Saturday afternoon. She didn't think she had any more tears, or anything left to give. She'd emptied her heart and soul and spirit onto the floor, as had all her small group individually. Fortunately, they were all helping each other through the process.

She was exhausted, and her eyes puffy from crying so much. She was totally spent and laying at the bottom of the well of total despair. Her whole life had been examined, as she had finally allowed it to be. At one moment early on, her counselor had gotten in her face and called her on her fakeness, her pretense. She challenged Jena to be real, and to give 110%. So, Jena gave it all. She dropped the imposter act. She laid it all out there for everyone to see… the anger, the sadness, the confusion, the despair. She emptied her guts to a room full of strangers who, by this time, were no longer strangers but sojourners on a path to find themselves again.

On Saturday night of Part Two, the counselors disappeared for ten minutes, then came back out and called Jena forward. She got out her chair and walked toward them. They smiled tenderly at her. Then they put her in a chair in front of a hundred of her sojourners and put her on simulated trial. But the charges and accusations brought forth were only the re-enactment of what Jena had been blaming herself for since the storm.

The charges were only indicative of the responsibility, fault, and shame she'd put on herself, for the loss of her family. The charges mirrored her own self judgement and condemnation.

It took almost an hour. It was grueling and heart-wrenching and powerful. At the end, the counselors called forth the entire group of her peers, her new friends and confidants of this retreat, to act as the jury.

She was found innocent of all the charges. The jury of her peers absolved her. Now, she only needed to forgive herself.

When it was all over, Jena was completely undone. Tears rolled unashamedly down her face. Snot flowed from her nose. Her hair was completely unruly. She was shaking and naked to the core of her soul.

Twelve of her team members came together and made two lines and locked their arms together to create a human cradle. They pulled her into the cradle and she laid outstretched in their arms, not knowing what to expect. Then the lights dimmed, and the song started to play.

Jena closed her eyes.

She'd heard this song before, somewhere.

Have faith and breathe, just breathe.

She wept as they gently rocked her back and forth in their arms. Their faces were so close to her and their voices quiet as the song spoke to her in words they could not say.

Have faith and believe in what you can't see.

Then the rest of her small group came and circled the human cradle, rocking in unison. They were crying, too, for they had walked with her for two weeks through the devastating revelations of loss.

What is before you is the greater yet to be.

She had truly endeared herself to them, and they all adored her for her courage and commitment, and finally her full transparency. She'd become their darling.

So, close your eyes. Have faith and believe.

The song continued and Jena was totally suspended in trust and held in the arms of love as the chorus of the song swelled and filled the room all around her.

Maybe not today and maybe not tomorrow.

Slowly, her cradle team extended their arms simultaneously and lifted her high in the air, in what she would later discover they called a sky cradle. She was totally at the mercy of their collective strength.

But there will come a time, when joy will heal your sorrow.

They rocked her back and forth, holding her suspended in the air with their arms and hands, and swaying with the music.

Maybe not today, and maybe not tomorrow.

Jena couldn't stop her tears. They were the pure raw tears she'd held at bay for almost a year. Now, she let them all free.

But there will come a time when love will heal your heart.

They brought her down gently, and set her down, wrapping her in their arms. When she finally opened her eyes, there were over a hundred people around her. The song gently faded.

Oh, love will heal your heart.

Everything changed for her in that moment. She finally understood. She couldn't do this alone. And she couldn't go back. Her life was waiting for her.

She went home that night and drank a cup of tea before falling exhausted into her bed, where she slept for twelve hours straight.

The next two weeks Rick and Katie hovered close to her, and listened while she talked for hours about the program and her journey through it. She shared the pain she'd harbored for so long, and cried in front of them when she talked about Pete and the girls.

But it was Part Three that brought down all her remaining walls. She did get her road map. But it was a road map she made herself as she sat cross legged on the floor, listening to heart-wrenching music about life and love and loss. The map started when she was born, and the road traced every major event in her life. Every milestone, adventure, benchmark and heart marker. She depicted the small achievements, the losses of those she loved, and the side trails of everyday living. When she got to the end of the road, she realized it had ended at today. Where would her life go from here?

It was up to her.

She had another chance at life.

The retreat small groups all went to lunch. And when they came back, there were ushered into a dark room, lit only by candles and counselors all dressed in black.

They gently invited anyone to the circle who had lost a child. A handful of the participants rose from their chairs and went to the place designated on the floor. They were asked to lie down and close their eyes. Then those remaining were invited to circle around them.

Jena found herself in the very middle of the circle, surrounded by others, men and woman alike, who'd lost a child. All their small groups stayed respectfully on the perimeter and listened as the lead counselor led them through a visualization of heaven. Soft music played in the background.

"Do you see your child?"

Jena did.

She saw them. It was a familiar vision, somewhat like the foggy dreams of her coma. Only this time, the vision was vivid and clear, and very real.

The girls were about three years old, with long curly blonde hair, and skinny little legs. Their faces were rosy and their blue eyes danced with joy. They were playing tag with a young husky guy in khaki shorts and a Texas Rangers t-shirt, bare footed, with light brown hair that curled like theirs. He stopped for a moment and stood tall, then turned and looked at Jena. Then he smiled so that her heart melted in the love. It was Pete.

They were playing in a field of flowers, running and laughing, and twirling with delight. And smelling the flowers one by one. The place where they were was radiant, and colors had their own personalities as they caught the prism of the light.

The girls stopped when they saw her, then ran full speed into her arms, knocking her over into fresh spring grass.

"Mommy! Mommy! We love you, Mommy! Kisses, Mommy!" Together they rolled in the grass, laughing and hugging and placing a thousand kisses on her face.

"Oh, my babies," Jena held them in her arms. "Oh, my girls! I love you!"

Then a much brighter light filled the day, in the place where they were. Another young man came and knelt beside them. He had long dark hair that fell past his shoulders, and was dressed in jeans and a white t-shirt. She'd seen him in the stupor of the coma. Now, his eyes spoke of unconditional love. He touched her cheek with his fingertips and spoke gently.

"Don't cry anymore, Jena. Your tears will turn to joy. For there is another waiting for you in your life. And many, many more to love."

Jena couldn't speak; she was so overwhelmed. So full of incredible peace. So full of awe. So full of this incredible, supernatural love that was the very oxygen in her lungs.

Then she was back on the floor of the healing retreat.

Many around her were quietly crying, and the muffled sounds of heartache filled the conference room.

The counselor let their emotions flow, reaching over to touch first this one, then that one, in a comforting touch. When she came to Jena, she bent down and touched her shoulder. Jena opened her eyes and looked up through her own tears. The counselor was silently crying, too.

She understood. In order to lead this drill, that counselor must have experienced the loss of a child. Their eyes locked and Jena was branded with an understanding so precious she couldn't breathe.

Jena closed her eyes again, and saw her little girls again.

"Your lost children have a gift for you," the counselor said over the quiet music. "What is the gift?"

Jana and Alexis were in front of her now. They smiled at each other, then placed little crystal balls of joy in Jena's hand. The balls were translucent and sparkling from light within. Barely the size of golf balls, they caught the prisms of color, and pulsed with a radiance of light not known on earth. The girls wrapped their tiny arms around Jena's neck and kissed her again. Then they were off, laughing and playing with Pete.

A song started in the background of the conference room, and slowly built-in volume.

"Open your eyes now," the counselor said. She looked back down at Jena and smiled tenderly. "Take a deep breath. Let it out. Then again. Let it out. Those of you who've been standing quietly on the side can now come in."

Jena's new friends found her in the circle and embraced her. It was more than she could take in.

That afternoon, they walked into a room full of helium filled balloons, and a table of paper and markers and ribbons. This was the goodbye drill.

Jena wrote a prayer for each of them. Pete. Jana. Alexis. She tied each prayer to a different balloon. She chose two pink balloons for the girls, and one royal blue balloon for Pete. She wrote their names on the balloons, and then, with the black marker, wrote another message for each of them.

On Pete's balloon, she wrote *The Rangers are winning!* On each of the girl's balloons she drew a heart and wings.

Everyone was led outside. The counselor gave quiet instructions. Let go of the balloons when they were ready. It was time to say goodbye. Everyone held their strings tight, and stood there for the longest time. And then, when it was time, each person let their balloon go. One by one the balloons drifted up. Then higher and higher. Ninety-nine balloons floated into the sky.

Some of the participants bowed their heads. Others looked up. After a few minutes, everyone had let their balloon go.

But her.

Jena still held the strings tight in her hands.

She was the only one with multiple balloons. Everyone around her knew of her tragedy, and how she'd lost her entire family that night last spring.

In some sweet and intimate way, she'd become the favorite of all the small groups, and of all the counselors, as well. Everyone had witnessed her walls, and cried with her as they came crashing down one by one.

The other balloons went higher and higher still, catching the wind and drifting toward the clouds. Some were almost out of sight.

Jena stood still. Silent tears rushed down her face. Holding on now she realized… she'd never said goodbye.

She'd been fighting for her own life when her husband and daughters were buried in the cemetery. She'd not had a chance to see them, or hold them, or kiss them one last time. They'd been lost to her in some great dark cosmos called death, and she had no way to find them. There'd been no closure.

Until now.

And now, it was time to say goodbye.

But it was alright. She knew how to find them. They were as close as her heart and only a breath away in the abode of light. She knew she'd see them all again.

Jena closed her eyes and remembered the crystal balls of joy, their gift to her. They wanted her to be happy again.

In this moment, Jena realized it was time for her to let them go, to say goodbye. It was the moment for her to step forward, with them in her heart. It was the moment for her to begin living again. Truly living.

Today the girls would have been eighteen months old. Today, of all days, was the anniversary of the storm. Today was a reminder. A mark of life, and of new beginnings. Perhaps today was not a coincidence. Perhaps today was, by perfect design, the very day for her to begin again. Slowly and deliberately, Jena opened her hand and let the strings slip through her fingers.

"I love you," she whispered, as, one by one, she let them go.

The balloons were not tied together, yet they floated upward as one. Their strings wrapped around each other, and the wind caught them and took them higher and higher. It was as though each balloon was dancing around the other two.

One hundred people stood mesmerized, looking upward, as the three balloons sailed directly into the brilliant sunlight. Jena shielded her eyes, straining to see them for as long as she could.

A moment later, they could not be seen with the human eye. The silence was deafening. No one moved.

Another minute went by.

The cool breeze touched her face.

Her heart pounded as the black alien mothership of grief released its grip and disengaged itself from her heart and soul and spirit. Then, it pulled away and followed the balloons into the brilliant blue sky.

Jena felt the release as it faded away.

For a few seconds, there was a huge void, a gaping emptiness deep in her soul where sadness had lived for so long. She felt the vastness and expanse of it.

And she sensed the holiness of it.

She felt a wisp of the breeze on her face. Then, ever so gently, hope came like a tiny white butterfly and rested on her shoulder, and filled the place where despair had been.

Jena took her hand from her eyes and smiled, then turned and slowly walked back into life.

Chapter Thirteen

Healing comes differently for everyone.

For some it comes from the shedding of a million tears. For others, it comes from the purging of lies. For yet others, it comes from the safe-keeping of precious memories, and the deliberate walking forward day by day. It comes from letting go. And for others, it comes from forgiveness.

For Jena, it was all those things.

In the weeks following the final weekend of the retreat, she found herself remembering more. But there were no more sudden flashback episodes like she'd had with Mark in the hotel. The memories came back in her waking moments. Not in a violent or traumatizing way, but in a gentle way, as though they were trying to find their way back to her on a path lit by candles and rose petals. And they were sweet, sweet memories.

One by one, they returned, and imprinted her heart.

And with each one, came a new breath of fresh air.

Jena started working out again.

And, she rescued a little puppy from the animal shelter.

She took on several new clients, and attended a new study group at church on Thursday nights.

She ate better, and started to gain back some of the meat on her bones.

She stopped drinking all together.

The deep lines in her face slowly melted away, and she went shopping for new clothes.

Five weeks after the end of the program, Rick and Katie asked her out to dinner. She met them at a quaint restaurant not far from her new home in the old part of town. They had not seen Jena since the end of the program. It was not an intentional neglect. But the kids had all had the flu, and both Rick and Katie were slammed at the hospital, working double shifts every other day to keep the staff numbers up. So many were out on sick leave, their children having the flu, or they themselves getting it.

Jena was dressed in a sapphire blue blouse, new jeans, and a simple set of classy earrings that matched her blouse and brought out the brilliance in her eyes.

It was warming again. May had just begun. So, they agreed to meet on the restaurant's patio that overlooked a pond with ducks. Jena saw them before they saw her, and walked toward them.

Katie looked up and her jaw dropped. She nudged Rick and he looked up from the menu he'd been studying. Seeing Jena, he stared, his eyes conveying his obvious shock. Her transformation over the last few weeks was astonishing. And she was smiling.

"Oh my," Katie breathed. "Look at you. You look fabulous!" She hugged Jena tight.

Rick rose from his chair and came over to claim his hug.

"Wow," was all he could say. "Just wow."

Katie recovered first. "How are you?"

"I'm good," Jena smiled again.

Rick and Katie exchanged glances and smiled at each other before all three of them sat down.

"Dinner is on me, guys," Jena proclaimed. "I want to thank you sending me to the weekends. You were right, Rick. It was amazing. Once I got over being angry for being there in the first place, things started unraveling. But you've gone through it, so you know what I'm talking about."

"Yes, we do," Rick said.

They ordered dinner, then sat on the patio talking for two hours. She shared with them about the third weekend, and about her experience during the many drills that encouraged self-disclosure and the processing of the pain, and new beginnings.

She told them about the sky cradle and the song, about seeing Pete and the girls in heaven, and about the balloons.

Rick and Katie teared up, but listened intently. They'd never known this Jena before. They'd only known the young woman brought in by Care Flight, half dead. They'd only known the stoic shell of the woman called Jena Parker. They'd only known the defiant recluse who'd become their charge to protect. They'd only known a sweet friend who carried depths of sadness in her soul.

Now, sitting with them on the patio, was a dynamic, gorgeous young woman with crystal clear blue eyes and a smile that radiated charisma and hope.

"Jena, I am amazed at you," Rick said, leaning back.

"It was hard," Jena admitted.

"But here you are," Katie beamed. "On the other side."

Rick and Jena shared a knowing glaze.

"I adopted a dog," Jena smiled. "She's still a puppy. I've named her Peaches. She's a little lab."

"Ah…" Katie responded.

Jena nodded. "And I bought a new car. A convertible like yours, Katie. Only it's dark blue."

"Really?" Rick leaned forward.

"And I have ten new clients as of this morning," Jena continued. "And two more contracts coming next week."

Rick watched her closely. She was radiant. He knew it to be a type of euphoria that comes from soul cleansing. "How do you feel?"

"I can breathe again," Jena admitted. "I now remember every moment of my life with Pete and the girls with a sweet sense of gratitude. I looked through the pictures again. I realized how they imprinted my soul…but in a beautiful way. And I cherish that."

Rick smiled.

"Pete and the girls blessed my life," Jena said, with a truly amazing look of joy on her face. "I will always love them. I will never forget them. They are alive in that place. I've seen them. But, I'm ready to go on. Not without them, but *with* them, forever in my heart." Jena reached over to them. "So, thank you both."

They ordered dessert and coffee and Rick and Katie brought her up to speed on the children and the neighborhood, and trip they were planning for their anniversary. Jena shared about the new renovations on the old house she'd bought, and a writing class she was registered for at the local junior college. They talked in circles around the one topic they all knew they all wanted and needed to talk about.

Finally, Jena broke the ice. "How's Mark?"

Katie glanced at Rick. "You haven't heard from him?"

"No," Jena replied. "But I haven't written or called."

She hadn't mustered the courage to reach out to him after they last parted. She'd left them both at an impasse. Yet she thought of him every single day. His face was so clear in her mind. And the memory of how he would have kissed her on that dance floor, had she let him, was still fresh in her heart.

Rick motioned for the wait staff to refill their coffees. "Mark misses you."

"…a lot," Katie chimed in.

"I miss him, too," Jena admitted.

"Look," Rick said. "I'll be frank with you. We don't know what happened between the two of you. It's none of our business. But something did happen. And it changed both of you. And for the better, I'd say. We watched it unfold before our eyes there in Galveston. You are good for each other."

"It was like," Katie began. "You were saving each other."

Jena glanced down.

"We are protective of you both, obviously," Rick continued. "We want the best for you. But I can't help think that you gave up too quickly."

"We weren't ready for each other," Jena confided. "We both realized that."

"And now?" Katie asked.

Jena swallowed. What words could she say that truly described all the thoughts and dreams and hopes and fears that were surfacing inside of her? There was no denying that there was something real and powerful and magnetic between them.

They both knew it from the moment they'd first met, and Mark had reached out to her in the ocean and pulled her back before her grief took her under the waves.

What began that night as a spark only grew with each day that they were together, and ignited into a firestorm on their road trip home.

But it was a fire that threatened to consume her at the time. So, she'd pushed him away and sent him off without ever telling him how she felt.

"How do you feel about him, Jena?" Katie asked.

"I'm afraid," Jena revealed, her eyes tearing up.

"Afraid of what?" Katie lovingly asked.

Jena knew, but she didn't want to admit it to them, or even to say it aloud.

Rick leaned back and watched her. Then he reached out and took Jena's hand. "She's afraid he'll die."

Jena looked at him. Rick had this art of nailing her exactly where she was. He had this uncanny ability and perceptiveness to read her mind, and her emotions. From the very first day when he'd come into her ICU room and gently given her a drop of water through that straw, they had bonded.

"And," Rick continued, quietly reading Jena's thoughts. "She can't again lose someone she loves."

Katie leaned forward. "You love him, Jena?"

Rick turned to Katie. "I felt the same way when I met you, Katie. You terrified me. The thought of loving someone and then losing them kept me from you for the longest time."

Katie smiled knowingly. "I remember."

"I was a hard shell to crack," he acknowledged.

"Yes, you were, dear husband."

Rick took Jena's hand. "I know what you've been through, Jena. And I know what you are going through now. But, like I said to you then, I'm saying to you again, it's about little steps. One day at a time. Push through the pain and fear. Take the risk."

Jena took in a deep breath. "It's the biggest risk of my life. I don't know if he feels the same way."

Rick nodded. "I know you question that now. But it could be that all of this is just the beginning of ten thousand wonderful days. I grew up with Mark. I know him inside and out. He's a good man."

"And good for you," Katie added.

"He won't hurt you, Jena." Rick looked her in the eyes.

"But what if I hurt him?"

Katie interrupted. "How could you ever hurt him?"

"You know the truth?" Rick said. "You're afraid of diving in. You want to stay in the shallow where it's safe. The bottom line is this. You're afraid to lose the people you love, so you hold back from loving at all. And you *do* love him. That's plain as day."

She looked at Rick a long time before she responded. "I think I've loved him from the very beginning."

"You told Katie and me that you are moving forward, out of the grief. We believe you. We truly see it in your face and in your actions. You've bought a new house, gotten a dog, bought a car that I never imagined you'd even consider driving, and launched back into your business. You're taking back your life." Rick paused and took a breath. "But in matters of the heart, are you?"

Jena glanced away.

Rick continued. "You told us, that in the lost child drill, the girls gave you a gift. What was it?"

"Little balls of joy," Jena whispered.

Rick nodded. "Their permission for you to be happy again. What will make you happy again, Jena?"

Jena choked back the knot in her throat.

"Are you going to accept their gift to you?"

She nodded.

"And, what will make you happy, Jena?" He softly repeated the question and his words penetrated her heart.

Jena reached for a napkin and dabbed at her eyes. She waited for the fear to show its face. But it did not. They gave her the moment, and she took it, allowing his words to filter down into her soul. She knew the answer so easily. It was who she was at her core. It was her purpose in life. "Being free to love."

Rick smiled. Katie dabbed at her own eyes. A passing waiter kept walking by.

After a few minutes, Jena looked back at him. "When did you get to be such a wise old shaman, Rick?"

He glanced over at his wife and smiled. "It comes from a heartache like yours, and the unconditional love of my beautiful wife who showed me what life could be like."

Out in the acre pond, the giant water fountain exploded, spewing water fifty feet in the air. The water streams danced in the colored lights around them.

Katie reached over and touched Rick's arm, then whispered. "It's time, Rick. Give it to her."

He nodded. "I almost forgot. We have something for you," he said, reaching inside of the backpack he always carried with him. He pulled out an envelope and handed it to her. "It's from Mark. He asked us to hold off giving it to you until we found the right time."

Jena slowly took it from him. It was a little crumpled, as though it had been handled by many on its journey to her. She opened it. It was a piece of typing paper with a handwritten note.

Come to me. Mark.

Stapled to the back of the paper was an airline ticket to Venice, with the date of the flight only two weeks away.

"Did you know about this?" she asked them, incredulously. "Do you know what this is?"

"No." Rick and Katie exchanged a puzzled look. "He didn't share that. What is it?"

Jena handed them Mark's note, and the airline ticket. They read it and slowly smiled.

"How did you know to give this to me tonight?" Jena asked. "Tonight, of all nights?"

"Mark told us that he trusted us to find the right time, the perfect time, he called it. And to give it to you then. And if we didn't, then there would never come the right time."

"Oh, my god," Jena whispered, examining the note again.

"Do you have a valid passport," Katie asked, holding back her own excitement.

"Yes, I do. From our trip to the Dominican Republic two years ago."

"We'll keep the damn puppy for you," Rick offered.

Jena was reeling.

She shook her head and tried to make sense of the sudden rush of freedom, and an overwhelming sense of anticipation. Her skin flushed. Her breath quickened. She read Mark's words again and touched the ticket with her fingertips.

"If not now," Katie said gently. "Then when?"

Jena couldn't answer. Where were her excuses?

Rick leaned toward her. "Are you going, Jena?"

He watched her eyes and read every thought racing through her mind and heart. He'd been there, in this same place. To stay put was safe, but lonely and oftentimes dark. But to jump off into a rushing river of the unknown took more courage than anything he'd ever done before. He watched as she weighed the options, opportunities, and the call of wild abandon.

Finally, Jena smiled.

She took a deep breath, and then another, and slowly released it into the evening.

"I guess I'm going to Italy."

***

Rick and Katie drove her to Dallas/Fort Worth International Airport. They hugged her goodbye, then waited long enough until she cleared security. She checked in, and stood in line to board. Once inside, she was ushered to first class. Her seat there was a strong reminder of Mark's generosity. She knew he was taking a chance, too, spending thousands of dollars on a ticket that he had no way of knowing would be used.

She flew from Dallas to Philadelphia, then over the northern route. She spent the night over the ocean. Now, she was within an hour of landing in Italy.

The Alps came up to meet her and the morning sun glistened off the new snow.

Once she landed, she would check through customs, then rent a car. She hadn't called or emailed Mark to let him know she was coming. Unconsciously, she had left herself room to back out. In the end, she called her clients and postponed their meetings for three weeks.

Now, at the end of the flight, she realized how much he had to trust in the power of what was between them.

The flight attendant offered her coffee or juice. She took the coffee and sipped it slowly as she looked out the window. Her hands were shaking slightly. A while later, the captain came on the intercom and instructed the flight attendants to prepare for landing. Then he shared the weather conditions in Venice with the passengers, assuring them it was a beautiful day for romance.

She finished the coffee.

She'd never done anything like this.

She'd always had a plan and worked the plan well.

Even her pregnancy had been planned, and arranged around her busy schedule as one of the most sought out business consultants in the area. But the tornado, and the deaths of her family, had completely knocked her off kilter. It wasn't until the day after the program's last weekend did she start to feel she was on solid ground again. The decision to come to Italy was spontaneous, and uncharacteristic of her. Yet, it was strangely right.

She felt the aircraft start its descent.

She knew he was at the airbase in Aviano. He had to be waiting for her. That thought, alone, excited her. She knew nothing about Italy, or driving in Italy, except that they drove on the same side of the road as Americans. She'd be sure to get a GPS with the rental car. Surely, it wouldn't be hard to find a town an hour away.

Ten minutes later, the Fasten Seat Belt sign lit up. The flight attendants walked up and down the aisle instructing passengers to secure their tables and bring their seats to the upright position.

She hadn't slept at all during the flight, and wasn't sleepy now. She spent all those hours thinking of him.

She remembered him climbing on his motorcycle and smiling handsomely at her as she climbed on behind him. She saw him walking toward her on the beach, and cupping her face with his hands, and taking her hand and leading her toward the dance floor at that hole-in-the-wall steakhouse on a backroad somewhere in East Texas.

She closed her eyes and imagined what it would be like to feel his lips on hers. She heard his voice softly comforting her, and felt his strong arms around her as she wept into his soiled shirt. She melted as she remembered how he looked at her with eyes that betrayed passion and revealed secrets from his own soul.

The wheels squealed as they hit the runway of the Marco Polo International Airport, and Jena felt the force of the jet's reversing thrust as it powered to slow the aircraft. Ten minutes later they were at the gate. The Fasten Seat Belt sign turned off. People around her rose and reached for their luggage.

Jena stayed in her seat.

Her heart pounded.

She was about to step out into the next phase of her life, a life she hadn't mapped out. A life unfinished. A new beginning. She was in unchartered territory now and it terrified her. She didn't know what to expect. But she was taking the chance.

She didn't know if the connection they had forged together in Galveston and on the road back would even hold true. But she'd made the decision to come to him and find out. No matter the outcome, she knew that she would, surely, someday regret not coming at all.

Mark had gambled that the right time, the perfect time, would come. Well, it was here. She finally stood and took her bag out of the overhead compartment.

She was the last to exit the plane. Her backpack was slung over her left shoulder and her jacket was draped over her arm. The walkway from the plane to the terminal seemed longer than it was.

She saw the bold letters of a hand-written poster board above the heads of the people inside the terminal gate area, long before she saw him.

Then she saw him, head and shoulders above the crowd. His face was tan and he was dressed in jeans. His muscular arms were holding up the sign that read *Limousine Pickup for Texas Bella.*

She laughed out loud. She walked toward him, never expecting that he would be here.

Then he saw her. He put the sign down, leaning it against a pillar, and pushed through the crowd toward her.

His eyes were alive with love.

Her soul was on fire.

They met half-way and stopped in front of each other.

"You came," he said.

"…I came," she answered.

Then he swept her up in his arms and hugged her, swinging her around, and burying his face in her hair. Neither one of them cared at all that a hundred Italians were smiling at them. He took her hand and led her away from the crowd.

"You had me worried! I kept seeing more and more people coming off that plane and you weren't one of them."

"You didn't know I was coming?" she smiled, jubilant to be with him again.

"No. You didn't text or call… or email."

"Rick or Katie didn't let you know."

"Nope."

"So, you came all the way to Venice…"

He nodded. "On faith."

"Oh, Mark." She reached up and ran her fingertips across his face. "I've missed you."

He looked at her with a strange expression.

"What…?" she asked.

"There's something different about you."

She smiled. "I trimmed my hair." She ran her own fingers through her hair, just imagining what it must look like after so many nonstop hours on a plane.

He shook his head. "No, that's not it. Have you lost weight?"

She laughed. "I've gained weight since you saw me."

But it was healthy weight that she needed to gain and, with her regular workouts, had left her slim and toned, and utterly gorgeous in the low waisted jeans and blousy top she'd worn on the plane over.

He continued just staring at her, memorizing every inch of her, as though she would suddenly disappear and all he would have of her would be this one moment, this one snap shot, of her as a keepsake in his forever. "It's your face. Your face is changed."

"My face isn't any different," she laughed.

"Yes, it is," he murmured.

"Is it?" She stepped over to a window and looked at her reflection.

"You have no idea, do you?" Mark asked.

"No idea of what?"

"How absolutely beautiful you are." He took her hand then and they went to retrieve her suitcase from the carousel.

He'd rented a black convertible with a GPS, and they drove the short distance to Venice. They parked at the edge of the historic center, in the parking facilities on Tronchetto, an artificial island that was designed for parking. From there, they caught the waterbus that took them down the Grand Canal. He'd made reservations at one of the few places in Venice that was remotely affordable, which was a fortune. The waterbus let them off at the stop, and they walked the cobblestone walkways to the hotel and checked in.

"I hope you don't mind, but I could only get one room," he said as they approached the reservation desk. "Everything else was booked. I'll be a perfect gentleman."

"You always are," she replied with a smile.

The room was incredibly small, but it had a bathroom with hot running water. Jena showered and wrapped herself in a towel while Mark went down to the restaurant and got them a light lunch. When he returned, she was asleep, still wrapped in her towel, and stretched on the side of the bed. Carefully, Mark put her under the covers before modestly removing the towel. And there he let her sleep until evening.

Chapter Fourteen

When Jena awoke, the room was dark. A side lamp was the only light. Mark was quietly reading in a corner chair by the window.

She felt strange and peeked under the covers. She was nude.

He detected her movement and looked up from his book. “Feel better?”

“Uh, Mark. Did you…”

“Didn’t see a thing. Just rolled you in, covered you up, and ripped out the towel.”

“I am so sorry. I didn’t sleep on the plane and I guess I hit a wall.”

“Apparently. Hungry?”

“I’m famished,” she replied. She hadn’t had a full meal in thirty-six hours.

“Why don’t you get dressed, and I’ll show you Venice at night. One of the magnificent wonders of the world.”

She pulled at the sheet and wrapped it around her. Then she retreated to the bathroom and dressed in jeans and an overly big sweater, as the temperature had dropped into the low sixties. She pulled on her flat boots and was ready to go.

They walked down the stairs to the waterway, and took a gondola to a quaint Italian family-owned bistro, hidden in the center of the city, away from all the tourists. He’d been here before and knew the lay of the city and its miles and miles of back streets, canals, and cobblestone walkways.

They ordered dumplings stuffed with ricotta and pears and lightly sipped on Tocai Friulano wine. In the distance, they heard the sad refrains of a saxophone playing in the night. The stars were brilliant overhead. The candlelight danced in her eyes, and Mark was mesmerized.

They took their time, and ordered more olives, bread, cheese, meats and fresh fruit. In this place of lights and romance, there was no need to rush anything, especially good authentic Italian delicacies.

They talked for hours, until finally the waiter came with their check. Mark paid, then pulled her to her feet and they left the same way they had come, through the back ways of old brick walls, and stone walks. They meandered, hand in hand, along the canal channels with the sounds of life and laughter and music around them.

Mark had splurged on the hotel, and asked for a room with a balcony that overlooked the bridges that were lit at night like a fairy tale Christmas in old Barcelona. When they got back, they went out on the balcony and leaned against the railing. Roving musicians played below them, and gondolas passed beneath, carrying lovers on their journeys of the heart.

"This is beautiful," Jena whispered.

"This is the Venice I wanted you to see. Venice at night. It is a different city than the day. In the day it is loud and busy and you can hardly walk because of the tourists and the vendors on the bridges and along the walks. And the waterbus blares its horn like a Mack truck."

"There aren't any cars here."

"There's nowhere to drive them. Everything is by boat or foot.

"Mark," she whispered, reaching for his hand. "Listen."

From beneath them by the canal came the haunting sound of the mourning saxophone.

"I think he's following us," Mark suggested. But he knew music was this city's voice at night. It was the sound of lovers parting and the long farewell captured in the minor key of the sonnet. And it was the song of lovers reunited after a lifetime apart.

They sat down at the table on the balcony. Mark opened a bottle of wine and poured a little in each glass. They silently toasted each other. The next few minutes they sat, savoring the exquisite Italian Pinot Grigio, catching up on their time apart.

Mark told her about the discharge process, and a little incident that happened on base. She told him about Rick and Katie and the children, her new puppy, and her work. He shared that he'd had another minor surgery on his knee, and would need to keep his activities in check. She told him about the house and the renovations, and her support group.

The evening was enchanting.

They talked on, and then sometimes would just silently sip on their wine, lost in their own reflections and the unspoken desires of their heart.

"This place is magical," she finally whispered.

He looked over at her. "Only if you are lovers."

She met his gaze. "Is that what we are? Lovers?"

"We've been lovers since that night in the ocean."

She didn't answer, but turned her gaze back out to the magical night.

He waited for her; a hesitancy shrouded in uncertainty. Then, he leaned forward in his chair. "Jena, what do you want?"

She took a deep breath. She'd thought so much about that over the last month. She knew they were about to embark on a different kind of journey. For so long she'd been afraid. But something deep inside of her had changed. "I want more."

He blinked. "More of what?"

She leaned toward him. "More of you. More of us." She watched his reaction, and saw it deep in his eyes. "What do you want, Mark?"

Mark was quiet for a long time before he replied. "I've been by myself all my life, Jena. I've played it hard core. Tough guy. I really haven't let anyone truly in, or let them see the man behind the fortress."

Jena wanted to reach out and touch him, but she didn't.

"I'm tired of war," he said. "I want tenderness in my life."

Behind them, in the Italian night, from farther in the heart of Venice, a violin answered the song of the saxophone. The music was sweet and melancholy, and familiar.

"Why did you come, Jena?"

She put her glass of wine on the table. "You asked me to come."

"Would you have come if I hadn't asked you?" He needed to know. He felt he'd risked it all by sending her the note and the ticket. The money meant nothing. But his heart had been suspended, never knowing if the time would ever come.

She watched his face, and the expression there. What did she see? A handsome Air Force officer. Yes, he was all that and more. But in that moment between them, she saw a vulnerability she'd never seen and slowly turned in her chair to fully face him.

"I would have come," she whispered. "Maybe not today. But I would have come."

"Why?" His face was stoic now, as though he were battling a war within and could not…would not…let her see.

Jena inhaled slowly, then let it out. "Because you imprinted my soul. No one ever has. Not even Pete, as much as I loved him. Not even the babies, who never had the chance. You branded me. And I haven't been the same since."

He stayed still. Silent. Watching her. Listening.

"You saved me from going under, Mark. You gave me a reason to live again. I don't know where any of this is taking us. But I know I had to come, or live regretting that I never did."

He reached out and slowly rubbed his hand down her arm. "I was scared. Still am." He laughed to ward off the intensity of what he was feeling.

"Me, too," she answered, reaching out to touch his heart. "Rick said I was afraid of loving, because I was afraid of losing again. He was right. It's hard sitting here right now with you. What I'm feeling is so very overwhelming to me. I'm excited, and confused, and afraid. My heart is racing."

"Mine, too." He reached for her hand and put it on his heart again. Jena felt it pounding through his shirt.

"Mark, you asked me why I came. Why did you ask me to come?" It was her turn for answers to her wonderings and what ifs.

"Because I love you," he said simply, without a hesitation. "It's sounds so quaint. But how else can I describe what keeps me breathing? From the moment I saw you in the ocean that first night, I felt like a mule had kicked me in the gut. I never thought of you as someone I had to have. But you are the one I want. I don't think I can live without you."

She felt her eyes misting over.

"We have this…thing…you and I…this bond between us," he continued. "It started on common ground. You losing your family. Me losing…that "Dear John" woman. We met there, on that ground, and it was equal ground. We shared it. And we suffered in it. And we fought against it. We fought through it. And we challenged each other, and held each other accountable, do you remember?"

She nodded yes.

"I had my moments just like you. And you talked me through them. And you cared for me, just like I cared for you. And then, one day, I just knew."

"When was that?" she quietly asked.

He smiled. "When you threw up on me."

"I'm so sorry about that."

"That did it for me." He touched her face.

"I knew it when you asked me to dance. When you sang to me."

"So why did you push me away?" he wondered.

"Because I knew that if you kissed me, I would surely fall all the way. And there would be nothing to catch me. I would love you. And if I loved you, I might lose you one day. And if lost you, there would not be anything to live for, ever again."

He watched her as she emptied the deepest part of her heart.

"So," he began. "The last day, when I dropped you off at your house, and we said goodbye, why didn't you tell me then how you felt?"

"I couldn't go with you. You couldn't stay. I was still fighting the ghosts. I felt like I was cheating on Pete. It would be closing the door on a past that I wasn't ready to let go." She smiled sadly.

He listened intently.

"But it was too late."

"You'd already given up on us?"

She shook her head. "I was already in love with you."

He leaned closer.

"When you lose someone, no one understands," she went on.

"No, they don't."

"They all just expect you to move on, away from it all, like it was a bad movie, or a disease, or a sad or unfortunate event. But we can't ever move on. We can only just go on, and keep what was precious protected in our hearts. The people we've loved and lost have made us who we are. You told me that once. We never stop loving them. But I had to discover that on my own."

Mark watched her, his heart beating faster.

"I will always have them with me, in my heart and soul. They will always be a part of me. But I am moving forward with them. They're just in a different place than they were before." She paused. "And I am a different woman than I was before."

He watched her intently. "So, what will happen if I kiss you right now? Will you turn away? Will you run away?"

She got up from the deck chair and came around to him, and slowly slipped into his lap. She looked deep into his eyes. "No more running."

She felt his body respond to her. His hands caressed her.

"…and if I kissed *you*?" she whispered.

"There would be no turning back." he said, so quietly she barely heard him.

"Mark," she finally breathed, her face so close to his. "I'm putting my heart into your hands. Be gentle with it."

Then Jena put her lips to his. It was a feather's touch, but his insides exploded in fire. Then she pressed her lips more firmly against his, and he answered with a passion born of longing and experience.

Then the lover in him took over, and he took her places she'd never ever known. His hands were everywhere, and she allowed them. In turn, she massaged his neck and ran her hands down his muscular arms. Their lips never left each other.

When they finally came up for air, they smiled at each other.

They held each other a long, long time on the balcony overlooking the City of Love. Then he led her inside and laid her across the made bed. He stroked her hair and caressed every outline of her face. Little, barely visible, wrinkles had appeared in the corner of her eyes since he'd last seen her, and he graced them with his fingertips. She cupped his stubbled face in her hand, then touched the side of his temples where there were wisps of gray.

They said no more after that, but fell asleep in each other's arms, fully clothed, yet each of them bare to the core of their souls.

***

She woke and found him staring at her with a lopsided grin on his face. The sun peeked through the curtains and showered them with soft beams of morning light.

"I love you, Jena Parker," he whispered.

She smiled at him.

"But," he groaned and pulled slowly away. "I need a very cold shower."

She watched as he left her side and walked into the bathroom and closed the door.

Jena laid there, as the fire raged anew and she felt herself burning up from the inside. She'd never felt this way, not even with Pete.

With Pete, love had been more subdued. It was contained within some unspoken boundary of respectability. It was never passion without limits. Their love always conformed to what they'd individually grown up with and witnessed. She and Pete had been mates, settling for a relationship and lifestyle that they thought was the norm. She loved Pete.

Oh, she did love Pete. That love would always be precious. But *this* love...this love was different. It transcended everything.

In one heart stopping moment, sitting here, she realized. She and Pete were never *soulmates*. She'd never known what that meant, until now. And that thought hit her hard, in so many ways.

She knew that Mark was going deliberately slow. She loved him even more for it, for it spoke of his respect and the depth of his commitment to her. But, for a long time, perhaps longer than she herself had known, she'd wanted more and more of him. She teetered between wise control and wild abandon. She knew he was concerned about spooking her, or going so fast that she retreated from him. But every minute with him confirmed that she'd made the right decision in coming here.

The shower shut off behind the closed doors. Jena rose and went out to the balcony. The city was transforming back again into a hustle and bustle of activity, tourists, and market vendors yelling and laughing. Five minutes later, Mark found her still there. He came up behind her and wrapped her in his arms. Together, they watched the city unfold into the new day.

"I have three more days," he said, kissing her hair.

"What?"

"I'm on a four-day pass, then I have to go back on duty until the discharge process."

"Then you'll be out?"

He laughed. "Yes, I'll be out. Retired, with full honors and a nice pension.

She turned to face him. "What are you going to do, then?"

"I have big, big plans."

"...really?'

He smiled. "Go shower and change. Then, let's get out of here and go find some food."

Jena showered and washed her hair, changed into worn jeans, a crimson blouse, and a pair of comfortable shoes. She put her hair in a pony tail and applied lipstick. But her cheeks were still flushed from thoughts of him.

They ate breakfast at a café on the canal, then strolled through the shops and market area. He bought her a white rose from the flower cart.

They wound through the city, discovering the heart and personality of a thriving city built solely on piers and tiny islands. They ended up in St. Mark's Square, and toured the Basilica there. They fed the pigeons out of their hand and, in a throwback to familiarity, they had lunch at the Hard Rock Café – Venice. Then they walked back to the hotel and checked out, and boarded the waterbus back to the parking area.

He put down the top on the convertible as they got back on the highway. She took down her hair and let the wind have its way. He kept glancing over at her, grinning ear to ear. He couldn't get enough of her.

"Where are we going, Mark?"

"On a road trip," he smiled, with mischief in his eyes. He drove the back roads and showed her the Italian countryside, where vineyards flourished everywhere. The towns were nothing like the towns in America. They were more hamlets and villages brought kicking and screaming into the 21st century. They stopped for gelato at an outside café, and he laughed at her as she tried to learn simple Italian phrases.

"How do you say I love you," she asked.

"Ti amo," he answered,

"And how do you say I have to pee?" she asked, innocently.

He laughed out loud and pointed to a door just beyond their table. "Devo andare al bagno."

When she returned to the table, he'd paid the bill, but was talking with a much older gentleman, who could have passed as his great-grandfather. He looked a hundred years old, if a day. They were speaking in Italian, and laughing, and using their hands to converse as much as their words. They both turned toward her as she approached.

The old man smiled a toothless grin, and his eyes twinkled as though he was the keeper of all the secrets of this valley. But in those wise eyes there was something else. He said something softly in Italian.

"Ciao, come va?" *Hello, how are you?*

Mark translated.

The Italian took off his hat, and spoke directly to her, gazing at Jena as though she was his sun and stars.

"He says you are the most beautiful woman he has seen since he wedded the preacher's daughter during the war, so many years ago."

The old man continued.

"He blesses you in love, and says you are a pure spirit." Mark grinned.

"…thank you," Jena replied. "Grazie."

Pausing, and leaning toward her, the old man reached for her left hand, raised it to his lips, and gently placed a kiss there.

Mark looked down, saw what was missing, then glanced quickly back up to Jena. She'd taken off her wedding band.

The old man murmured one last message.

"He says he wishes to marry you if…"

"…if what?" Jena smiled at the two of them.

"He says he wishes to marry you if I do not."

"Cosi bello," the old man said. *So beautiful!* "Andare con Dio." *Go with God.*

Then he put on his hat and took up his cane. He looked back only once, then he walked out the door. To Jena, she felt as though she just been visited by an angel.

Back on the road, Mark drove slower, pointing out landmarks and telling her the stories of the German occupation of Italy and old handed-down stories of lovers in the war. It was late afternoon when they arrived in Aviano. She felt the slight sunburn on her skin from the day in the convertible. It was becoming on her, and pulled the rose into her cheeks

Mark pulled into a quaint family-owned hotel close to the center of the small town. "It's not fancy, but it is clean. The owners are friends of mine."

He asked for two rooms on the third floor, and they rode the old elevator up. Her room had a king bed, and a couch, and huge bay windows that opened overlooking the Dolomite mountains, the foothills of the Alps. In the distance could be heard the sounds of life. He closed the door behind them and set her bag on the bed.

"This is nice," she said, looking around. She went to the open windows and breathed in the fragrance of a thousand flowers blooming in the window planters outside. She quietly scanned the mountains tops beyond.

Mark came to stand behind her.

"Mark, we don't need two rooms, do we? It's so expensive."

"I don't mind."

She turned to him. "I do. We have so little time before you have to go back."

"I could sleep on the couch," he said, hopefully. "I can give you your space, if you want."

Suddenly, a roar filled the air and an F-16 raced by them outside the window, just a hundred feet above the trees, its jet engines ablaze as it banked sharply and climbed into the sky.

"There go our boys to protect and defend," Mark said. "It's beautiful to watch, isn't it?"

She turned to him. "Mark, go turn in the other room key. We're both adults. I want every moment with you."

He nodded. "Ok. Be back in a few minutes."

While he was gone, Jena sat on the couch and looked out the window. It was so beautiful in this country. Time marched to a different pace, and people took the time to enjoy the moments. People here spent hours at dinner, eating and drinking and talking and laughing. They lived life to the full. Missing were the man-made distractions of commercialism and status. Families here had been here for hundreds of years.

She'd missed so much of life The last few days had made her realize that. There had always been more than she'd never known.

This land was a land of passion. She could feel it in the air, and see it in the vineyards and flowers, and hear it in the echo of the bells ringing from the bell tower of the centuries old chapel around the corner from where they were.

In two days, she'd fallen in love with Italy, and fallen deeper in love with the man who'd brought her here.

Mark returned with his bag and briefcase and placed it on the bed next to her bags.

He wasn't going to rush anything. Not with Jena. He'd had women before. But this woman was Jena. His best friend. His soulmate. The love of his life. She was so different than any woman he'd ever known. And he treasured her. So, he could go slow. He *would* go slow.

"Let's go to dinner," he reached for her hand. They walked out of the hotel and strolled along the sidewalks. The dusk was a Picasso painting in and of itself.

They reached a restaurant where music played and the wine flowed, and vines hung from a hundred baskets throughout. They ate on the patio, ordering five courses and took their time through each one.

"Tomorrow, I want to show you Lake Barcis. It's not far from here. Before I sold the bike I had here, I'd go every week."

She listened to him talk of Lake Barcis, and the mountains, the trails and the waterfalls in the area.

They stayed until late, talking and sharing of this and that, of their childhood and their dreams, and the things they cherished the most. They were so comfortable with each other. They always had been, from the moment they'd met in the ocean. Jena wondered if they'd been lovers in another lifetime, and were finding each other again. She mentioned it out loud to Mark.

"…maybe," Mark replied. "To lovers, then." He raised his glass. "May we always find each other."

She raised her glass and touched his. "…may we always find each other."

"Oh, that reminds me," he said, reaching into his coat pocket. "I have something for you. I saw it in Venice. I thought you might like it." He handed her a long velvet box.

She opened it, and her heart caught in her throat. It was a sterling silver necklace, with two tiny white pearls embedded in a perfect heart.

"For the girls," he whispered.

"Oh, Mark."

He stood up and draped the necklace around her throat. Gently, she fingered the heart, touching each pearl.

"Jena," he breathed. "I don't want to overstep. But I feel like, because they are forever yours, they are forever mine, too."

She was touched beyond measure. She looked up at him with the tears glistening in her eyes.

They fell asleep in each other's arms that night, mirroring the night before. Their love was pure, and they both knew what was happening between them was a holy thing to be cherished and honored. The breeze came in from the open windows as they lay together talking and kissing deep into the night. They finally fell asleep to the song of the nightingale.

Chapter Fifteen

He took her to Lake Barcis the next day, stopping at each hamlet along the way. They were tucked into the mountain as gems, hidden from the real world. Each hamlet had a small chapel and bell tower, and every hour on the hour, the bells reverberated off the mountains and echoed across the valley below.

Lake Barcis was its own storyland, with chalets and open-air cafes, and Italians sunbathing by the lake. The lake was small and mirrored the Alps in the clear turquoise waters. They'd packed a picnic and had lunch on the grass. While they were dining on bread and cheese, fruit and jam, they heard the sound of race engines. They looked up as twenty-seven Lamborghinis came winding down from the mountains. They slowed and squeezed through the one lane thoroughfare through the mountain hamlet. The locals and tourists alike stood up and walked toward the road to better view the parade of race cars.

"Be still my heart," Mark said.

Jena smiled at him. "Only in Italy would I ever see this."

The race cars slowly ambled through town, weaving through the cobblestone streets. Then they went on their way down the mountain.

"I wish I could buy you one, one day," Jena said.

"Ah, I don't need one. I have all I want right here in front of me," he said, winking at her.

"What else do you want, Mark? Surely there are things you've thought about."

He popped a piece of cheese in his mouth. "To tell you the truth, I haven't really thought about it. A year ago, I had some plans. But those changed."

"When you get out of the Air Force, where do you want to live? What do you want to do? What other wild adventures do you want to have?"

He thought a minute. "I like Texas. East Texas. I like the piney woods and the forests."

"What else?"

"I want us to be together. I want a family. Two or three kids. Maybe four kids. A dog or two. A house with a workshop. I'm not particular. As long as I'm with you, nothing else matters."

Jena took in a small breath and looked down.

She hadn't told anyone. But now, he needed to know. It might change everything, or nothing at all. But she owed it to him to always be honest.

"Mark." She hesitated. Then looked up at him.

"Yes, Jena?"

"I don't know if I can have children again."

"What?"

"Carrying a child to term won't be the problem. It's getting pregnant in the first place. There was a lot of damage done. Rick said that the chances were slim to none. It would take a miracle."

He looked at her for a long time then. He hadn't known. She hadn't told him. He took a minute to process what she'd just said before he said anything.

The silence between them was deafening, before he finally spoke.

"Do you think, Jena," he finally asked. "That me knowing this now could ever change how I feel about you?"

"I thought it might. And, you should know."

He shook his head as he wrapped up the cheese. "And if I came back tomorrow from the war zone, and had only one arm, would that change how you feel about me?"

"Of course not," she whispered. "You could come home to me a quadriplegic, and I would love you."

He put the cheese in the basket and closed the lid. Then he turned to her. "Talk about miracles. Well, you're the walking miracle, Jena Parker. I never thought, that in my lifetime, I would ever know a woman like you. Or ever be loved by a woman like you. So, I believe in miracles."

She sat still on the blanket. The sunshine cascaded all around her, and the breeze touched her hair.

"But like everything wonderful and good and true," he continued. "Miracles come in their own time, and when we least expect them, and sometimes at the last possible moment."

Behind them near the lake, a child laughed.

"This thing we have, Jena," he reached over and cupped her face in his hands. "This love of ours gives birth to miracles."

They held each other's gaze.

"And if we can't have children of our own," he continued. "We can adopt a brood of them, or get more dogs."

She smiled, and the sun came out again.

"I just want to grow old with you, Jena. I want to watch your hair turn gray and watch your teeth fall out. I want to fight you over the hearing aid. I want to bring you coffee every morning of every day. And, most of all, I want to be able to kiss you every single day. Every single hour. Every minute."

She laughed out loud.

And, in that moment, Jena knew for sure she'd lost her heart to him, completely. She didn't need more time, or proof that this was right between them. The signs were everywhere. Every time he spoke or touched her or looked her way confirmed what she already knew. Perhaps she'd known from the very beginning.

She loved him.

"Just one question, though," he said tentatively, gently. "With the damage done to you, can you still…"

She touched his lips with her fingertips, as though to silence his concern. "I lost an ovary, and almost lost the other one. So, to answer your question…." She smiled at him then. Her voice went suddenly very sexy and he felt like he was going to fall over.

"I can still…very much so."

That moment said more than any of her words had before. All doubt between them fled. She knew he wanted her. And now, he knew she wanted him.

He took a long deep breath, then cleared the frog in his throat. "I'll take you anyway I can get you, for however long, Jena Parker. Just say the word." Then he bent over and kissed her.

And she answered.

"Jena?"

"Yes?"

"Did we just have the making love, having children, dogs or cats conversation?"

"I believe we did."

He grinned. "How did it go for you?"

She wrapped her arms around his neck, and kissed him sweetly on the lips. "Does this answer your question?"

"Yep."

They packed up the food then, and gathered their things.

"Let's go back a different way," he suggested. He grabbed the picnic basket with one hand, and her hand with the other and led her back to the convertible. "I want to show you more before we head back." He steered the car in the opposite direction of where the Lamborghinis were headed. In a few minutes they were gingerly ambling across a very small bridge that ended at the mouth of a tunnel. Mark entered the tunnel very slowly, as the walls pressed in from the sides, coming within inches of the doors.

"I hope you know what you are doing," she said, holding her breath as they threaded the entrance to the tunnel. Then they were in it, and Mark slowed to a crawl.

At first, Jena thought they might be entering a cave, and the thought frightened her, as there seemed no way out. Then she saw the circle of light far beyond. At the same time, the hair on her neck stood up, and her arms broke out in goosebumps.

"Mark."

"Shhh," he whispered.

"What is that?"

He turned to her, and smiled.

"I hear marching," she whispered. "The sound of men marching. And, tanks rolling."

"It's the sound of history."

"We're in a time warp."

"The imprint of time." He smiled. "There are imprints everywhere. People who've come and people who've gone." He looked at her. "There is a power to the love they brought and what they did. Even across all these years we can still feel them."

"I still feel them… Pete and the girls."

"And you will always feel them. Because their love was so powerful in your life. It's not something to be afraid of but, like this moment now, it is something to be treasured and to hold in awe and reverence. It's good to remember, and never forget."

Slowly, the echoes of time faded from around them.

Mark drove carefully through the tiny tunnel, and then they were back out in the sunshine and in a beautiful forest.

"Beautiful, isn't it?"

She was speechless. Towering trees created a canopy over them as they drove the small curves of the one lane that switch-backed up the mountain. They drove in silence for ten minutes, in awe of the beauty. The sunlight filtered through the trees and lit up the gorgeous colors of the leaves.

Halfway up the mountain to Piancavallo, a thunderstorm came over the mountain and the downburst of rain caught them by surprise. Mark put the top up on the convertible, but not before the rain soaked them both to the skin. It was hard to see and the wipers swished back and forth on high speed, but to no avail. Then the front right tire blew as they ran over a fallen tree branch. The car swerved and a second later, the back right tire blew, as well.

Mark hit the brake and quickly pulled over to the side of the road. He prayed there were no big trucks barreling down the narrow mountain road toward them. The visibility was almost zero, and the road wasn't wide enough for any encounter. Yet it was obvious they needed someone else on this road to help them.

Mark popped the trunk and opened his door. "Be right back." A minute later he was back, rain running down his face.

"Two flats. One spare." He said as he climbed back into the driver's seat.

"That's not good," Jena said, handing him his jacket.

He wiped his face with his jacket and slung the water from his short hair. In his mind, he ran down the list of possible scenarios and the dangers threat. He mentally listed possible resources.

He dialed a number on his cell phone, put it to his ear, then pulled it back and glared at it. "No cell phone coverage." He tossed the phone on the console, then he sneezed.

Jena looked at him and burst out laughing.

"What?" he growled.

"You. You look like a drowned bear."

"Well, if you have any ideas at this point, I'd love to hear them. Or, are you going to keep laughing at me?"

"Oh, my god," she laughed. "I've had more adventures with you than in my entire life."

"So, what do you suggest, my darling?" he said, still wiping water from his head and face and arms.

"How far is Piancavallo?"

"A few miles. No less than three. No more than five."

She leaned back and closed her eyes. "So, we wait until the rain stops, walk the rest of the way, and call a tow truck."

"And, what do we do in the meantime?"

She smiled.

***

It was almost dark before the rain stopped. Mark saw headlights in the rearview mirror and got out to flag down help. It was an old truck clanking up the road, and it slowed when it came near them. The truck stopped, and a young man in his twenties reached across a young woman and rolled down the window.

"Mark! My friend! What are you doing up here this time of day?" It was Antonio, from the mechanics shop in town.

"We were on our way to Piancavallo and ran over a tree."

Antonio raised his eyebrows.

"What are you doing up here?" Mark asked, leaning on the door of the old pickup.

"Coming from Barcis. I went to pick up my girlfriend," he said, his Italian accent heavy. "This is Vittoria." The young woman smiled at Mark and glanced over at the car sitting half off the road.

"We've got two flats and one spare. If you're headed up to Piancavallo, can we get a ride?"

Antonio looked over at the car, the driver's door open. "Who is that woman with you? She is beautiful, si?"

Mark nodded. "Very beautiful."

"Oh," Antonio smiled, knowingly. "She is the one, si?"

"Si," Mark replied, glancing over his shoulder at Jena as she sat quietly waiting.

"Get in. We are going to my parents' home there. They are celebrating love tonight! Fifty years! There is a party. You must come. Tomorrow, we will come back for the car."

Mark glanced back at the car. He had no choice. "Grazie, my friend." Then he walked back over to the car and leaned in. "We have a ride. We'll come back for the car in the morning."

He went around the side of the car, stepped over the tree branch that was lodged underneath the car, opened her door and helped her out. They crammed themselves in the front seat of the truck, and Mark laid his left arm on the bench around her shoulders.

The old truck spit oil, then kicked into gear and rambled back up the mountain road.

"There is a party tonight," Antonio said to Jena, his face lit up with excitement. "You and my friend Mark will come and celebrate with my family, yes?"

Jena smiled, remembering Mark telling her to never turn down an invitation from an Italian. It was bad luck. And Italy was a place of good fortune.

"We'd be honored," she answered.

"Mark has become part of my family over the years," Antonio said. "He's had many dinners with us, and knows my family."

"All of them," Mark laughed. "I even know the names of the horses and pigs behind the barn."

"My mother and father have claimed him as a son. So, you both will stay with us tonight. The weather is bad. And, it is a big house with many rooms." Antonio cleared his throat. "I have seven brothers and sisters. But there is always room!"

"Grazie, Antonio. I owe you," Mark said.

"Si. Tomorrow, we will fix your car. But tonight? Tonight, we drink and dance and celebrate life!"

The trip up to Piancavallo took thirty minutes, partly due to the old truck and partly due to the slick road. Jena listened as Mark and Antonio bantered in Italian and English, going back and forth. Finally, they pulled onto a long dirt road, and the truck sloshed through the mud to the giant hundred-year-old farm house. There was light in every window and they heard the music before they even got out of the truck.

The unmistakable sounds of a mandolin, accordion, and a guitar filled the night as they walked along the path to the front door. The music was festive and light, and Jena smiled.

"Ciao a tutti," Antonio called, coming into the room filled with thirty people. Young and old, children, teens, and adults. "Ho portato amici!" *I brought friends*.

An older woman, her face weathered but filled with joy, came out of the kitchen, wiping her hands on an apron. "Benvenuto!" *Welcome*! She embraced Mark.

Her husband, Antonio's father, followed her out of the kitchen. "Più siamo, meglio è!" *The more the merrier!* He, too, took Mark in a hug. "Good to see you, my son!"

Antonio showed them to a large bedroom on the second floor. "It is drafty in this old house, but there is warmth enough," he said, motioning to the fireplace. "After, I will bring dry clothes and dry wood and you will be warm tonight." He showed them the bathroom and gave them towels. "Come down when you are ready. We will eat and dance and sing all night, so there is no hurry."

"…only in Italy," Jena murmured, a smile gracing her lips.

"Grazie!" Mark said, thanking his friend. Mark would miss Antonio when he left Italy for good.

The party was in full swing when they finally descended the creaking stairs and joined the family. A young woman placed a glass of wine in each of their hands and ushered them toward the dining room table. They had brought the tables and chairs inside when the rain began, and now they crowded the large living area.

The table was laden with salads, and breads, cheeses, open bottles of wine, bowls of fruit, and platters of meat and roasted potatoes. Jena had never seen so much food in her life!

The family gathered round and took their seats, still talking loudly and laughing. The younger children sat at tables by the kitchen and picked at each other playfully.

Mark took his seat next to Jena, squeezing in the smaller space caused by adding two more chairs.

The patriarch reached over and took a piece of roasted lamb and popped it in his mouth.

"Papa!" his wife scolded. "La benedizione!" *The blessing*!

"Si!" he replied, playfully patting her plump behind.

When everyone was seated, and quieted down, the Papa stood and bowed his head. His family followed his lead.

"Benedici, Signore, noi e questi tuoi doni, che stiamo per ricevere dalla tua generosità. Per Cristo nostro Signore." *Bless us Oh Lord, and these thy gifts, which we are about to receive, from thy bounty, through Christ, Our Lord. Amen.*

"Amen," his family answered, crossing their hearts.

Then the Papa raised his wine glass. "A tavola non si invecchia." *At the table, you don't get old.* "Not with so many beautiful women!" His English was broken but his words brought a warm glow to Jena as Mama leaned over to kiss him on the cheek.

His family chuckled.

"Chi si volta, e chi si gira, sempre a casa va finire." Papa looked around the table of his family, nodding to each of them, including Mark and Jena. *No matter where you go or turn, you'll always end up at home.*

Then he turned to his wife of fifty years. "Sei la mia casa, Tesero. Ti amo." *You are my home, my darling. I love you.* Then he leaned over and gave his wife a deep and sloppy kiss.

The family rose as one and clapped, laughing, and slapping each other on the back. "Congratulazioni, Papa! Congratulazioni, Mama!"

"Congratulazioni," Mark said.

"Mangiamo!" Antonio exclaimed. "Let's eat!"

Mark and Jena were famished and ate and laughed for hours. Jena found that the language barrier was not all that difficult, and she started picking up on the conversations and jovial bantering around her, especially when Mark leaned over and translated. The wine never ended and the food just kept coming. As did the toasts.

"To life!" Antonio yelled across the table, as he filled his mouth with roasted potatoes.

His brothers followed, with their own toasts to their parents and to each other. Sometimes the toasts were touching. Others were totally inappropriate and brought scolding from Mama. Yet they brought laughter as the brothers slapped each other on the back.

Mark offered a toast to Papa and Mama, and all cheered.

Then Antonio rose and toasted Mark. "Many women. Many loves. But true love comes only once in a lifetime. You have found yours, my friend. May you be blessed."

Mark nodded and raised his glass in response of gratitude. "Grazie."

Antonio raised his glass to Jena. "Bella donna. Beautiful woman. May you dance through the storm… and may you be held in the arms of love all the days of your life."

Jena was deeply touched, then smiled brilliantly. "Thank you, Antonio."

Mark felt his heart leap inside his chest.

Everyone joined in and toasted their family and friends, and drank deeply again of the wine of life. Several of Antonio's brothers rose from the table, and started playing music again, this time singing slower songs of amore.

After a while, the younger children were put to bed. The other children followed soon after.

Jena was happy but exhausted as she rose from the table and helped clear the dishes. Then she joined Mark and they sat on the stairs together, his arm around her, and listened to the music and watched the family together.

"Is it always like this?" Jena leaned into him.

"Every time I am here, it is just like this."

When it was apparent that everything was winding down, they thanked Antonio and his parents, said goodnight to his siblings, and made their way up the stairs to their room.

Antonio had gone ahead of them and was starting a fire in the fireplace. "This old house has been in my family for generations," he said quietly, stirring the flames. "It is cold at night. So, we try and keep the fires going. I've left wood here for you."

"Grazie," Mark said.

"Goodnight," Antonio answered. Then he was gone.

Jena crossed the room, took the blanket off the bed, wrapped herself in it, and went to sit in the big chair by the fire. Mark sat down on the bed and took off his shoes.

The house creaked as the family settled in the rooms around them. A baby cried, then quieted. A log cracked in the fireplace.

Jena felt strangely at home in this place with this family. They made it warm and happy and had included her, now, as one of their own daughters.

She wanted a family like this one. She wanted a love like Papa and Mama. Perhaps fate, or faith, was offering just that. A love kind and warm and enduring for a lifetime. And maybe children. Mark said they could adopt. As she sat quietly by the fire, she tried to imagine what that might look like now.

She'd watched him with the children tonight, putting them on his shoulders and bouncing around the living room and down the halls. She'd seen him rescue the crying toddler and swoop her up in his arms to soothe away the tears. She'd witnessed his laughter and his playfulness with Antonio and his siblings, and with Papa and Mama.

And more than once, she'd caught him staring at her with eyes that spoke volumes of a lifetime.

It was moving so quickly, this healing of the heart, and it seemed to catapult her into the arms of a safe and real love of which she'd never so fully experienced. There were things moving in her heart and soul which surprised her, but that she so welcomed. She was waking up from a lifetime of only wishing.

She'd held to a past of lost loves to which she would never let go. And Mark had a past of loves lost, from which he'd moved on. But here they were, together, on this night high up in the mountains, surrounded by love and laughter and the making of memories that lasted a lifetime.

"Mark," she said quietly.

"Yes?"

The last two days with him had rocked her world, and transformed every hurt into hope for a future again.

"Antonio's toast to you," she began, gazing into the fire. "Is it true?"

Mark slipped off his socks. "Is what true?"

She was silent for a moment. The fire crackled.

"That you've known many women, and had many loves."

"…my friend knows me well."

She watched as embers floated upward in the fireplace. "…and that I was your true love."

He watched her from across the room. Then he rose and draped his shirt on a hook on the wall.

The rain began again, lightly, and the sound of raindrops hitting the window echoed across the room. Jena stared into the fire. Behind her, Mark stood still by the door.

"You are my true love, Jena."

"…and you are mine," she whispered softly, still staring into the fire. He barely heard her.

But he did hear her.

A minute later he came to stand quietly in front of her. Then he took a knee. He looked into her eyes and watched as the reflection of the firelight dance in them.

"Jena. Luce mia. *My light.* Vita mia. *My life,*" he said slowly…reverently.

Jena turned her gaze from the firelight and looked at him.

"Anima mia. *My soul,*" he continued. "My beloved."

Her eyes filled with tears.

He gently took her hand in his. "Per sempre. *Forever.*" He drew in a shaky breath. "Per sempre, ti amo."

She reached up and touched his face. The look in her eyes said all he really wanted to know.

Then Mark slowly reached into his pocket. "I've had this for months, hoping and praying you'd come to me." He opened his hand. Laying in his palm was a diamond ring.

"Jena Parker...will you marry me?"

She looked at the ring, then back at him.

There was a moment when time stood still. Mark couldn't breathe. Those silent seconds became a lifetime.

The fire crackled in the hearth.

The final rumble of the storm rolled off into the distance.

Then Jena smiled.

"Yes…" she whispered.

Chapter Sixteen

They spent the night in each other's arms holding each other, laying in front of the fire, wrapped in blankets just trying to stay warm. Their heads rested side by side on the pillows, and they whispered quietly for hours until the early morn.

They woke to the aroma of Italian expresso and freshly baked pastries.

Jena slowly stretched and looked at the ring on her finger. "Was I dreaming, or did you ask me to marry you last night?"

Mark pulled her closer. "I did. You said yes." He went up on his elbow and looked strangely at her. "You don't remember?"

"Oh, I remember. Like it was a moment ago."

"Changing your mind?" he wondered.

"My mind was made up before you asked." She kissed him.

"We can get married when we get back to the States."

She looked into his eyes. "Why not here?" she asked.

"Marry in Italy? We need time to do the paperwork."

"How long does it take here?"

"A month or more." He touched her hand and fingered the ring he'd given her the night before. "I don't want to rush you. We don't have to hurry."

"One month," she said softly. "We have to wait one month?"

"At least, from what I've heard." He sat up and pulled on a sweater, then stood up and pulled on his socks and shoes. "Don't you want a big church wedding back home?"

Jena was quiet for a moment, then she shook her head.

"No," she whispered. "I don't want a big church wedding."

She remembered marrying Pete, and the fiasco that wedding was. His mother had invited two hundred of their friends, and she and Pete had spent a fortune on the traditional expectations. In the end, it'd been a huge party for their country club friends, as Jena had no family, save an aunt and uncle who didn't even stay for the reception.

He came to sit down beside her. "What do you want, Jena? Anything. Just ask."

"I love you." She declared, so innocently, and yet her words carried the passion that surprised them both. "I don't want to wait to marry you, Mark."

Mark sat quietly. He'd waited for her for what he now knew had been a lifetime. And suddenly, in the span of a few days, here she was, declaring her love for him. He'd gone slow on purpose. To honor her, certainly. But more so, to give her the time and space to discover everything he already knew. They belonged together. As friends. As lovers. As man and wife.

"I want to marry you here, in Italy," she gazed at him. "I don't want the fanfare or the circus of a big wedding. I've had enough drama for one lifetime. I just want to be with you."

He wrapped her in his arms and kissed her. "Then I will move heaven and earth to make it happen, Jena."

They came down the stairs and Antonio was entering the front door! "Good morning, lovers!" he said good naturedly. "We are ready to go. Good thing we rise early and my brother has a tow truck. We have your car outside. And we put on spare tires."

"Thank you, my friend," Mark said.

"Grazie, Antonio," Jena replied.

"Ah, bella," Antonio reached out for her hands. She placed her hands in his. "My brothers have asked to marry you." He glanced down at her hands, then looked, surprised, over at Mark. Antonio raised her left hand to his lips and kissed it.

"But I shall tell them your heart has already been stolen away," he smiled. "Yes?"

She smiled. "Yes."

"Mama! Papa! Come quick! Our brother has found his love. Our brother has captured his joy!"

Mama and Papa came quickly from the kitchen, steaming cups of coffee in their hands. They saw Antonio holding up Jena's left hand to them, and the diamond ring on her finger.

"Lodare, Dio!" Mama cried. *Praise God*!

Papa took her hand and kissed it, as well. "Tanta bellezza da amare!" Then he kissed her full on the lips and twirled her around.

Jena laughed.

Mark hugged her.

"What did he just say," Jena asked, as Mama and Papa yelled up the stairs for the whole family to come down and celebrate again.

"He said *such beauty to love*," Mark whispered in her ear.

"When did this happen, my friend," Antonio demanded.

"Last night," Mark smiled.

Mama and Papa came back over and stood before them. "Benedizioni su di te!" *Blessings on you*!

What was meant to be a quiet morning, a quick cup of coffee, and uneventful trip down the mountain turned into an hour engagement celebration. Mama and Papa and several of Antonio's sisters created a breakfast feast of laughter, fruit, cheeses, pastries, pastramis, pancetta, and prosciutto. Papa even went down in the basement and came back up with bottles of champagne. Everyone toasted Jena and Mark, and the rounds of kisses and hugs began all over again.

"Many babies," Mama cried, joyously. "Many babies!"

Jena looked over at Mark, but he just smiled at her.

It was after nine thirty that morning before they finally were able to get on the road. But not before Jena and Mark were passed around one last time and showered with kisses and hugs. They'd endeared themselves to this family, somehow, and were assured that they were part of the family now and welcomed always.

"Go with God," Mama yelled in broken English as they drove away.

Papa stood on the porch and put his arm around his wife.

"Ah, Mama…loro sono noi." *They are us*. He gave her a sloppy kiss.

"Si, mia caro."

***

They got the car down the mountain and back to the rental car place. By noon, they were driving away in another rental.

"I want you to have something to drive this week while I'm at the base," Mark said as he pulled into the parking lot at the hotel. He shut off the engine and looked over her, his eyes filled with love.

She smiled back and reached out for his hand. The silence between them was filled with the electricity of their chemistry together, and the hope of a future. It was broken only by the occasional sound of a car passing by.

"Jena," he began. "I've been thinking about what you said this morning. I want you to marry me."

She laughed softly and held up her left hand, and the diamond ring caught the sun. "I am."

He glanced at her, then looked out over the parking lot. "The paperwork required would take a month, maybe more to go through the Italian system. I checked. To get married in Italy, an American Citizen must present two documents. A Nulla Osta (or affidavit) released by the American Consulate in Italy and legalized with an Apostille, and Atto Notorio released by the Italian Consulate in the USA or by an Italian Court."

She shook her head, confused. "I have no idea what you just said."

"There is a lot of paperwork and it takes a very long time. My discharge date is in two weeks, and I have to go back to duty tomorrow morning."

"So, what are you saying, Mark?"

The thought of waiting weeks or months to marry him upset her. It had taken a while for her heart to start healing, but once it had, she'd thrown her whole heart into the relationship with him.

They were already one in so many ways, save one. They'd made love in every facet of their beings, except with their bodies. Now, she wanted to be with him more than ever, and he with her.

Yet a silent promise to wait until they were married hung suspended in the air around them. It was something unheard of these days. But their friendship and love and respect for each other had demanded it.

"Let's get married in the chapel we saw yesterday, driving up the mountain to Barcis."

"The one with the old bell tower, and the flowers all around it?" she asked.

Mark nodded.

"When," she whispered.

"Tonight."

"But I thought you said it would take two months to get the paperwork approved."

He turned his full body to her in the seat. "What is a wedding, but the exchange of holy vows before God. I want you as my wife in every way. We leave for the states in two weeks. We can have a ceremony again there, before a judge, or whatever you want…a church wedding, maybe. I'll make sure, on my honor and on my life, that everything will be legal as soon as possible. But you want to get married in Italy. And I just want to marry you."

She looked at him, weighing his words.

"Once we get back to the States, it will take less than a week. If we wait for the paperwork to clear here, we'll be here for another eight to ten weeks. Is that what you want?"

"…no, I don't."

"What do you want, Jena?"

"Tonight?" she said to herself.

"I have a friend on base. He'll do it."

"Without a marriage license?"

Mark smiled. "It happens all the time in the military and for the same reasons. There are too many moving parts. Time is not a luxury. There are too many unknowns."

He saw the unexpected hesitation in her eyes. "But we can wait until we get back to the States and do it all at the same time, if you want. I've waited so long for you, Jena. I don't mind waiting a few more weeks."

Her mind raced. Get married tonight, in the chapel with the bells, and the flowers surrounding on all sides. With the moon in the sky and the sounds of music filling the air. With Mark beside her, and the future before her.

"What do you want, Jena?"

"I want to marry you, Mark, before we go back home. I want to marry you here, in Italy. Tonight. " Her smile took his breath away. "What do you want?"

He took her hand. "You."

The day suddenly got busy.

They drove into Pordenone. Jena went shopping for a dress. Mark went shopping for a wedding band. He also bought a bottle of expensive Italian champagne. Then he stopped by a little florist shop and had them make a small bouquet of white roses and baby's breath, which he placed in a Styrofoam cooler to keep it from wilting, and keep her from seeing it.

Mark was on the phone the whole time, calling friends and calling in favors.

Then he picked her up and they drove back to Aviano, light hearted and excited, and both of them talking a mile a minute.

He drove them on base, and they went to the PX, where he picked up his dress uniform while Jena grabbed a few groceries and stopped into the gift shop. By then it was 4 p.m., so they went back to the hotel.

"I'm leaving you off, here," Mark said, reaching over her and opening the door.

"Why?"

"I think the bride might need some time alone. I'll meet you at the chapel at six."

"But we only have one vehicle, and I don't know the way."

"That friend I told you about will pick you up and bring you. His name is Jon Harris."

She reached over and kissed him. "You do move mountains, don't you, Captain Riley?"

"Only for you, mia caro." He was quite proud of himself. She had no idea what he could produce on a short deadline. He wanted to surprise her. "Tonight, then. Six o'clock. Jon will be here at 5:15 p.m. to pick you up. It's not a lot of time." Then he kissed her and left her breathless.

She took the things she'd bought, got out of the car, and watched him drive away. She went into the hotel and up to her room. The windows were still wide open and the breeze was cool. She left them open while she showered. Then she wrapped herself in her robe and put her hair up in a towel, and went to sit for a moment by the window.

She was getting married in less than two hours. It was crazy and spontaneous. But Mark always called that out in her. After so many months of grieving and healing, life had suddenly become wildly unrestrained.

She should be nervous, but she wasn't. She was more at peace than she'd ever been in her life. And, that was the sign to her that this was the right decision. There were no regrets and no second thoughts. Nothing close to the anxiety she'd felt at her first wedding. Oh, she did love Pete. She'd always cherish him.

But she felt something now she hadn't felt in so very, very long. What was it? Excitement? Anticipation? She curled her legs beneath her on the couch and looked out the window. She smiled to herself when she realized what it was.

It was joy.

Suddenly, she remembered the visions of Pete and Jana and Alexis, and the crystal balls lit up from within.

In that moment she realized the freedom that had come, not from leaving them behind and moving on, but going forward with them always in her heart.

And now here she sat, about to dive off into the deep, into her own happiness. She was going to marry a wonderful man that she would grow old with…have adventures with…dream with. She was not starting over. Starting over was when you made a mistake the first time. Oh, her life with Pete was a not a mistake. It was a gift. Not to be put aside, but to be embraced and never forgotten.

Now, her life would be with Mark.

That realization lit a fire in her soul as she remembered the vision of Antonio's Mama and Papa slow dancing cheek to cheek in the kitchen when they thought no one was watching. How he caressed her plump derriere, and how she rubbed the back of his neck, whispering into his ear.

She was about to marry a gentle man, who'd only ever shown her unconditional love, friendship, and tender passion. A man she knew loved her, and respected her, and never once asked her to be someone she was not, or give up what she believed in or held in reverence. A man who held her while she wept, and shared her pain and grief and fear, and offered to protect the precious memories of a young marriage, and of her two little girls.

Jena reached over and took a sip of water.

She wanted children with Mark, but she might not ever be able to conceive again. Everything was still there, but damage had been done. But Mark knew that now, and wanted her anyway.

In the few minutes that Jena sat by the window, a thousand thoughts passed through her head, and her heart. He was the only man she'd ever known that made her laugh out loud, or weep uncontrollably, or dream again. He brought out the best in her. He brought out the truth in her. He brought out her true personality and allowed her to be herself… raw, beautiful, afraid at times. From the first moment, she'd been real with him, and he with her. They'd never been who they were not. There'd been no need to impress, no need to pretend, no need to hide.

He had never asked her to leave her past behind, or sweep what had happened that night of the storm under the rug, or even diminish what she and Pete had shared as man and wife. Mark had always honored that, for he knew that it was cherished by her, and always would be.

He was a man with flaws, she knew. And a man with history, and fears of his own. Yet, he'd never hidden those from her or lied to her or made her think something other than what truly was. Perhaps that alone was what first endeared her to him…his simple honesty and transparency and compassion.

He was an authentic man of integrity, steel…and velvet.

He was a pilot. A soldier. A warrior who would protect her with his life, if it came to that. She was sure of that in her heart, and he had told her the same on several occasions. He was a man fortified in courage, and not one to easily let his emotions get away from him. He'd never, not once, given her a reason to fear him. Yet he'd given her a million reasons to trust him. And she did.

She was going to marry him, and give herself completely to him for a lifetime. She'd decided that last night. By the fire. In one moment of clarity and conviction.

She was going to marry him.

Today, in the light of day, she knew there were no guarantees. And there were a thousand risks. But she was willing to take them, now, and to commit everything to him.

Most likely, people would talk back home. Especially people in her church. Maybe some in her professional circle would lift a judgmental eyebrow to the widow taking a husband so soon after such tragedy. And Esther would be torn, out of allegiance to Pete, and the girls.

Let them talk, she thought. Let them all wag their tongues if they were going to. It wasn't their life.

They didn't really know her, or anything she'd been through since the storm. They certainly didn't know Mark. Because if they did know him, they would see that he'd saved her life and given her a reason to live again. They would understand the preciousness of it all. And, perhaps, they might see a divine hand in it all.

Jena looked over at the dress hanging from the door. It was a simple ivory dress, a classy and elegant dress. It was the third dress she'd seen walking into the bridal shop in Pordenone. It revealed just enough skin and curves to make it alluringly sexy. She'd bought high heels to match, and an ivory lace wrap for her shoulders. The dress seemed designed just for her.

Was she ready to marry Mark tonight?

Yes, she was ready. More ready for happiness than she'd realized. Her darkness hours had given way to the sunrise, and her heart, although never completely as it was before, had transformed into a vessel capable of holding even more and more… love.

Jena stood up and let the robe drop from her naked body. The air was cool on her skin. She unwound the towel from her head, and flung back her blonde hair. She glanced at the clock on the bathroom wall. Jon Harris would be here in a while.

She misted a soft fragrance across her skin.

She dried and fluffed her hair into a wild and wispy style that spoke of elegance and a freed spirit. She applied light make up and a rosy lipstick, and applied a light layer of mascara.

She took her time.

She finally slipped her tight-forming dress over her head and carefully zipped it up in the back. She smoothed out the wrinkles over her hips and caressed the smoothness across her thighs. She cupped her breasts and lifted them so they pushed up against the open cleavage of the dress. Then she sat carefully on the bed and slipped on the high heels.

Finally, she stood and looked at herself in the long mirror. The woman looking back at her was beautiful. Jena felt herself staring.

For the first time in years, perhaps the first time ever, Jena saw herself. She truly saw herself. Her deep and poignant soul, the fire of her spirit, and light in her eyes. The light in her eyes was the same as the light her daughters gave her that day of the healing retreat. The light was joy again.

And she knew. She was free. Now, she could love without fear, because the love she knew now could never die.

Someone knocked on the door. She went to answer it. It was Jon Harris, a man not too far away in age from Mark. He was tall and handsome, dressed in Air Force blues, his hat under his arm. He stood at a dignified attention. She apparently took him by surprise because he was momentarily speechless.

Finally, he spoke. “Ma’am. Lieutenant Jon Harris. I’ll be your escort this evening.”

“Good evening, Lieutenant. Let me get my things.” She walked back into the room and closed the windows. Then she gathered her purse and shawl and walked toward him.

He stepped aside and she came out and closed the door behind her. “Ma’am,” he began.

Jena reached in her purse for the room key and then locked the door. Her hands were slightly trembling. “Yes, Lieutenant?”

“If I may say, you are the most stunning bride I have ever laid eyes on. And I’ve done a few weddings in my time. The captain is a very blessed man.”

She smiled and took his offered arm. “Thank you, Lieutenant. But honestly, I feel I am the one marrying up.”

He held her hand in the crook of his arm, donned his uniform hat, and led her toward the elevator. They went down and out of the hotel and he held the car door open for her as she gracefully climbed in. Then he circled around and got in on the driver’s side.

“Captain Riley asked me to give this to you, Ma’am.” He reached back and took a cake size white box and handed it to her.

“Thank you, Lieutenant.” Then Jena lifted the lid. Inside was a small, but beautifully designed bouquet of white roses and baby’s breath. And there was a card.

Come to me, Mia Caro.

She swallowed the sudden lump in her throat. Mia Caro. *My darling*. She took the bouquet out of the box and held it in her hands all the way up the mountain to the tiny village where he was waiting for her.

Chapter Seventeen

The Lieutenant pulled off the mountain two-lane road and into the quaint town square. The sun was just starting to lower toward the evening tide. The sound of a violin playing met her as she slowly walked up the cobblestone path to the chapel. The scents of flowers filled her senses and she suddenly felt a wave of euphoria. She glanced up, and saw the snow-covered mountaintops being kissed by the sunset.

The chapel doors opened. The violin music paused. They lingered at the doorway and Jena looked over at the Lieutenant.

He smiled, then offered his arm again, and she took it. She could feel herself slightly quivering. The Lieutenant placed his other hand over hers and smiled down at her.

The violin began to play again. Only it was to a beautiful Academy Award winning song, *Shallow*. She'd seen the movie and wept. But the song was beautiful and she had memorized the words, and now it seemed the perfect song at the perfect time, here in this perfect place.

The Lieutenant softly urged her forward and she took a step, and then another. As she entered the tiny chapel, she hesitated and let her eyes adjust from the sunlight. Then she caught her breath.

There were a hundred candles lit, and a hundred white roses. A cross hung above the altar, as it had for hundreds of years. The stained-glass windows reflected the waning sunshine, and her heels softly echoed on the beaten wood floors as she walked forward…slowly…deliberately…one step at a time…

The Lieutenant kept her locked arm in arm.

Jena saw three people standing at the front and wondered. Then they turned around. It was Antonio, and Mama, and Papa. Papa took off his worn hat and nodded sweetly to her.

"...witnesses," the Lieutenant whispered.

Jena was brought to tears. But she pushed them back and breathed deeply and slowly, blew it out, then breathed again.

The music echoed throughout the chapel. It seemed to have an old soul of its own. It was about lovers diving into a place they'd never known. Jena silently mouthed the words as she remembered them.

Her step faltered slightly, but she regained her balance and kept walking forward. The melody soared around her. Then she saw him. He was walking out from the side shadows. His face was lit up with love and his eyes had tears in them from the moment he'd seen her step in through the door. The closer they got to each other, the harder her heart pounded, and the quicker her breath came. She'd never felt so alive in her life!

Mark reached out for her hand, and the Lieutenant placed her hand in his. Then the Lieutenant went and took his place in front of the altar as Mark and Jena turned toward each other.

Mark bent his face close to hers and whispered. "We're far from the shallow, now, mia caro. But I've got you."

She smiled through her tears.

Behind them the violin faded and Antonio and Mama and Papa slowly sat down in the old wooden pews. From the back of the chapel a guitar started softly playing, and a mandolin joined in. Antonio's brothers.

The Lieutenant quietly cleared his throat. "Dearly beloved."

Papa sniffed from the first row.

"We are gathered here tonight, in the presence of God the Father, His Son Jesus Christ, and the Holy Spirit...to join this man and this woman in holy and sanctified marriage."

Mark reached out for both of her hands.

"I don't think there is an objection within a thousand miles, so I'll skip that part," the Lieutenant said.

Mark and Jena smiled.

The Lieutenant just held his Bible. "God created true love. It is a force so pure and so strong and everlasting; it transcends time and space and all comprehension."

Jena looked up at Mark.

"If part of it is separated from itself, it will search high and low across all oceans and skies and lands until it finds its other part, so that it can be whole again. That is the essence of true love."

Mark reached over and gently wiped a tear from Jena's cheek.

"True love is not a feeling," the Lieutenant continued. "It is the destiny of two hearts brought together by pain and passion, who are somehow joined in some magical, sometimes mystical connection neither one can explain. It is two broken hearts coming together as one, and healing as one heart. It is two souls melding together in the fire of adversity, and coming out stronger and inseparable, one vessel that now contains the grace and mercies of life."

It took everything for Mark not to wrap her up in his arms and hold her with every ounce of his being.

"Mark and Jena, you stand here now, wishing to be joined as husband and wife in the sight of God and these witnesses. Now I know the license is coming…"

Mark nodded, and Jena smiled.

"And while we wait for that to materialize, all that means, Jena, is that you don't have access to his money yet."

Mark and Jena laughed. It was the perfect timing to lighten the moment.

"Do I have your word, Captain Riley, that all of this will be made legal within a few weeks when you get back home to the States."

"You do, Lieutenant."

The Lieutenant continued. "Holy marriage is not meant to be sanctioned by man or any government. It was created by God, to be blessed by God. A hundred years ago, in simpler times, you didn't need the permission of the government to get married. All you needed was a judge or a roaming preacher."

Mark and Jena smiled at him.

"So," the Lieutenant continued, more seriously, tapping himself on the chest. "Here is your roaming preacher."

From the back the guitar and mandolin music faded.

"Marriage is not something to be entered into lightly, but with much thought, with honor, your word, and your commitment. So, we stand here now in the presence of the Creator of Love, accountable to Him and to the heavenlies for what you are about to say and do."

Jena had stopped quivering. Her breathing slowed. Her heart was no longer racing, but was beating steadily in her chest. She was going to give him all, without any reservations, and step into a lifetime of loving him.

"Do you have your vows?"

Mark nodded. He held her hands in his, and looked her in the eyes. "Jena. You asked me once who God was to me. I know now. He is love, embodied in you. So pure and good. So graceful. Radiant and beautiful. There has never been another who has had my heart. And there will never be another. You stole my heart that night in the ocean, and I never got it back. Please keep my heart always, because you are my soulmate … and my true love."

The only sound in the chapel were their heartbeats.

Jena looked up at Mark. She hadn't even thought about her vows, what she would say to him, what she would promise him. But when she opened her lips to speak, the words flowed softly and eloquently out, like oil being poured out as an offering.

"You saved me," she whispered. "You gave me back my life. You taught me how to live again, and how to love again. You are self-less, strong, giving, and amazing love. I trust you with my life, and I give you all my heart, my mind, my body, my spirit, and my soul. You are the very air I breathe. And I… I love you."

Mark smiled down at her, his insides turning upside down.

"So, now the vows, " the Lieutenant began. "Do you, Captain Mark Fitzgerald Riley take Jena Elizabeth Stratton Parker to be your wedded wife, to have and to hold, from this day forward, for better, for worse, for richer, for poorer, in sickness and in health, to love and to cherish, till death do you part…"

"No," Mark turned to the Lieutenant, interrupting him. "Not until death do us part. Get rid of that part. I will love her forever."

The Lieutenant smiled. "My bad. Let's try this again. Do you, Captain Mark Fitzgerald Riley take Jena Elizabeth Stratton Parker to be your wedded wife, to have and to hold, from this day forward, for better, for worse, for richer, for poorer, in sickness and in health, to love and to cherish… forever… according to God's holy ordinance; and thereto, forsaking all others, pledge yourself to her?"

Mark beamed down at her. "I do."

"And do you, Jena Elizabeth Stratton Parker take Captain Mark Fitzgerald Riley to be your wedded husband, to have and to hold, from this day forward, for better, for worse, for richer, for poorer, in sickness and in health, to love and to cherish forever… according to God's holy ordinance; and thereto, forsaking all others, pledge yourself to him?"

Tears of joy were running down her face. "I do."

"Do you have the ring?"

Mark pulled the band from his pocket and held it between his fingers.

"Place the ring on your bride's finger and repeat after me."

Mark turned toward his friend. "Let me take it from here, will you, Jon."

The Lieutenant nodded and stepped back.

Mark stepped closer to Jena and took her left hand in his. He gently removed the diamond engagement ring. In the next moment, he slid the wedding band onto her left ring finger. It fit perfectly. "This is the ring I want closest to your heart. It is my love, never-ending. My honor. My vow. My promise to you forever. Don't ever take it off." Then Mark slid the engagement ring back on, and smiled.

The Lieutenant closed the Bible. "Then in the presence of God and these witnesses, and by the authority vested in me as an ordained youth pastor, licensed chaplain in the United States Air Force, and officially on the payroll of the First Baptist Church of Daffodil Hills, Alabama…"

Mark and Jena glanced over at him.

"…I do now declare you husband and wife. God has so obviously joined you together…so ain't nobody breaking this one up. Sir, you may now kiss your stunning bride!"

Mark bent down and kissed his stunning bride, and kept kissing his stunning bride, as the bells in the tower above them rang out across the valley.

***

An hour later he was fumbling with the hotel room card.

"We're on the wrong floor, Mark," Jena laughed as she lay draped in his arms.

"No, it's fine."

"Do you want to put me down?"

"I've got you. Just be still." He slid the room key one more time as he shifted her in his arms. This time the lock clicked. He kicked the door open and carried her across the threshold backwards.

"Mark, this isn't our room," she laughed.

"Yes, it is," he argued. He set her down and turned her around.

She was right. It wasn't their room. It wasn't even a room. It was a suite for kings and queens.

It was all painted white, with a massive king-sized bed against the far wall. Huge French doors opened onto a baloney overlooking a small lake. White rose petals lay in a trail on the floor from the door to the bed, and covered the white lace coverlet. There were newly lit candles on every table and window sill. A bucket of ice sat chilling a bottle of champagne on the dining table at the far end of the suite. To the left, and through the doors, Jena saw a bathtub built for four people.

"Oh, my god," she whispered. She saw their luggage and bags in the closet, and walked over and ran her hand along the soft velvet of his and her robes. "When did you do this?"

"I had help. I called in a few favors. My friends like me."

"Apparently," she smiled, her eyes still roaming around the room. "It's all so beautiful, Mark."

He walked over and placed his uniform hat on the dresser. "I thought you'd like it."

"It must have cost you a fortune."

"I've got money," he grinned. "I've saved my entire career. Of course, you can't touch it yet."

She laughed out loud, as she turned around. And when she did, he melted at the knees.

"You… are… so…"

"What?" she whispered, suddenly caught in the intensity of his stare. She was standing in front of the bed then.

"Precious," he said, simply. Then he started walking toward her as though not to scare her off. But his gate was set and he moved with a quiet power, his intent very clear.

"What are you doing, Mark Riley?" She had butterflies in her stomach.

"You know what. So, don't move."

She didn't. Her shawl was still wrapped around her shoulders, and her hair was all wild from him carrying her in his arms all the way up from the car.

He stopped a foot away from her. His gaze started at the top of her head and then went to the blue pools of her eyes, then the wet rose of her lips. Then his eyes traveled down to her neck, where the necklace he'd given her lay perfect on her skin. He followed the nape of her neck down to her shoulders, then across to her breasts. He watched as her breath quickened. Then his eyes moved downward across her stomach and across her hips, then down the dress until it quit just above the slender calves. He looked down at her feet and saw her toenails painted with a soft mauve.

She stood completely still, her heart now racing.

He reached forward and took the shawl from around her and carefully laid it across the chair. Then he bent down on one knee, and gently removed her high heels. He ran his hand up her calves and kept going higher. The tight dress kept him from going where he really wanted to go. So, he stood and looked down at her with eyes that made her feel like the most beautiful woman in the world.

Then, he slowly turned her around. And like a ticking clock, unzipped her dress one link at a time. It seemed forever until she felt the cool breeze on her back. There were no more barriers now.

He kissed her shoulder from behind, and the kisses followed her spine downward to where the zipper ended. Goose bumps broke out across her arms and breasts, and at the same time, fire ignited in the deepest parts of her body. She turned in his arms.

"My turn," she whispered.

He dropped his hands away from her.

She helped him slip off his uniform jacket. And then his tie, followed by his shirt. She rubbed her hands across the hair on his chest and bent to kiss him there.

He groaned in response. "That's dangerous territory you're exploring there, Jena."

She smiled and continued. The belt came next. She started to bend down and take off his shoes. He beat her to it and kicked off his shoes and wiggled out of his socks. All that he had on were his dress slacks.

She slowly rubbed her hand over his shoulders as she circled him, taking in every detail of his muscular shoulders and then his arms. She felt him shiver slightly and shift his weight.

Then he turned around and met her face to face.

"My turn again," he said boldly. Then he slowly slipped the beautiful dress from her body and it slid to the floor. There was nothing beneath but Jena.

He stared at her for one full minute, and swallowed several times to dislodge the lump in his throat.

"Why are you stopping, Mark?" she quietly asked.

"I've waited so long," he whispered. "And now, here you are."

She smiled. "Here I am." She remained perfectly still.

He touched her breasts, and smiled as a blush cascaded across her chest. He looked into her eyes. She met his gaze with a boldness he'd never seen before.

"You think me shy, Captain Riley?" she whispered.

"At one time, I would have thought so," he answered, taking his time again now to run his fingers from her neck downward and then lower still. "Now, I see how wrong I was to even imagine it."

He felt her fingers at his waist, and tried to relax as she skillfully unzipped his pants. They fell to his ankles and he stepped out of them. He was left standing in his boxers.

She looked down and smiled. "Hearts? Really?"

He shrugged, good naturedly. "For you. They were on sale."

She pressed her body up against his. He came unglued. Yet he forced himself to remain in control and let their first time be something they'd always remember.

She reached up and cupped his face in her hands. "Is it always going to be like this," she breathed.

"Like what," he whispered, his body tensed as the fire raced through every vein.

"Candles. Roses. Champagne." She kissed him after every word, in different places as she moved down his body. "This. Incredible. Breathtaking. Heart Stopping. Mind altering. Body on fire…"

"Yes," he replied, suddenly wrapping his arms around her, and lifting her in the air, and gently placing her on the bed. He followed, coming on top of her, and covering her with his body. Then he bent down and kissed her.

They made love all night, like two ravenous animals, afraid there would never again be enough to satisfy them. At three in the morning, they came up for air, and sat up looking at each other. Then they looked around the room, or what was left of it, and burst out laughing.

"Oh my god!" Jena laughed. "They're going to kick us out."

"I'm starving," Mark said, standing up in all his glory.

Jena smiled. "You're always hungry."

He growled at her.

"In the cooler," she pointed.

He made them both a sandwich and climbed back into bed with her. His sandwich was gone in four bites. She took her time. He watched her intently, savoring the sight of her.

Her hair was disheveled, her lips were slightly puffy from his kisses, and her skin was flushed. When she was finished, he reached over and took her plate away.

Then he loved her again.

Chapter Eighteen

"Jena?"

She moaned and opened one eye. He was dressed in his uniform and standing over her.

"I have to go."

"No," she whispered.

"I have to report back by 9 a.m." He kissed her on the lips, and she pulled him toward her. He pulled away. "I can't, Jena. I'll call you."

She opened both eyes. And came fully awake. Slowly, she sat up in bed. "When?"

"It will probably be after three or four o'clock." He picked up his laptop. "Here are the keys and my credit card. I have a ride."

"Mark? Thank you."

He turned to her. "For what, Jena?"

"For marrying me. For loving me."

He came and sat down on the bed beside her. "Loving you is the easiest thing I've ever done in my life."

Then he kissed her and the sparks flared anew.

"You know," she smiled. "If we do every night what we did last night, one of us is going to get hurt." She looked around at the room. The bed covers were all over the floor. The chair was upside down. The bucket of champagne and ice was lying on the floor where it had been knocked from the table.

He laughed. "I have medical insurance." Then he blew her a kiss and was gone out the door.

Jena lay in bed for a long time, just enjoying the quiet and the memories of last night. It was all so beautiful. The wedding, the music, the lovemaking. He was strong and gentle and aggressive and kind, and her heart melted when she thought of him kissing her.

Eventually she got up and took a shower. Then she wrapped in one of the robes, made herself a strong cup of coffee, and took it out on the balcony. The air was crisp and the morning was bright, and the mountains in the distance were white with a covering of snow.

She thought of checking her emails, but didn't. She hadn't checked them since she'd landed in Italy. Nothing was that important anymore. If anyone really needed her, the important people had her cell number.

She sipped the coffee. It was strong, but she liked it that way. She ran her fingers through her hair, and then pulled the robe a little tighter against the cool air.

She heard the roar of the jet before she saw it.

It blasted past her in the valley and shot upward in the sky. Another followed a minute later. And then another. She counted seven jets in three minutes, their engines fiery red as they shot past her, hell bent on getting somewhere fast.

By lunchtime, she was famished, and moseyed down to the family-owned restaurant and ordered salad and a glass of tea. Then she strolled downtown and window shopped at the quaint little family shops. When they all closed from one to four in the afternoon, so shop owners could go home for a few hours, she walked along the streets where houses had mini gardens and vineyards. She took in the sight of a dog and her puppies sauntering across an alleyway to get back to their home.

She kept checking her watch.

Time was going by so very slowly.

It was only ten minutes past three.

He had said he wasn't sure if he could stay with her tonight. He had to clear it with his commander. But he didn't foresee a problem.

So, Jena stopped at a small grocery and picked up some food so they wouldn't have to eat out tonight. She wanted him all to herself, to pick up where they'd left off at 7 a.m. this morning.

At 5:40 p.m., he called.

"Hi," he said. He sounded exhausted.

"Hi, back." she replied, her heart beating faster just at the sound of his voice.

"Jena, I've got some bad news."

"You can't come back tonight…"

"Worse."

She held her breath. "…ok. I'm listening."

"Are you watching the news?"

"No, not at all. I've been around town, and made us dinner."

"Turn on BBC. Iran shot down one of our $130 million-dollar drones. We're on high alert. The President might retaliate."

She paused and forced herself to stay calm. "I saw the jets take off this morning."

"They're going out to the carriers."

"What about you?"

"Well," he stalled. "That's the thing. They suspended my discharge date and are keeping me on active duty."

"What does that mean, Mark?"

"I don't know, except that I have to stay on base and be ready to fly at a moment's notice."

"Fly? Where?" Jena bit her lip.

"I can't tell you that. If I'm called up, I can't call you again until I get back to a military base. We go silent on these types of things. So, don't worry if you don't hear from me for a few days." She could tell from his voice that he wasn't happy about any of this.

"…ok," she whispered in the phone.

"Stay close in town," he commanded. "And if you don't hear from me after a week, go ahead and make plans to get on back to the states. The plane tickets are in the briefcase in the closet. I won't be far behind you."

"Mark, I'm not leaving here without you."

"Jena," he snapped. "Please do what I ask. I know you don't want to, but I will need you to do that. I want to know you are safe."

"Are we going to war, Mark?" The thought exploded in her head.

There was silence on the other end of the line. Then she heard him take a breath. "I live with this possibility every single day, Jena. This will probably blow over. But right now, it's a volatile situation, and we are sworn to duty."

"I know…"

"I love you."

"I love you, too, Mark."

"I've got to go. They're calling us into a meeting. Don't worry about dinner. Just take care of yourself. Promise me."

"I promise."

She heard him talking to someone on the other end, then the call went dead.

Immediately, she stood up and walked over to the TV and turned on BBC. They were giving more detail than she really wanted to know. The carriers were pulling in closer to the coast. Surveillance satellites were being repositioned. Military bases in Germany, Italy, and Israel were on high alert and launching F-16s in the direction of the U.S. carriers.

She nibbled at the food, then pushed it away.

He didn't call again that night.

Only because she was totally exhausted, did she fall asleep and sleep until the next morning. She'd left the TV on, and woke up to the updates. They weren't good. Things were escalating.

Three more jets raced by and kicked into supersonic speed before they even crested the mountain tops. Five more followed them in successive order. Then four more.

Mark had been a jet pilot since he first began his career. He'd done his basic training in San Antonio, then trained with the Navy in Pensacola. He never talked much about the missions, but he had more metals than he could put on his dress uniform.

He didn't call that morning, either. Or any time that day. By one o'clock, Jena was starting to really worry. Was he the pilot in one of those planes that flew out this morning?

She went for a walk just to push back the cabin fever and boredom. Then she came back into the hotel and sat down in the bar and ordered a glass of tea. The TV was on, but the sound was off. There was video of F-16s flying over Saudi Arabia.

That night, she called home, and left a message on Rick's phone. She wasn't sure, because of the time change and his work schedule, if or when he might call her back. He called in the middle of the night, Italian time.

"Well, hello there," he said brightly. "Long time no hear from. I assume you are still in Italy, where you were supposed to have called us and let us know you are still alive."

"Hi, Rick. I'm very much alive. Have you heard from Mark?"

"No, isn't he with you?"

"He got called back up yesterday because of the Iran deal."

"That really sucks," she heard him say.

"You haven't talked to him at all?"

"No" Rick replied. "I haven't talked to him since before we gave you the letter." The call started to deteriorate. The cell coverage in Aviano was intermittent. "I can't hear you well."

"Will you let me know if you hear from him?" she asked.

"I will. Where are you staying? Are you in Aviano?"

"Yes."

"Are you enjoying yourself?" he asked.

Jena paused before answering. "A lot has happened."

"Tell us all about it when you get home. Hey, I'm being called into surgery. Give Katie a call later and fill her in on all the details."

"I will," Jena agreed. Then the call went dead.

After that, she couldn't go back to sleep. BBC kept replaying the same footage of the military escalation.

The next day dragged on and on and on. There was no new information being shared by the news outlets. But there was no call from her husband, either.

She prayed for an hour. Then, she went down to the café and ordered a soda.

She went back upstairs to tidy up the room, but room service had already been there. So, she got in the rental car and went for a drive.

On her ways back into town, she pulled over at a gas station and just sat by the side of the road. One by one, four F-16s flew in low and landed on the runway just beyond the fence line.

She looked at her phone.

No calls. She looked toward the direction of the entrance to the base, and saw the flags lowered to half-mast.

She was fighting not to panic, at this point. She started up the car and drove to a tiny family-owned grocery store where she picked up a salad, some cheese and fruit, and some bottled water. Then she went back to the hotel and sat out on the balcony as night fell again in Aviano.

After an hour, she went inside and made herself a cup of tea. Then she grabbed the quilt off the bed, wrapped herself in it and went back out on the balcony.

She looked up. There were no stars out tonight to wish upon. The breeze had died down to nothing. From way off in the distance, she heard the echo of a mandolin and a saxophone in duet, playing a slow lament of lovers.

A light mist began to fall. It dusted her covering and alighted on her hair. Sitting there quietly, she realized there was a possibility that Mark might not be coming back.

She had no way of knowing where he was, or if he was alright. She contemplated bargaining with God over this one. But it hadn't worked before. The last time she'd tried hadn't brought Pete back. It hadn't brought the girls back. She looked up into the sky.

She thought she believed. Sometimes she knew she did. Yet there were other times when she so questioned God's motives, and the madness behind what He allowed or who He chose to heal or save.

Tonight, she was wanting to believe. In what, she wasn't so sure. In divine protection? In mercy?

Why would He let her live and go through all she had, only to bring her back again to the place of Job. He'd lost everything. He'd lost everyone, all his family, every one of his children.

Was she being tested?

The rational in her spoke calm and patience, and urged the making of plans to leave Italy. The fear in her spoke death again. But, the heart in her just kept beating, waiting, hoping that tomorrow he would call or come through that door.

Sitting there, with the mist falling on her, Jena chose to follow her heart.

After a while, she rose and went back in. She closed the French doors behind her, took off her shoes, and climbed fully clothed under the covers.

From the TV came the news that the President had called off the retaliatory attack, saying it was not proportional to the shooting down of a drone. But the military was strong, and on alert, and urged Iran to take full responsibility.

***

Her days turned into a forlorn routine of waiting, checking her watch, and pacing holes in the hotel room carpet.

She tried to keep her mind occupied, but there was nothing to do but wait. She was in limbo.

The first day without him had become two. Then the two became three. Then the three days became four. She lost count after that.

He'd made her promise to use her ticket home if he wasn't back in time. He'd purchased their tickets home on the same day he'd bought her ticket to come to Italy. That was months before. He'd purchased the tickets hoping, that after his discharge date, they would be going home together.

He'd risked so much, believing in her, and in love, and in what they had together, without much evidence from her. But he'd believed in her all the same.

He'd made her promise to use her ticket if he wasn't back. Because, if he wasn't back, it meant one of two things. He wasn't coming back. Or, tensions in the region were escalated to the point of military engagement and the threat was very real. If that was the case, he would be on active duty for a while. As much as she didn't want to admit it, especially not knowing his fate, she knew she could not live out those lonely days of waiting alone in an Italian hotel. She had somewhat of a life back home, with responsibilities and a mortgage, and a company to run.

But the thought of leaving him ripped her heart out.

She'd gotten into the habit of waking up each morning, making herself coffee, watching BBC for any news, taking a shower, and then roaming the town around the hotel. She didn't eat much. She tried to read to keep her mind off her biggest fear. That didn't work well, so she started journaling.

Every afternoon, she would drive to the base and sit in the car just outside the gate. She attempted to enter the base and find someone who could give her information, but was stopped by Security Forces at the gate. She had no clearance. The young airmen who guarded the gate with rifles and their lives got used to seeing her after a few days. They knew who she was waiting for. So, when they saw her, they came out with hot coffee and a few words of encouragement. They had no information, and even if they did, they couldn't share it without being court martialed. So, she sat quietly by the gate for an hour at a time, watching the planes take off and land.

She called Katie one day, asking if they'd heard from him. They hadn't. So, she kept the call brief and thanked her. Jena hadn't yet shared all that had happened since she'd arrived in Italy. It was almost as though she wanted those days held secretly protected for a while longer. If he never returned, she could never claim his name, or even make sense of it to anyone else, that they'd forgone all legalities and secretly married.

The hotel staff became familiar with her, and brought her hot pastries from the kitchen in the early mornings. They even stopped to talk to her in the hallways as they went about their duties.

The sounds of jets taking off and landing became so routine, she stopped noticing. Mark was never in them.

When evening came, still without him, she would go outside and sit on the balcony and watch the dark skies. Sometimes there were stars. Sometimes not. She would pray that God would bring him back to her. After a while, she'd go back in and close the doors. She tried to sleep, but it alluded her.

Sometimes she would drift in and out, or dream. Most often, she'd lie awake through the long nights thinking of what she'd do if he never came back.

She was lying awake tonight. Thoughts rolled inside her head. It was midnight. The flight back to the States was scheduled for less than forty-eight hours from now.

She was still in her jeans and a sweater, and still had her shoes on. She got up from the bed and pulled on her jacket, then picked up the car keys off the table. She glanced at her phone on the table, still plugged in. It was having a horrible time holding a charge. And when it did, she couldn't get more than a bar or two. She left it laying where it was.

She went downstairs and outside, and got in the car and drove toward the airbase the short distance away. It was within walking distance, and sometimes she did walk there. But it was in the middle of the night now. She pulled into the parking lot near the gate entrance and sat there.

The night was very dark, and there was little movement on base except for the armored Hummer that occasionally drove by on the other side of the fence. She sat there for an hour. After a while, she broke down and began praying to God to bring Mark back to her. If for no other reason, than for out of His grace. But she heard nothing in her heart. So, she wrapped her jacket closer.

Then she saw something out of the corner of her eye and turned to look across the valley. Flashing lights from an incoming jet pulled her attention away from her thoughts of finally having to leave him. She watched its approach, as she had watched a hundred other jets over the days.

Hoping each time had proven to be a waste of energy.

The lights of the runway flared brighter, guiding the jet home. It came in at tree top level and cleared the boundary fence before touching the wheels to the runway. The jet engines reversed and the tires screeched. She watched as the jet decelerated away from her down the mile-long runway to end its mission.

Jena sat there for another ten minutes, then started the engine and drove back to the hotel.

The night dragged by. She tossed and turned. In the early morning hours, a storm rolled in from over the mountains. The thunder pulled her from a dream. She opened her eyes. The room was dark, save for an occasional flash of lightening.

She'd made her mind up to keep her promise to Mark. She would leave and go back to the States. But she would leave her heart and soul here, in Italy, until Mark brought them back home to her.

There was another flash of lightening, then a loud rumble followed closely behind. The rain came then, and unleashed a deluge of water against the windows. With the rain came a torrent of her tears, washing over a heartache she wondered would ever end. And so it was that she cried herself to sleep in the middle of the storm.

***

A soft knock came at the door. *Tap. Tap.*

She stirred, and covered her head with a pillow.

A louder knock. She rolled over and looked at the clock. It was five a.m., too early for the staff to bring pastries. Someone had the wrong room. She ignored the knock again and curled under the covers, embracing a pillow and pulling it close to her breasts.

The knock came again, this time as a banging.

Jena pushed back the covers and rose. She was dressed in sweat pants and a thin t-shirt. Her hair was unruly from the tossing and turning all night.

She walked across the room and unlatched the lock. But she waited to open the door.

"Who is it?"

"Jena."

Her heart leaped. She recognized his voice immediately. She flung the door open.

And there he was. Soaking wet, still in his flight suit.

"Hi," he said, smiling ear to ear. "I'm back."

She bounded into his arms with such a force it knocked them both back against the wall of the hallway. He kissed her and she kissed him. Not gently or tenderly, but with a hunger that took both their breaths away.

With his arms around her, holding on for dear life, he pushed her back into the room and kicked the door closed behind them.

Epilogue

They came home together on a commercial flight, a flight also deemed an Angel Flight, as it carried the remains of an airman from Texas. When the aircraft landed at the DFW airport, everyone waited in silence as the casket was taken off the plane and transferred to a waiting hearse.

Mark and Jena watched with reverence as a young widow with a baby on her hip and another young child in hand approached. She bent down and kissed the flag draped coffin that contained her love. Jena bit her lip, and reached for her husband's hand.

It was bittersweet, and the passengers remained seated and quiet until the casket was loaded into the hearse and the hearse slowly drove away.

Mark and Jena were the last to disembark the plane.

The Air Force had pushed back his discharge date a month. But the base commander, having known Mark for years, personally signed off on an emergency leave that allowed him to escort his bride back to the United States. In the same sweep of the pen, the commander had also ordered his honorable discharge be processed through the base in San Antonio. It was the least he could do for a man who'd served his country so well for so long.

Rick and Katie were waiting at the gate for them, and greeted them. Rick embraced his brother.

Katie reached out for Jena's hands and brought her close. She felt the diamond before she saw it. Looking down, she saw the ring, and the wedding band behind it.

Katie's mouth dropped open and she looked quickly into Jena's eyes. "You're married?"

Jena smiled. "Yes."

Rick turned around. "What?!"

Mark wrapped his arms around his wife, beaming. "We did the deed."

"Oh, my god!" Katie screamed. Then she wrapped Jena in her arms and hugged her. "Oh, my god! You got married in Italy?!"

"We want to make it official in the States, so will you two stand up with us?"

"When?"

"This weekend," Mark answered.

Rick nodded in surprised wonder. "I'll be, big brother. All I can say is that it's about damn time you claimed this woman!"

The marriage license took an hour to obtain, and it was the first thing they did. Three days later they were standing together in another chapel, this one in the backwoods of East Texas. There was another preacher. And there were music and flowers, and a more formal repeating of vows. But the vows that Mark and Jena had shared in Italy were so precious and so holy they didn't need repeating for the sake of others. But they did promise again to love each other forever, forsaking all others. Rick and Katie and Esther were there to share in the celebration. And Mark and Rick's mother and stepfather came, as well. It was intimate and beautiful.

Mark moved into Jena's house, and made fast friends with the puppy. Within two weeks, he found a job with the county's emergency services department, and a second job with Care Flight as a standby pilot. It was a surprisingly smooth transition into civilian life. Jena rebuilt her consulting business. She stepped down from the Junior League, and got trained with the Red Cross.

They spent most of their free time hiking, and going on short motorcycle rides across the countryside, stopping now and then to savor the simple pleasures of a beer and a burger. Sundays were spent with Rick and Katie and the kids… eating Italian food, drinking wine on the patio, telling stories and laughing until they cried.

Their nights were spent loving each other in ways that lovers hold precious, and whispering together into the early hours of the morning.

Every morning, Mark made coffee and brought it to her. Every night, she rubbed his shoulders until he pulled her into his arms and kissed her with a passion she'd never known before him.

Jena laughed a lot, mostly at Mark and his antics. They wrestled over the last piece of pie, and played gin rummy during the rainstorms. Together, they built a greenhouse behind the old house and started a garden of vegetables and white roses.

Christmas came, and they walked through a tree farm up by Sulphur Springs until they found the perfect pine. They took it home and decorated it together with Christmas carols playing in the background. Jena put up angels on the mantel. And, on Christmas Eve, they gave each other their gifts by firelight.

Esther came for a visit now and then, and seemed at peace. She was truly happy for Jena, and pledged her affection for always.

Winter turned into spring, and the powerful bond between the two soulmates grew ever stronger. He lived for her smiles. She cherished his tenderness. They found a church they loved, and became life group leaders, and starting working with teenagers.

Jena started writing a book.

Mark turned the detached garage into a shop and man cave, replaced the worn fence, and painted the outside of the house.

That next summer, they took a much-needed vacation, and drove to Galveston, renting the same house where they'd first met. Rick and Katie and the children were joining them in a week.

They cherished the time alone, and together. They went swimming, and laid in the sun, and made love. Sometimes, they just sat on the sand and held hands, looking out to sea. They read each other's minds, and often finished each other's sentences, laughing when they did. They explored the town, and ate dinner at the hole in the wall he'd taken her to before.

On the evening before Rick and Katie were to arrive, Mark grilled shish kabobs and Jena made salad, and they ate outside on the deck above the ocean beach.

After they finished, they cleared the dishes, turned off the outside lights and came out to stand on the deck by the railings.

Dusk was exquisite and painted the sky the color of red roses. The lanterns on the deck flickered and created a romantic glow of romance and old-world charm. One by one, a thousand stars appeared and twinkled above them, reminding them once again how vast and wonderous and unfathomable was the meaning of life, and what could not be seen or comprehended with the heart. The glow of the thousand stars reflected off the sea.

"It's beautiful tonight," Mark whispered. "I love you."

Jena leaned up to kiss him.

He put his arm around her as he looked out over the calm sea and expanse of sandy beach. Then his eyes focused on the beach. "I love them, too. They were the ones who brought us together."

"Who?"

"Them," he nodded toward the beach.

Jena turned to look out toward the ocean and saw them, slowly walking down the beach. There they were. All of them. Pete. Jana. Lexi. The girls were grown now, with long curling blonde hair and a gentle sway to their hips. Pete seemed older, with a touch of gray at his temples.

The three of them slowed and waved at her, then lowered their hands and stopped. They looked a long time in her direction, as though they were memorizing her face, or offering her one lasting imprint for her heart. Then they turned and started back down the beach from where they'd come. The three joined hands and kept walking, gathering sea shells here and there in the waning light of the evening.

"Oh, my God," Jena breathed.

She opened her mouth to call them back. Then she paused.

They were walking away from her into another time and dimension she could never understand…beyond the veil just out of sight. She took in a small breath, then pressed her lips together.

No, she would not call them back.

Instead, she watched until they faded into the late evening mist of ocean spray.

"I won't see them again, will I?" she whispered.

"Not until you are very, very old." Mark slowly took her in his arms, and kissed the top of her head.

The silence of the moment was beautiful, reverent, and profoundly sacred.

"Are you ok?" he finally asked. He could see the mist in her blue eyes and the slow swallow.

She nodded.

"It's all amazing, isn't it?" Mark whispered.

"Yes…it is," she answered quietly. So much had happened. So much death. So much grief. So much healing. So much love again. And, so much life yet to be lived.

Perhaps God *was* real, after all. He'd been real all along, quietly making the way for her to live again.

But she'd never understand or comprehend how it all fit together, or the mysteries of life…or life beyond. Maybe she didn't need to. After all, wasn't life a series of little steps taking you on a journey of choices and risks and beautiful moments, and ten thousand days of joy you never expected. There were no guarantees. No safety nets. Life was a journey of faith.

Perhaps life was the journey into love itself.

She took a deep breath. "Mark, do you remember what you said in Lake Barcis? About our love giving birth to miracles?"

He smiled. "I do."

"I need to tell you something," she whispered, looking up into his incredible eyes.

He pulled her in closer in his arms. "What is it, Jena?"

She was so gorgeous, especially here in the glow of the lanterns, with her blonde hair gleaming and her body supple in his arms. He was captured by the love and a lifetime of keepsakes shining in her blue eyes.

She looked up at him with an expression so precious it took his breath away. "I'm pregnant."

He didn't respond.

He tilted his head slightly in stunned confusion.

She sweetly smiled in answer.

Then, Jena saw tears in his eyes. They welled up and then spilled over and slowly ran down his stubbled cheeks…big thick salty man tears.

He was speechless. And so very still. Then he finally found his voice. "How long have you known?" he whispered, his voice choked with emotion.

"A few weeks. I was waiting for the right time to tell you."

He leaned back and looked at her with eyes that spoke of his wondered amazement and his every adoration of her.

"We're having a baby?"

Jena nodded her head up and down, feeling the joy explode around her. "You're going to be a daddy."

He cupped Jena's face in his hands and held her so very gently. Then he bent down and kissed her with such sweet passion her knees almost buckled. Then he wiped two lone tears away from her cheek.

He smiled through his own tears. "Ti amo, mia caro!"

The starlight glowed above them.

The waves softly lapped against the shore.

From inside the house, a country song came on the radio. It was the first song they'd ever danced to on that night at that Texas roadhouse, when she first knew that, out of the blue, love had quietly come again, and offered her heart hope for a future.

This was her second chance.

Perhaps, this was her destiny all along.

"And I love you," she whispered. "Forever."

Then Mark wrapped her in his arms, pulled her close to his heart, and they slow danced to what had become *their* song.

Three seagulls appeared then and soared over them in the new moonlight, their wings outstretched, having caught the wind. Then they banked and sailed into the stars.

About the Author

The author has a Ph.D. and an extensive background in business consulting, executive coaching, higher education, and non-profit organizations. While most days are filled with writing and consulting, spare time is spent with family, friends, grandkids, and on the farm.

www.ingramcontent.com/pod-product-compliance
Lightning Source LLC
LaVergne TN
LVHW010613100826
845148LV00014B/2944

9798218566005